instructions for a broken heart

kim culbertson

sourcebooks
fire

Published by Sourcebooks Fire, an imprint of Sourcebooks, Inc.
P.O. Box 4410, Naperville, Illinois 60567-4410
(630) 961-3900
Fax: (630) 961-2168
teenfire.sourcebooks.com

Library of Congress Cataloging-in-Publication data is on file with the publisher.

Printed and bound in the United States of America.
VP 10 9 8 7 6 5 4 3 2

PRAISE FOR *SONGS FOR A TEENAGE NOMAD*

"*Wow!* Rich, beautifully detailed, extremely well written, and completely real people in a real world coping, just as we all cope. Calle is a female kind of Holden Caulfield…Brilliant work."

Ben Franklin Award judge

"This is a novel that you will want to experience over and over again, just like a great song."

— Becca Boland, Teensreadtoo.com 5-Star Review

"Culbertson has crafted a world true and honest to the teenage experience, with characters you love immediately."

—Loretta Ramos, MFA Producers Program, UCLA School of Theater, Film, and Television

"I can't imagine anyone not liking this book. Using music in a teen book contributes to the authenticity of the story. I think there are many, many teens that will see themselves in this book, and it will help to validate who they are."

—Ben Franklin Award judge

"As if being a freshman in high school isn't hard enough, Calle Smith has to endure a rootless life with a mother who can't seem to settle down in one town or with one guy. Told through a blend of prose, song lyrics, and musical references, *Songs* tells the story of a girl whose life resembles a random-shuffle playlist struggling to become comfortable in her own skin."

—*azTeen Magazine* Book Club selection

"Culbertson writes with great respect for teenagers. Her literary yet accessible prose is both thoughtful and entertaining, an engaging blend of humor and heartbreak. The book speaks not just to teenagers but also to their parents—to anyone who has been young and searching for their own soundtrack."

—Rebecca Kochenderfer, senior editor, Homeschool.com, coauthor of *Homeschooling for Success*

"In *Songs for a Teenage Nomad*, Kim Culbertson expertly captures the tumultuous adolescent experience."

—*Maui Time Weekly*

"Culbertson gives an independent voice to the teen genre."

—Tyler Midkiff, *Sedona Red Rock News*

FOR
PETER AND ANABELLA

Also by Kim Culbertson

Songs for a Teenage Nomad

All through his boyhood he had mused
upon that which he had so often thought
to be his destiny and when the moment
had come for him to obey the call he had
turned aside, obeying a wayward instinct.
—Stephen Dedalus

A Portrait of the Artist as a Young Man

before the envelopes

The costume barn wasn't much to look at. Just an old, rusting shed out behind the theater. Years ago, some realtor guy in town had donated it. Hauled it over on a flatbed trailer, depositing it to its final resting place. White paint peeled to gray on its exterior, its eight-by-ten-foot frame was starting to cave on one side, and the door never latched quite right, leaving a smile of an opening above the entrance.

But inside, it was a portal to endless worlds.

Jessa hurried toward it. Having just spent every afternoon last week organizing it with three other girls from the Drama Academy, she knew right where the hat was that Mr. Campbell had been asking about in class last period, the black felt derby that Kevin wanted to wear in a scene he was doing with Lizzie for class tomorrow. She'd just grab it for them so they could have a chance to rehearse with it. In fact, since her Community Club meeting was canceled, maybe she'd spend the extra hour giving them a few notes before heading to her SAT tutor at four-thirty.

Swinging the key chain around her finger, she clicked through the double doors that led out to where the barn squatted on a patch of black asphalt; it looked tired and worn in too much spring afternoon light. She could hear the baseball team practicing on the field out beyond the parking lot, that clean crack of the ball against the bat. It was warm for spring, the air full of cut grass and the easy tilt toward the break coming up the following week. Heading toward that smile of the barn's door, she could already feel the calm that greeted her every time she stepped through it onto the barn's spongy flooring.

Over the past few years, she had spent countless hours in the barn's shadowy rows of dresses, suits, capes, and robes. She melted into the chaotic order of the place—the velvety suits in the back, the Dr. Seuss hats resting atop wide, angled jackets from the musical version of *Horton Hears a Who!* they'd performed for the nearby elementary school last fall. Jessa would lose herself in the dusty air, the material bin oozing bolts of velvet, satin, denim, and a seemingly endless length of silver tulle. In the feathery light of the bare, swinging bulb, she would run her hands along the rack of satin pajamas they had all worn for *A Midsummer Night's Dream*, the gossamer fairy wings still attached to the backs.

The buzz that seemed always in Jessa's ears emptied during those hours, took refuge somewhere else, leaving her head clear and vast, a landscape for dreams or, better yet, for nothing at all. She could just let her mind empty, drain all those equations from chemistry, forget her horrible time at the last track meet, or ignore that stupid thesis statement she just couldn't get quite right for honors English. She just floated in the haze of the place, buoyed by the number of worlds around her waiting to explode onto a lit stage—each costume a possibility.

The barn held a log of her friends. The ice-blue dress Carissa wore for the Shakespeare festival where she won a gold medal. The gold-threaded tunic Hillary wore as Polonius. Christina's silver pajamas for Titania in *Midsummer*. And there was a whole rack of Sean, her boyfriend of nearly a year. The velvet Hamlet suit, the *Oliver!* knickers with the funny bows at the knees to keep them from gaping, the letterman jacket he wore in *The Breakfast Club*. He'd been in that Hamlet suit for their first kiss—stage left, behind the sway of a heavy, black curtain. When Jessa worked in the costume barn alone, she would run her eyes over all those costumes, reading the map of her high school days so far, knowing some of those empty, hanging clothes were just waiting to make new memories for her.

As she held the key out to the lock on the barn door, she frowned. It was open and dangling from its funny hinge. Stupid beginning drama class. Mr. Campbell shouldn't let them anywhere near the barn. She tucked the lock in her pocket and heaved open the door, inviting the cool whoosh of dusty air into her nose.

At first she thought a cat had crept into the barn again. That big, sweet tabby that had a habit of making a nest out of the poodle skirts and petticoats. She could hear him toward the back rustling around.

Jessa swore under her breath, hoping he hadn't turned the chiffon into a giant frayed mess. She swiped at the dangling cord for the light.

It wasn't the tabby.

There, on top of the *Oliver!* knickers box she had worked so hard to pack, Sean froze, his arms wrapped around Natalie Stone. It took Jessa only seconds to focus in on the red dress tangled haphazardly around their legs, binding them to one another. The dress she'd worn to play Kate in *The Taming of the Shrew*, the one they'd had to take the bust in on, the costume mistress with pins in her mouth, her eyebrows all scrunched up, sighing to Jessa, "I just have to take this in even more."

Jessa's eyes fastened themselves to that red dress mostly because she couldn't bring herself to keep looking directly at them. Like the sun. Or a blinding light from an alien spaceship. More like that.

Because what she was seeing could not in any version of Jessa's universe be happening to her. Sean twisted into some sort of human pretzel with Natalie Stone. Or as Carissa always called her, the Boob Job.

Jessa must have let out some sort of sound, some sort of small, injured animal sort of sound, because they untangled themselves at the same time, tripping over that dress, the fabric tearing.

The alien spaceship started landing on Jessa's dress-needs-to-be-taken-in chest.

"Jessa, wait…I," Sean stumbled, that dress tripping him up, for probably the first time he even realized he was tangled up in it. He frowned at it, kicking at the fabric, then caught his balance against the rack of suit jackets Jessa had spent an hour sorting by size and color. Green, taupe, gray, black, pinstriped. He leaned mostly into the pinstripes, the jaunty double-breasted section, the section with his Hamlet suit. With her breath coming in jagged bursts, Jessa's eyes pinballed around the now-mussed-up barn, lighting on the spilled box of shiny men's dress shoes, the overturned tub of ties, the box of bright feather boas spilling onto the neatly swept floor—what had they been doing in here?

"I thought you had Community Club today." Sean's voice rasped across what felt like miles but must have been only feet. She could have reached out and touched his arm.

"Canceled," Jessa said, her own voice sticky, thick, sounding like she'd swallowed cotton. Or maybe a red dress.

The cotton migrated to her ears, everything muffled, far away.

"Jessa, did you find that…" Mr. Campbell's voice trailed off as he stepped inside the barn behind her. "Oh."

The floor creaked beneath his weight. A breath of air from the open door fluttered a rack of druid gowns, empty ghosts shuttering in the stale air. Like sad angels.

No one said anything.

• • •

"What did you say to him?" Carissa's voice crackled into the phone. She must be out at the stables. Her phone got crap reception at the stables.

5

"Nothing." Jessa huddled on her bed, her clean laundry piled on top of her belly and legs, its clean, lemony scent a force field. She switched her phone to her other ear. *Les Mis* blared from her stereo, the music bathing her.

"Nothing?"

"Carissa, you don't understand what I'm saying. You should have seen them. I think I said 'canceled.'" Jessa watched a fly crawl across her weekly calendar board. Monday: "Community Club 3 pm—don't be late!" Her stomach turned. She pulled a folded pair of socks across her eyes.

"Canceled? Like your relationship?"

"No. He asked why I wasn't at Community Club."

Carissa blew a wind tunnel of a sigh into the phone. "That's so humiliating."

"I'm aware of the humiliation factor, thank you." Jessa sat up, laundry tumbling around her. She scribbled her blue dry-erase pen through "Community Club 3 pm—don't be late!" Then quickly scratched out "SAT tutor, track, chem study group." She hadn't gone to any of it.

"Turn off *Les Mis*." Even Carissa's voice could roll its eyes. "You're just making it worse. You don't need to spiral into some Éponine-On-My-Own-pity-pool."

"Supportive. Thanks." Jessa snatched a gray Williams Peak volleyball T-shirt from the pile on her legs. She rubbed the shirt across her white board, erasing most of Tuesday's activities along with the fateful Community Club. She paused at Wednesday: "Leave for Italy 9 pm bus!!!"

Carissa wind-tunneled again into the phone: "Don't be pissed at me. I wasn't kissing Sean in the costume barn. And I'm not continuing this conversation until you turn off the pity-palooza!"

Jessa clicked off her music, then threw her shirt at her laundry hamper. Missed. "Why are you being so bitchy? You're supposed to be consoling me right now. I can't believe I have to go ten days in Italy with both of them there. I wish you were going."

Silence on the other end.

"Carissa?"

"Yeah?"

"Oh, I thought the phone cut out or something." Jessa flicked a piece of hair from her eyes.

"So you're still going to go?" Carissa's voice sounded small, quiet.

"You think I shouldn't go?" Jessa rubbed her pulsing temple with her free hand.

"Do *you* really think you should go?" Carissa was feeding her horse. Jessa heard the crunching.

"Could you not feed Jumper right now? It's kind of obnoxious." Jessa studied her packing job—her clothes lined up in little piles on her dresser; her small tubes of shampoo, moisturizer, toothpaste all organized and ready to go into her suitcase. "No, I'm going. I don't care. He doesn't get to take Italy away from me too."

"Well, I have to baby-sit for the Jensens all week," Carissa reminded her. "To help pay off Santa Cruz."

"I know," Jessa sighed. "I just wish you were going."

"Sorry." Carissa was feeding Jumper again. The crunch, crunch, crunch of the carrots sounded like a trash compactor. "Jess, I gotta go. No *Les Mis*—I'm serious. It's hazardous to your general emotional health right now."

"Right." Jessa clicked off her phone and turned the music up well past the agreed-on limit her dad had notched onto the stereo knob with a Sharpie.

• • •

Panic attack. One minute Jessa was staring out the airplane window into the dawning sky and the next she was sweating, her chest squeezing against her sweater like it might implode and that bag of butter toffee peanuts would make an encore. The seat belt was splitting her in two. She had to get out of here. Had to get somewhere, anywhere but this seat. Staring at the back of their two stupid, lying, cheating heads. OK, his lying, cheating head and her stupid, over-dyed, bad-highlights head.

Jessa pulled her iPod earbuds out, cutting off Carol Burnett's "Shy" from *Once upon a Mattress* in mid-yowl, snapped open the buckle of her seat belt, and stumbled across a still-sleeping Tyler and down the aisle to the back of the morning-hushed plane.

Breathe.

She pushed her way into the bathroom, avoiding the mirror at all costs. She already looked like she had the stomach flu from crying so much and not eating right, and airplane mirrors just made her look all blue and washed out. Last thing she needed was a reflection like that right now, like a Smurf with the stomach flu.

What had she been thinking, getting on this plane? It wasn't so bad flying through the night, the eye mask firmly clamped across her tired eyes, but now, with the plane starting to wake up, with everyone starting to move and shift and the small plane windows letting in daylight, she couldn't believe she had actually thought this was a good idea.

She took another breath. Her dad would tell her to evaluate the situation. Very practical. Assess the scenario. Look at assets and obstacles. OK, good. Her breathing was normalizing. Scenario. Somewhere behind her, the sun would soon rise over her own little town in the northern California foothills. Her dad would head to the office. Her mom would tell her sister Maisy, sprawled in front of the Disney Channel eating Oat Swirls from Trader Joe's out of the box, to turn off the TV and put on her school shoes. And Jessa was here, suspended in blue sky, flying to Italy for spring break with fifteen other members of her Drama Academy. She'd wanted to go to Italy since she was six and had seen her grandmother's pictures of a trip to Florence. It had taken until junior year, but soon she'd land on Italian soil—well, after connecting in Washington, D.C., and then flying another eight hours. But it was still a good scenario.

OK, now assets: eight hundred dollars on a Visa card she'd earned from saving birthday money, baby-sitting, and filing at her dad's law office. A very cute new pair of jeans that fit exactly the way jeans should fit. Her iPod full of all her favorite Broadway musicals and as many songs as she could afford to download from the various *Glee* soundtracks. Her journal and a new black pen. And Tyler let her have the window seat, albeit after playing a rigorous game of rock-paper-scissors. Best three out of five. Still, the window seat. Actually, Tyler Santos sitting in the plane seat next to her was a huge asset; at least she had one ally on the trip. All good. All assets.

OK, obstacles. Two huge ones. Seats 12C and 12B. Sean and the Boob Job. How could he? And with *her?* The summer before their sophomore year, Natalie Stone had been flat as a board, not even training-bra material, and then suddenly at the start of tenth grade she showed up with a pair of Jessica Simpsons. Even the teachers stared. "I hit a growth spurt," she told Kara Jenkins during volleyball tryouts. More likely, she hit up a plastic surgeon.

Someone knocked on the door. "Excuse me?"

Jessa slid the door open and the heart-shaped face of the flight attendant appeared, her eyes heavy with taupe shadow. "Hey, honey, we're going to land in D.C. soon. You OK?" Her words sent a whoosh of spearmint gum into Jessa's face.

Jessa blinked back at her. "Not really."

"Can I do anything?" The attendant adjusted the collar of her crisp white shirt, and Jessa wondered briefly how the flight attendants stayed so pressed and polished when just sitting on an airplane put wrinkles into every inch of Jessa's own clothes.

"Can you make the guy in 12C not be a lying-jerk cheater?"

"I could drop a drink in his lap." She ushered Jessa out of the bathroom. Clearly, a line had been forming and that man in the Baltimore Ravens cap looked annoyed.

"Sorry," Jessa mumbled as she moved past him toward her row, noticing with some vague satisfaction that the line of passengers appeared just as wrinkled and wilted and red eyed as she felt. She paused in the aisle.

Tyler was sitting in her seat.

"No fair."

"Don't whine. I was just sitting here until you got back. Just think, only ten hours left." He slid back over into his middle seat, the buckles on his leather jacket jingling.

"Ugh." Jessa inched into her seat. "I'm not going to make it."

"But I have a gift."

Jessa noticed the large, bulky envelope in his lap. "What is it?"

"It's from Carissa, and it's nonnegotiable." He flipped his black hair out of his eyes. Probably on purpose since Tyler always seemed halfway committed to an Elvis impression. At least, before Elvis got fat and started wearing jumpsuits.

Jessa frowned. Tyler was using his stage manager voice—that mix of patience, attentiveness, and condescension that made Jessa feel both safe and three inches tall, like at any moment he would usher her in perfect time onto a lit stage or give her a graham cracker and a cup of apple juice. Right now felt like the latter.

Tyler patted the empty seat next to him. Condescending.

Jessa didn't budge.

"Come on. Sit down." He smiled at her, that smile he had that shot through his dark eyes and made his face gleam. Patient. Attentive.

Thing was, Tyler was a really good stage manager.

She sat.

#1: the polka-dot incident

Outside, the sky was losing the flashes of pink that had been streaking the sky.

"Open it." Tyler motioned to the envelope in Jessa's lap. "I think it will make your day."

"Promises, promises." She turned the package over. The front was labeled:

Top Twenty Reasons He's a Slimy Jerk Bastard:

Instructions for Getting Over

One Pathetic Excuse (Key Word Ex) of a Boyfriend

Jessa couldn't help but let a smile sneak out. Under the title it read:

Open it, Jessa!

She slid her finger under the half-sticky film of the opening, then peered inside. More than a dozen small white envelopes peered back.

"What is it?"

Tyler raised his eyebrows. "Instructions are in there."

Jessa dug through the sea of envelopes and extracted a piece of pale-blue binder paper covered in Carissa's neat print:

> This has an order—a method to my madness (see…I paid atten-
> tion, even if I didn't get the part I wanted in the stupid play)…
> anyway—digressing! The envelopes. They're numbered 1–20,
> enough to open two a day on your trip but the IMPORTANT
> thing is that you read and think about each reason and THEN
> do the instruction before moving on to the next envelope—no
> skipping ahead! Pinky swear with Tyler right now that you won't
> skip ahead! I'm waiting. Do it!

Jessa held her pinky up to Tyler. "Pinky swear I won't skip ahead." They locked pinkies and shook their hands three times.

> And make sure you save the last two envelopes for the plane ride
> home. Each envelope has a reason why he's a jerk and not worth
> the dirt on your shoes. And each one has an instruction, some-
> thing you have to do—NO CHEATING. Tyler knows he's to be
> ON TOP OF THIS! I'm doing this for your own good—you're
> in no state right now to argue. Ciao!—C.

"What a nut." Jessa folded the paper and handed it to Tyler.

He tucked it back into the package. "She thinks she's helping."

"No wonder she's getting a D in chemistry. She spends all her time doing stuff like this." But inside, Jessa felt the tight knot around her heart loosen a bit.

Tyler fished around in the package until he found the #1 envelope. He peeled it open and pulled out the thin sheet of paper.

Reason #1: The Polka-Dot Incident: Remember in third grade when Sean had that birthday party and his mom hired the clown and he punched the clown in the face because he was wearing polka dots instead of stripes and his mom cried? This is Sean Myer—a kid so disturbed, he has to punch a clown in the face and make his mom cry. You dodged a bullet, Ms. Gardner. A bullet! Who wants to be with a clown puncher who's mean to his mom?

Tyler started cracking up. "He punched a clown?"

Jessa rolled her eyes. "He was eight. And in Sean's defense, that clown had serious personal-space issues."

Tyler passed her the letter. "Says a nice thing about you."

At that same party, you hugged the clown and told him that polka dots were your favorite kind of clown outfit.

"I was eight. And polka dots *are* the best kind of clown outfit." But Jessa knew about that part of Sean that reacted when he didn't get what he wanted. Her eyes strayed past the rows of airplane seats. She could just make out the crown of his head, his dust-blond hair, see the edge of his elbow in its tan jacket on the armrest, one white curl of his iPod cord. What was he listening to? It better not be one of the mixes she made him. That was the problem with the digital age: she would never have the satisfaction of snapping any CDs she had made him in half. You can't snap in half an iTunes playlist.

"So are you going to do it?" Tyler studied the paper.

"Do what?"

"Your instruction." He motioned toward Carissa's letter.

"What is this—*Mission Impossible 5: The Teen Years?*"

"I'm sure she's starting you off easy."

The instruction for this one was easy. List five things she hated about him. She could list more, she was sure of it. Of course, she was suddenly struck dumb with images of all the good stuff. Sunday mornings at Ridge Café for breakfast and studying. That hair, those green eyes, the way he smelled like spice after a shower, the way he said he suffered from Jessaplexy—a known disease to cause serious shivers (OK, that one was totally lame and she made fun of him for it, but she secretly loved it)—the note in her locker each morning just to say "Morning!" because he had a zero period and she didn't. *Hate, hate, hate him,* she repeated over and over in her head.

"He doesn't like Broadway musicals." She looked at Tyler hopefully.

"Insensitive jerk. He's a disgrace to the entire world of theater."

"You don't really like Broadway musicals either, do you?"

"Not so much—no."

Jessa leaned her head against Tyler's shoulder, the black leather of his jacket cool against her skin, and listened to the hum of the airplane. Seriously, what had she been thinking coming on this trip?

• • •

Somewhere over the Atlantic Ocean, Tyler grabbed an edge of their drama teacher's sweatshirt as he headed down the aisle toward the bathroom. "I'll ask Mr. C."

Her teacher stopped and leaned against the side of the seats. "What's up?"

Mr. Campbell was in his second year as drama teacher at Williams Peak. Twenty-six and fresh out of an MFA program for playwriting. He was a great teacher, nimbly walking that hazy line between teacher and sweet big brother. Right now, he seemed sort of rumpled and tired, though planes seemed to have that effect on most people—except flight attendants.

"Do they have liquid soap in Italy?" Tyler blinked up at him.

"Is this for the book?" Mr. Campbell tugged absently at a string of his hooded sweatshirt. Tyler was always saying he would write a book: *Stupid Questions and Other Ways to Pass the Time.*

"Sure." Tyler hooked a thumb at her. "Little Miss Small-Town USA here doesn't think they have liquid soap in Italy."

"I'm just saying that liquid soap seems like an American construct, that's all." Jessa glanced at Tyler. "This is not book material."

"I think they probably do." Mr. Campbell smiled at them. "But it's not a stupid question."

"Diplomatic, Mr. C." Tyler flipped open a copy of *Rolling Stone*.

Mr. Campbell pointed out a band he liked to Tyler in the glossy pages of the magazine. Then he said, "I like that book you gave me, Jess."

"I just know how much you liked *The Bean Trees*," she started to explain, but then Sean shifted in his seat up ahead, leaned in toward Natalie, and suddenly any and all coherent thought vanished from her brain.

Mr. Campbell was smiling down at her, his brown hair sticking out the way it always did, but as he turned to follow her gaze, his smile dimmed. She remembered how he had come up behind her when she found Sean in the costume barn, had wrapped an arm like a blanket around her, led her back to the theater. He'd seen them, a jumble of limbs and bare skin. He knew. He knew where her head was right now, which was actually more than just a little embarrassing.

Jessa shook her head as if she could clear the image of Sean and Natalie like the Etch A Sketch app on her dad's iPhone. She tried to regain the thread of conversation with her teacher. "Anyway, the book has the Southwest plus it has all the acting stuff in it too." She'd given him a novel called *Catching Heaven*, a woman fleeing her acting life in LA for a small southwestern town, a woman fleeing herself.

Mr. Campbell ran a hand through his thick hair. "I think we can all relate to wanting to run from something," he said, fiddling again with the string of his sweatshirt hood, his eyes shadowed as they slipped back to Sean and Natalie.

Jessa didn't respond, couldn't seem to find her voice. The head shake hadn't worked. She couldn't get the image of Sean and Natalie out of her head. It sunspotted her, burned behind her eyes, and it took her a few minutes before she noticed that Mr. Campbell had wandered away back up the aisle.

• • •

Without warning, the sunspot was standing over her, and Jessa thought for a minute that she was having a nightmare, the one with the looming black shadow that struck her sometimes, left her shaking and sweating in the middle of the night.

This was something like that.

"Hey, Jess." Sean tucked his hands awkwardly in his pockets, two quiet tucks of guilt.

"Keep it moving, Sean. Nothing to see here." Tyler surprised Jessa with the growl in his voice.

"I was just going back to see Devon," Sean started, but something in Tyler's look must have stopped him. Jessa memorized the first half of the safety instructions poking out of the seat's back pocket.

"Yeah, well, I didn't want to just walk by and not say anything."

"Yeah, well, nobody's going to accuse you of good judgment." Tyler's hand settled on Jessa's shoulder.

She studied the long line of Sean's body out of the corner of her eye, his legs in his jeans fidgeting as if they weren't sure whether they were staying or going. *Going*, she willed them. *Going.*

Staying. Using muscles she was sure she grew yesterday, she forced her eyes to his face. And, of course, his mouth. She had kissed him for what would be the last time Sunday evening, a soft, quick afterthought of a kiss, before he got in the green Honda she'd named Frodo. They'd been studying, and she'd walked him outside. Such a silly nothing of a kiss. A sort of half kiss, half laugh because they'd been laughing at something. Something on the Funny or Die website. It made her smile a little even now, and he mistook it for an invitation.

"Jessa, I wanted to say…" he started, his hand finding a place on the seat rest behind her head.

Tyler saw the tears before she realized she had spilled them. "Sean…" he stood up, ducking a little to avoid the bag storage. "Just go. I don't think the flight attendants will like it when I punch you in the face."

"Five things," Jessa blurted, staring straight ahead, the words tumbling out. "You never wash your car. Your cologne smells like possum pee. You overcommit to all your lines, and it is so, so annoying—you think you're Marlon Brando in *On the Waterfront* and you're *not*. You don't like my dog, and you always pick Junior Mints at the movies when you know, you *know*, I like Raisinets." She turned, almost panting, to Tyler. "Is that it? Is that five?"

"Close enough," Tyler laughed, sinking back into his seat. Sean was already moving away down the aisle, other passengers' eyes slipping from him to her. "And I don't want to know how you know what possum pee smells like."

#2: the audition

Jessa blew a strand of hair from her eyes and surveyed the tiny hotel room. She rolled her suitcase across the cool blue-and-white tiled floor and hefted it onto one of the two small beds. She needed a shower. Where was the shower? Her mind churned with the drive from the airport, the way the light hit the stone and terra-cotta buildings, everything here warm and buttery. *Italy, Italy,* she had mouthed into the expanse of bus window, making tiny patches of steam on the glass. Julius Caesar, Michelangelo, Seneca, that guy that Russell Crowe played in *Gladiator.* Jessa had wanted to burst open the window and drink it all into her lungs. Now, outside the hotel window, framed in a gauze of pale curtain, a freeway buzzed and she caught a glimpse of a hazed linen sky just turning pink at the edges.

A rustle at the door turned her. Natalie "the Boob Job" Stone stood frozen there, a blue-jeaned statue, eyes locked on the white square of paper Ms. Jackson had handed out in the lobby. Jessa held her breath as she watched the other girl check the iron number affixed to the blue door and check her paper again. Natalie had taken off the sweatshirt she had on the plane and a white T-shirt strained across that chest. Jessa stared at the red lace of one peeking bra strap, then checked her own paper, her fingers starting to shake. Nine—underlined. Room nine—with the underline of death that made sure that girl standing three feet away hadn't flipped it by mistake, to make a six a nine.

Five hours might have passed. Or five seconds. Time had suddenly failed Jessa, crawled inside her eardrums, a hissing monster. She blinked again, started zipping and unzipping the outside zipper of her black suitcase. Black suitcase with a green slip of hair ribbon tied around the handle—Maisy's ribbon. Natalie's suitcase was red, of course. And still there. Still there in the doorway.

"Oooh, problematic." Tyler's head appeared over Natalie's shoulder. She recoiled as if burned, still clutching that stupid scrap of white. He laughed out loud. "You two are not rooming together—it's not that kind of show."

"I got nine?" Natalie had one of those voices that always seemed like it was asking a question. Always. Even if she was telling you something, she wasn't totally sure about it. It made improv scenes with her an absolute nightmare because she always seemed to be getting permission for the next beat.

"Come with me." Tyler grabbed Natalie's arm in one hand and her suitcase in his other, and steered her out of Jessa's throbbing sight line. Listening to their retreating steps, the roll of the red suitcase echoing away, she pressed her fingers against her eyelids, took a breath. The room smelled suddenly of mold, of old green things and wet paper. She needed a shower more than ever.

Then she noticed the showerhead on the wall. She squinted as if the light was wrong, as if there were not in fact a showerhead in the middle of the bedroom, and her eyes moved to the ring on the ceiling, to the bunch of curtain pulled into the wall. She was supposed to take a shower in the middle of her room? Her eyes went again to the tile floor, the curve of it toward a drain.

She fell backward onto the small bed.

• • •

Within minutes, Mr. Campbell was standing over her.

"Roommate trouble?"

She sat up. "Can't I just room with Tyler the whole time?"

Mr. Campbell sat down on the bed next to her. "Listen. I get why you can't room with Natalie. I mean, what are the odds of her pulling that number? Sick universe."

"Par for my week."

In the midst of what must have been a sympathetic glance, Mr. Campbell got caught in a yawn. "Sorry." He rubbed his eyes with the palms of his hands. "Here's the thing—one of the goals on this trip is to grow as a community. We want you guys to have different roommates so you don't clique up on us the whole time."

Jessa took a deep breath. Somehow, the thought that it was Italian air cycling through her lungs helped lift the weight a little. "I'm sorry. I'm really not trying to be a drama queen."

"You think I don't know a thing or two about drama queens?" He tried to catch her eye, coax a smile out of her.

A rustle at the door—Jade Evans stood there, her bright, multicolored, woven duffel over her shoulder. "I switched with Natalie." Her jangling earrings glinted in the late-afternoon light.

The weight lifted entirely. Jade had that calming Earth Mother effect, with her wide, dewy face and thick curls, her mood-ring eyes that shifted between hazel and green and brown. Being around Jade was always a bit like being glazed with fairy dust.

Mr. Campbell moved toward the door. "Thanks, J." He patted Jade's shoulder on his way out. "Dinner's in an hour. Meet us in the lobby."

• • •

Jessa reread the text on her phone from Carissa and then checked the slip of paper again. She gazed out over the red rooftops, watched the far dot of a man walk the smaller dot of a white dog along a riverbank on the other side of the whirling freeway. Tyler had somehow gotten a balcony with his room. She got a showerhead.

"I can't get this SIM card to work." Tyler frowned at his phone. "What'd she say?"

"Still blaming Sean for not getting to play Hamlet last spring."

She passed him Reason #2, her eyes still following the man and his dog:

> He STOLE my part! Do I need to say it again!? STOLE IT! What kind of jerk docs that?

Tyler read it as he bit the end off a Snickers bar. "That play was already a nightmare to manage—would have been a train wreck with Carissa in the lead." He pretended to strangle himself. "Still, rumor has it he jacked her monologue."

Jessa frowned. "It was not Sean's fault he got cast as Hamlet over Carissa. It wasn't the direction Mr. Campbell was taking the play. It has nothing to do with them doing the same monologue."

"But he knew she was doing that one. Dubious." Tyler picked a piece of chocolate and caramel from the end of the wrapper.

"Thanks for offering me a bite by the way." Jessa grabbed the envelope back from him.

He held the last blob of candy out to her. "They didn't have any gummy bears at the airport."

Ignoring him, Jessa reread her instruction in Carissa's purple pen. "She wants me to write a fake audition character description. About Sean and his sly, manipulative ways." A few weeks before auditions, Mr. Campbell would tack up rows of multi-colored index cards outside his office with descriptions of each character in the play, so they would know who to audition for.

"What ways?" Tyler tossed the wrapper in a garbage can and wiped his sticky fingers on his jeans.

Jessa held the phone out for him to see. She had asked Carissa the same thing. The text read:

U know! Dont ask again

Tyler gave her a funny look. "The audition?"

Jessa nodded.

He sat up in his chair. "It's true?"

Jessa tucked the paper back into the envelope, avoiding Tyler's dark eyes. "It's true."

• • •

For dinner, they dragged their jet-lagged bodies toward a small restaurant near the hotel. Tomorrow, they would start their tour of Rome, and Jessa felt it simmering under her skin, like roiling water. They would see the Forum and the Sistine Chapel, something extra special because they were being granted a tour on Good Friday. She could stare up at Michelangelo's arched ceiling and suck in all that history through her pores—all the people who were there before, and she could breathe into the people who would come after her.

Tyler walked slowly beside her, staring into shop windows. She had told him about the audition, about how Sean had switched his lineup ticket with Carissa so he could go before her, how he'd swiped it right off the metal seat where she'd left it to go talk to Christina about costume ideas, since she was helping Christina with costumes. He'd been twelfth and she'd been fifth, and he switched them. His sly, manipulative ways. Jessa sure related to that stupid twelfth ticket, left on a metal chair for a newer option.

Tyler held the door of the restaurant open for Devon and Jade, and then he and Jessa stepped in behind them. The restaurant was candlelit and smoky, with a few burning wall sconces. Tables sat snugly together in the main room, and they settled into chairs near a fireplace, a low flame going. The stone walls of the room made Jessa think of fantasy novels or Shakespeare. Small prints hung here and there, line drawings of Rome, a few watercolors of buildings she didn't recognize. Several other patrons dined quietly, a salty, low buzz of Italian all around. She watched her friends find seats, giddy with sleep deprivation and excitement, chatting, clutching menus. Hillary pulled out her Italian dictionary and was translating back and forth for Devon and Tim.

"What an idiot," Tyler finally said, scanning his menu.

"Well, yeah." Jessa's eyes fell on the penne all'arrabbiata. Yum.

"He switched the order?"

Jessa shushed him.

He just shook his head. "And you're mourning this guy?"

"It was humiliating, Tyler." Jessa said, studying Sean, who was cuddling with Natalie at a corner table. "It still is." Jerk. Jerk. Jerk.

Tyler snapped his menu shut and leaned across the white-clothed table. "I get that. I do, Jess. But he's done some seriously bonehead things. Not at the top of the list, switching his audition order so he was the first to do that Hamlet monologue, and, I mean…" His eyes strayed across the room. "Natalie? She's nice and all, but she's kind of like a Barbie with a speech impediment."

That got a hiccup of laughter out of Jessa. "You should design T-shirts."

He settled back in his chair, scanned the cover of the menu. "Not to be a dick, but he really traded down."

"Thanks, Ty." Then she was suddenly sick again, watching them there at that table, her eyes feeling like they'd been rubbed with sand. Breakups were hard enough without having your own personal reality TV show in front of you just days after you found your boyfriend half naked in a costume barn with the Barbie in question. Not that Natalie wasn't a nice-enough girl. She was. Until Monday, she really hadn't been much on Jessa's radar. Carissa couldn't stand her, but Carissa couldn't stand a lot of people. Still, how nice of a girl steals someone's boyfriend?

Jessa pushed back away from the table and found her two teachers sitting a few tables away. "Ms. Jackson?"

"Yeah?" Ms. Jackson placed her hand on Jessa's arm, almost instinctively, to keep her from fleeing. She must have that look in her eyes. Like prey.

Jessa cleared her throat, tried for a light, clear voice. "Can I go back to the hotel, please?"

Mr. Campbell sighed, his face slipping a bit. He glanced at Ms. Jackson and then back to Jessa. "I'm sorry, Jess. We all need to stick together."

Tears welled in Jessa's eyes.

"You know what?" Ms. Jackson stood. "I'll walk you back to the hotel." She pointed to her menu. "Ben, order me anything that doesn't have lamb."

• • •

The air had grown cool and a light wind rustled the leaves in the trees lining the narrow street. Jessa pulled her denim jacket close to her and glanced sideways at Ms. Jackson. She'd had Ms. Jackson for English for the past two years and couldn't actually remember standing this close to her before. She was a terrific teacher, maybe thirty, knife-blade sharp, always calm, and she came up with interesting projects for the English section of their drama academy, always talking about feminist theory or literary symbolism, and totally into the students' insights about what they read. She was polished—bohemian meets Banana Republic clothes—and her short blonde hair seemed always in place, her black-rimmed reading glasses perched on her head or dangling from a beaded chain. Still, there was a coolness to her, something distant in her, not at all like the warm big-brother light Mr. Campbell pooled onto them. The air between them now seemed tight and strange.

"Thank you for walking me, Ms. Jackson." Jessa wiped at a stray tear.

Ms. Jackson seemed to be weighing something, hesitating. Finally, she said, "It was brave of you to come, Jessa. No one imagines for a moment that this is easy for you."

Jessa started to tell her it was fine, that she had saved for ten months for the trip and that no stupid, cheating boy was going to keep her from the experience of a lifetime—and besides this was going to look really good on her college applications—but she stopped. She stopped on the street and looked at her teacher, felt a melting in the air between them. "I don't think I can do this."

Ms. Jackson's smooth brow furrowed, and Jessa immediately regretted her words, wished she could just stuff them right back into her mouth like a big chunk of bread.

"Yes, you can." Ms. Jackson's usually muted eyes glittered. "You can. But you can't half ass it."

"What?" Jessa took a step back, her eyes finding the hem of her jacket.

"Jessa. You know how Mr. Campbell talks to you guys about auditioning?"

"Yeah?"

"How you start your audition the second you walk in the door, the second you take your seat. Not just when you get on stage?"

Jessa nodded.

"Think of this like that."

This was one of those things English teachers did when they wanted you to find the deeper meaning, when they wanted you to seek out the metaphor. Jessa was missing the metaphor.

"I think I'm missing the metaphor."

Ms. Jackson laughed, a deep, surprised laugh she sometimes got when one of her students said something unexpectedly funny in class. "No, honey, you're not. This is about impressions. How you're seen. You don't want him to see you moping around, leaving restaurants and sulking. You want him to see you having a blast, living it up, not needing him. Don't come all this way and then blow your monologue. Now there's a metaphor."

Jessa thought about Carissa's audition for *Hamlet*, her meltdown when Sean switched their lineup tickets and then marched on stage with his "O, what a rogue and peasant slave am I!" What a rogue? For sure. But Carissa had flipped and then sulked her way through the rest of auditions. She had blown her audition before she got on stage.

The street darkened, tiny bits of lamplight pooling from the windows of restaurants and bars, the haze of evening settling over the city, this city she had come so far to see.

"You know what, Ms. Jackson? They had some pretty good-looking pasta on that menu."

"Good girl."

. . .

The next morning, Jessa sat cross-legged on the smooth floor inside the belly of the Pantheon. She still couldn't believe she'd walked through those massive gray columns and into the heart of this ancient temple, the huge dome above her head with its bright, light-spilling eye. She breathed in the cool air, tried to close up her ears as if they had eyelids. For a quick moment, she thought about her iPod—she craved *Rent*. How perfect would "Seasons of Love" sound right now? But she didn't want to drown out the sounds of Rome around her completely. She was sitting in the temple of the gods, this great sweeping place where all the people in their tourist shorts and swinging cameras seemed out of place, seemed like they should be wearing togas or draping gowns laced with ivy. No, an iPod would just be tacky. Looking up, she followed the smooth marble walls peppered with Latin rising around her, her eyes sliding across the high ceiling, the dome lit with sky. She willed away the sounds of all the tourists around her. She began to sing under her breath about all those thousands of minutes that made up a year. The gods probably sang, right? Even if they didn't sing Jonathan Larson.

She rubbed her eyes—so tired. Stupid Tyler and his stupid rock-paper-scissors he made her play to see whether or not she'd write Carissa's character description. He knew Jessa had made a personal commitment to never turn down a legitimate RPS request. No fair. And she had lost—paper to Tyler's scissors. So she'd stayed up and written it, surprised it had taken so long.

The first draft was just too mean; the next rewrite wasn't mean enough, wasn't close to accurate. But Jessa had spent a good deal of her relationship with Sean defending him. It was a hard habit to break. Finally, she'd landed on it. She sent it to Carissa at breakfast after a pretty lengthy argument with Tyler to include "dresses like an Aberzombie":

Audition for World's Suckiest Boyfriend

Name: Sean Myers, age 16. Tall, good at sports, good looking but not in an obvious sort of way

Character traits: Charming, big ego that he covers with afore-mentioned charm, CHEATER, only half listens when someone talks, selfish, eats too fast, gets what he wants, likes pizza a little too much, average student, great soccer player, decent writer when he tries, demanding, flashes of romantic behavior (can make up for all bad behavior above), dresses like an Aberzombie (Tyler's contribution)

Now, watching Sean and Natalie holding hands several yards away, both peering up at that great eye in the ceiling, she wished she had sent the meaner one—the one that called him an ass-kissing mediocre bastard. Her eyes welling up, she sang softly to herself, something Sean used to love about her, her Julie Andrews instinct he'd called it. "Seasons of Love"—all those minutes that made up a year, all those moments.

A year—almost a year ago, she was kissing Sean in the faint backstage lights of *Hamlet*, swathed in her Ophelia costume, that incandescent, cascading dress she had thought about borrowing to wear to prom. Now she was sitting in the temple of the gods watching Sean nuzzle Natalie's ear, rubbing his hand up and down her narrow back. She jerked her eyes away. It would suck to puke in the temple of the gods.

She searched the room for Tyler. No sign of him. Mr. Campbell stood near the entrance, checking his watch. They were waiting for the other school to arrive with the tour guide. Because Williams Peak had such a small group, only eighteen including Mr. Campbell and Ms. Jackson, they had to partner with another school for the trip to share all the tours, bus trips, and hotels.

"Don't worry," Mr. Campbell had assured them the night before, right before lights out. "We told them we're a theater program. I'm sure they'll find us a good match."

There was commotion at the entrance. A pack of teenagers stomped their way in, talking loudly, pushing and jostling one another. Jessa counted the swarm, twenty or so students. Two men, probably teachers, were with them, both wearing versions of the kind of shirts you buy in travel magazines, the kind that say they don't wrinkle.

"Oh my God," Jessa heard a girl in huge black sunglasses say. "It's so filthy." The girl planted her hands squarely on the hips of her designer jeans. She was very blonde, a polished chrome-bumper of a girl—all gleaming and photo-shoot ready. "Gross." Sniffing, she checked her pink BlackBerry.

A shorter redhead in skinny ankle jeans next to her nodded and snapped a picture with an expensive-looking digital camera. "Twenty bucks." She snapped another picture. The heels of her shoes looked like ice picks.

"Your dad is such an idiot." The blonde was now checking the skin beneath her eyes in a sleek, glittery compact. "I can't believe you get twenty bucks a picture."

"I know, right?" The redhead had a laugh like a howler monkey. "But only if it's 'culturally relevant'—whatever the hell that means."

"It means 'old.'" The boy who had sidled up suddenly, winding his arm around the blonde, was over six feet, with dark creamy skin. He put his free hand in the low pocket of his baggy pants. "And he's only doing it to make sure you actually look at some of this junk and not just abuse the discos." The redhead swatted at him, then stood on tiptoe to plant a kiss on his mouth.

"Oh my God, Madison. You're such a slut!" The blonde snapped the compact shut and tucked it away in a small gold bag.

Jessa frowned at Tyler as he settled in next to her. "Oh goody," he said, pulling the hood of his black sweatshirt over his head. "Our traveling partners."

Then the frog appeared.

At first, Jessa thought she was imagining something or that she saw someone's silly hat, or maybe even some sort of sign for a nearby restaurant. Then, as it closed in on them, bobbing over the heads of tourists, she realized it was a plastic frog on a stick.

#3: dead dog

"Buongiorno, I miei amici!" Their tour guide, Francesca, blinked out at them with bright eyes much like the frog's she was toting on the stick they were supposed to follow. Standing outside on the shallow steps of the Pantheon, dwarfed by a massive column behind her, she assembled the group. Jessa studied Francesca's wide, cropped linen trousers and the charcoal cape that seemed a nod to the togas on so many of the statues that dotted the city landscape like secret service agents. Her outfit had no right angles, all sweeps and folds. Her hair seemed its own creature, something wild and reddish brown and curly; its tendrils down her back, draping her shoulders, swept back away from her wide O of a face. Her looks were exaggerated and windswept, strikingly beautiful.

The two men from the other group had noticed immediately.

The taller man quickly positioned himself close to her, watching her, her every word the key to something he couldn't quite open. He was six feet tall but shorter somehow, as if the world's hands constantly pressed his shoulders into downward slopes. Close-cut hair, not blond or brown, a travel shirt with flaps and pockets and on the sleeve some sort of buckle. Probably a history teacher, or earth science.

Francesca surveyed the group. "Are we missing some?"

"Um, Francesca?" The man with sloping shoulders laughed nervously. "My wife and a couple of our students went to do a bit of shopping. Hope that's OK. Not holding us up?" He had a mustache that Jessa hadn't noticed at first, a mess of straw beneath his nose that looked like something Carissa might feed Jumper for a snack.

Francesca frowned, adjusted her cape. "Certainly, certainly." She checked some papers she had fastened to a clipboard with a large jeweled clip. "Actually, no. You must fetch them. We have to meet the bus."

The shoulders slouched off in the direction of the boutique shops across the way.

A low murmur arose from the group, side whispers that were suddenly allowed to grow and shift. Jessa spotted the blonde girl with the BlackBerry snapping her gum. The redhead snapped a picture of her snapping her gum and got a manicured middle finger as a reply.

Francesca spoke suddenly into a cell phone in fast Italian. Mr. Campbell and Ms. Jackson pulled the Williams Peak group over to a nearby fountain to wait for the wayward members of the other school.

Tyler sat on the ground next to Mr. Campbell, reading a

packet of what looked like stapled-together index cards. As Jessa crouched down next to him, he shoved them into the inside pocket of his jacket.

"What was that?"

"Nothing. Travel stuff." Tyler cleared his throat and nudged Mr. Campbell. "OK, so this is dubious." Tyler's new favorite word— lately, everything mildly annoying or suspicious was dubious.

Mr. Campbell slipped on a pair of sunglasses. "Come on, it's not that bad."

Tyler flipped his hood off. "Correction. It wasn't that bad until the whole cast of *The Hills* showed up."

"Be nice." But Mr. Campbell was smiling.

Jessa longed to go park herself at one of the small café tables lining the plaza, sip an espresso, and read a book. But instead, they waited. Tim attempted handstands and Devon tried to knock him over without stepping on the pigeons. Jade sang quietly, strumming her travel guitar.

"How do you say 'bored' in Italian?" Tyler asked.

Jessa brushed some hair from her eyes.

Mr. Campbell motioned to the inside of her left wrist, the long iridescent skinny trail of a scar. "Where'd you get that?"

Jessa laughed, pulled her cuff up. "Didn't you know? I'm Harry Potter's crazy half sister."

Chuckling, Mr. Campbell pushed on the nose of his sunglasses as if they didn't quite fit and went back to studying the whole group. Jessa used the tiny pocket of time to fish her iPod out of her sweatshirt pocket and plug herself in. She found *Les Mis* and started from the beginning.

Tyler peeked at her screen, reached over, and clicked it off.

"Hey!"

"Carissa's orders." He handed Jessa a white gummy bear, her favorite.

A moment later, Francesca ushered them back into a pack, the frog a bobbing, floating thing.

"Come on, Éponine," Tyler said, pulling her to her feet.

The shoppers returned, their arms full of shiny bags. They wore cropped jackets and strappy heeled sandals, designer denim, and round, smoky sunglasses. Jessa frowned. The whole lot of them looked lacquered, shiny, and windproof. Jessa stared down at her Chaco sandals and tan shorts that might as well have a neon sign reading "Tourist" on them.

Francesca snapped her phone shut. "Yes, yes—we are all here? Follow the frog!"

• • •

Reason #3: Remember when we found that dead dog? Someone had hit it on your road, and Sean was all pissed that you wanted to wait until animal control got there. Told you we'd waited long enough, that we had to get going. I know you hate it when I bring up the dead-dog story. But it's a solid reason. Had to bring it up.

Jessa showed Tyler Reason #3 as they made their way toward the Roman Forum. She shivered. Every once in a while, she'd still dream about that dog. He wasn't too old, no gray in his muzzle, black and mutt looking in a little crumple by the side of the road. At first, they thought he was sleeping there in the dirt shoulder, the sky above them aglow in sunset wash. But he wasn't sleeping.

Tyler popped open another bag of gummy bears he'd picked up at a kiosk and ate a handful. "I don't know the dead-dog story."

"It's so gross that you eat them all together. They're different flavors."

"Grosser than a dead dog?" He shrugged, holding the bag out to her.

Jessa frowned at him but selected a white gummy bear. She told him the story. They'd been walking to get ice cream from the market at the bottom of Jessa's long road. Found the dog there. Carissa called animal control immediately. Bless the iPhone of all knowledge. Jessa stood there, tears wetting her face. Somehow, she couldn't peel her eyes from his strange parenthesis of a body, its little arc, his head tucked beneath one leg. There wasn't even any blood. Sean had kept tugging at her sleeve. "Let's go," he'd said. "The store closes at six. We've been here long enough." But Jessa hadn't wanted ice cream anymore.

"Did you read the instruction?" Tyler asked.

Instruction: "Long enough." I personally think you put up with his crap for long enough. But what does "long enough" mean to you? Write a poem and read it out loud. Not just to Tyler.

"She wants me to write about what it *means?*"

"Like your interpretation of that phrase." Tyler chewed another handful of bears.

"Helpful."

"You know, that kind of self-reflection, self-aware stuff you're always trying to avoid doing unless it's for some scholarship you're applying for." He rattled the bag to dislodge the ones clinging for their lives to the sides.

"I don't try to avoid self-reflection."

"OK."

Jessa watched people hurrying by her on the street. She made her face all dreamy. "Long. Enough. What does it mean? See, this is me…reflecting."

"Impressive."

"What does it mean to me?" she mumbled again. But the landscape around her took over, invaded her mind. All the color and age of the place. What must it be like to have all this history around all the time? To wake up to a view of the Pantheon outside your apartment window each morning, to walk by St. Peter's on the way to work? Jessa stared at the McDonald's sign looming next to a crumbling column. Weird. Tyler stayed silent beside her.

When they came to a stop outside the Forum, Francesca dove into a discussion about Julius Caesar, his orations, his betrayal, his cremation. Jessa couldn't believe the crazy, open beauty of the Forum, its deteriorating sprawl—the columns shooting up from green ground, the crumbled stone, the way the remaining skeleton of the place stood out against the cloudy sky. Francesca walked them down into the ruins, and Jessa felt herself descending into history. They stood silently near the place where Mark Antony held Caesar before he was cremated.

"Interestingly," Francesca told them, her arms poised like a conductor, "the group of senators who assassinated Caesar on the Ides of March wanted to bring a sense of normalcy back to the republic, but their betrayal really lead to another Roman civil war." She clucked her tongue and stared out at them, dropped her arms to her sides. "Any questions?"

No one had questions. A girl from the other group in a Stanford sweatshirt yawned loudly.

Holding back what appeared to be a sigh but could have been a yawn of her own, Francesca released them. The frog on a stick took a break, propped against stone and grass. The group spread out to wander the Forum, to run their hands over its ancient remains. Jessa pressed her face into a slab of white, breathing in the cold dirt smell of it. She pulled her earbuds out of her jacket and started to put them in her ears.

"Et tu, Brute?" Mr. Campbell motioned at her ears.

She stuffed them back in her pocket. "What?"

"I'm just teasing you. It's not like my generation's any better with our constant need for a soundtrack."

Jessa felt her face grow hot. "I don't *need* it."

"OK, I'm just teasing you." Mr. Campbell motioned to the grounds. "So what do you think?"

She hesitated, stuffing her iPod back into her pocket. "It's pretty amazing."

"And?"

"Old."

He laughed and put his hands in his pockets, his eyes sweeping the angles and shadows of the place. "Yeah. It's amazing to think of all these people who walk around every day with their world grown from all these ruins, you know?"

"Makes me feel small." Jessa pulled her jacket closer. Across the Forum, Sean and Natalie groped each other with little notice of the couple trying to take a picture of the historic spot the two of them were currently disrespecting.

Mr. Campbell nodded, still staring out over the grounds. He frowned as his eyes fell on the gropers. "Tomorrow, and tomorrow, and tomorrow… Life's but a walking shadow, a poor player, that struts and frets his hour upon the stage, and then is heard no more. It is a tale told by an idiot, full of sound and fury, signifying nothing."

"Is that from *Julius Caesar?*"

"*Macbeth.*"

"It's kind of depressing."

"Yes it is." He shook his head, as if trying to pop himself from a trance.

"Can I ask you a question, Mr. Campbell?"

"Shoot."

"Why didn't Katie come?"

His eyes grew sad. Jessa had never noticed before how dark they were. His eyes, all milk- and dark-chocolate swirls. He cleared his throat. "Katie and I broke up. Last month."

Jessa kicked at a small tuft of grass at her feet. "Oh, I'm sorry. I didn't know that." The first time Jessa met Katie had been at the dress rehearsal of *The Breakfast Club*. Jessa had been a freshman, co-stage managing the show with Tyler. Katie brought them pizza, taking a break from the dissertation research she had just started. She had been studying something with sociology, something about the way girls group themselves. She told Jessa about it over a slice of pepperoni pizza, her short, dark hair lifting with each passionate statement. She came to every play Mr. Campbell directed, and always brought him flowers and a metal thermos of coffee, but she usually left at intermission.

A breeze picked up through the Forum. Jessa shuddered. Each breeze here seemed to carry spirits of the ancients prodding her with their wise, skeletal fingers. "Are you OK?"

Mr. Campbell swallowed, his hesitation lowering like a curtain. Then his eyes settled on her. "Not really."

. . .

Waiting in line for the Sistine Chapel viewing, Jessa tried not to roll her eyes at the woman from the other group, but seriously, could one person really ask so many stupid questions in one hour? Earlier, they had climbed their way out of the Forum and headed to the Piazza Navona for lunch. Over cannelloni with spinach and ricotta, they watched a mime perform near Bernini's sculpted fountain, where the light and water played like imps. The woman had wondered loudly, waving her arm for Francesca's attention, why there was a clown. Why was he dressed like that? Why were there so many pigeons? Jessa had tried to tune her out, but her voice had that high, nasal quality, like her Aunt Sally's, that could somehow break through all other sound to become the only noise in the room.

At the café table next to Jessa, an Italian couple had shared a cigarette over tiny cups of espresso, kissing and laughing, their ankles laced together beneath the table. It pressed in on her senses, picked at her eyelids, stuffed itself in her ears—the whole damn country in love. She couldn't look anywhere without seeing some couple kissing or groping or pressed in a desperate embrace. Even a huge *straciatella* gelato did nothing to help, and now she just had a stomachache.

Finally, she'd written Carissa's poem. Not because she thought it would help or because she had any idea what "long enough" could possibly mean, but because at least it would distract her

from the love fest all around her. She'd written it quickly—
without rereading, pressing the ink onto the pages—before
burying the journal deep in the bottom of her bag.

Now she forced her attention back to Francesca, her lecture
on the history of St. Peter's, and the absurd woman from the
other group, who Jessa suddenly realized looked an awful lot
like a trendy, modernized version of Cruella De Vil, without the
white streak in her hair.

"Why are they all so busy? Why are there so many people?"
Cruella waved a manicured hand toward where the men reorga-
nized palm fronds and candles.

"It is Good Friday," Francesca patiently explained. Again.

Jessa leaned into Tyler. "That woman could provide all the
content for your stupid-question book. Seriously, you need no
other sources."

Tyler shook his head, his eyes never leaving Cruella. "Dubious.
I mean, do you think she knows she sounds like that?"

Shrugging, Jessa stifled a yawn, her eyes scanning the group.
Everyone was starting to wilt around the edges, sag like flowers
left too long without water. Christina and Rachel were texting on
their phones. Maya's head bobbed along to the unheard music
on her iPod. Erika whispered to Blake quietly behind her hand,
probably filling him in on all the details Francesca was leaving
out, all the gory history details, probably secret beheadings
and such. Erika was always grossing them all out with all her

horror-history trivia. Jessa yawned again, resisting the urge to plug herself into *Spring Awakening* and drown out all else. Then she suddenly realized how inappropriate it would be to listen to *Spring Awakening* on sacred ground—she'd probably be struck by a bolt of lightning. She tuned back into the guide. Francesca was managing to work in some interesting stuff around all of Cruella's stupid questions.

One boy from the other group, dressed in a Tim Burton sweatshirt and standing a bit off by himself, caught Jessa's eye and raised his eyebrows. He made a little talk-talk-talk sign with his hands, a little Cruella shadow puppet, and then pretended to strangle it. Jessa suppressed a giggle.

Fifteen minutes later, they waited on the cusp of the chapel's entrance. Ms. Jackson made sure the girls had their shoulders covered and that all hats were stashed in back pockets and bags.

"No pictures, guys." Ms. Jackson motioned at Devon and Tim. "That means your camera phones too. And no talking." She shot a look at a giggling Rachel and Lizzie, and the girls clapped hands over their mouths. "This is a pretty special thing, to view this place on a holiday like this one. Act like it, please."

"Um, why can't we take pictures?" Cruella again. Tyler widened his eyes and made a low gagging noise. Francesca explained about the delicate artwork, the respect for the space. Cruella adjusted the huge sunglasses atop her head, then parked her hands on her hips over the two twists of gold cord she wore wound around her waist. Belts? A noose should she need one? Jessa wasn't sure.

"They shouldn't show it to us if we can't take pictures of it." Her voice rang out over their heads like a living, breathing thing of its own, a specter.

Jessa felt her group shift, send out a bubble of space between them and the other school. Tim whispered something to Devon, who started to laugh.

Cruella's eyes swiveled his direction. "Is something funny?"

Silence from Tim and Devon, eyes on the floor.

Cruella's eyes narrowed. She waited.

Drop it. Drop it. Jessa waited for her teachers to say something. Mr. Campbell glanced at Ms. Jackson, who was chewing her lip. Jessa watched Cruella from under her lashes.

"Ready, please." Saved by the frog. Francesca waved the students one by one into the chapel, the frog giving a quick little nod on the end of the stick each time one passed. Mr. Campbell shook his head at Tim, who shrugged, sheepish, and then Jessa stepped inside.

• • •

The flayed skin on the mural followed Jessa with its hollowed out eyes. The Sistine Chapel was actually much smaller than she'd thought it would be—dramatic and haunting but smaller. She couldn't seem to escape that image of the flayed skin. Turning her back on it, she scanned the pages of her Italy book, tried to look somewhere else, at the South Wall with its crossing of the Red Sea, the ceiling arching with the events of man before Christ. The North Wall, the temptations of Christ in broad, rich colors. Michelangelo had painted his soul into these walls with each brushstroke; the emotion, the vision, seeped through them, permeated the air. The silence. Around her, coats rustled against each other; shoes shushed along the floor. Somewhere a guard said, "Shhh," though Jessa hadn't heard anyone say anything.

She could feel the skin watching her. Her eyes slipped back to it.

Behind the altar, Michelangelo had painted *The Last Judgment*. Francesca had said the work showcased his maturity, as he'd been in his sixties when he finished it. Jessa's eyes fell on the powerful central figure of Christ, one hand allowing the rising figures to ascend, the other keeping those souls down who would not rise. Two times Michelangelo's self-portrait appeared in the Sistine Chapel. Once in a small figure watching the souls try to rise from the grave, and the other in the flayed skin that St. Bartholomew held like a sack of dirty laundry, a screaming sack.

Jessa felt suddenly cold, felt the grip of the saint at her neck, stripped of bone, peeled from ligament and tissue, left an empty, gaping thing. Sweat collected on her upper lip. There were too many people pressing in all around her. She hurried toward an exit.

Outside, a breeze caught her, cooled her. The sky had gone gray with rain clouds, casting the world into a cool, blue light, and making the sweeping stone of St. Peter's look like weathered bone.

It had been raining the night of her first fight with Sean.

One of those strange late-April rains that hit suddenly and soaked through your clothes. They had been waiting outside the movie theater, waiting for Carissa and her flavor-of-the-week boyfriend to show up so they could choose a movie.

Sean had gotten mad at her because of the end of the year fund-raiser Scene and Be Seen. She and Carissa wanted to do a scene from *The Women,* but he wanted her to do a scene with him from *A Streetcar Named Desire.* She would suck as Blanche, and she didn't want to do it, but he really, really wanted to play Stanley. Mostly, he wanted to scream a lot so people would think he was an amazing actor. Jessa said as much—huge fight.

The poor guy in the box office hid behind a copy of *The Hunt for Red October.* By the time Carissa called and said they weren't coming, Jessa was already heading off down the street, calling her mom for a ride home.

When she turned at the corner, waiting for her mom to pick up, she had seen Sean duck under the shelter of the theater. He had seen the movie anyway.

• • •

Tyler found her standing alone outside of the chapel in the looming shadow of St. Peter's. "Where did you go?"

She pulled her hair from her neck, her pulse returning to a steady rippled river through her body. "I was having a religious moment or something."

"Well, this is the place for it." He looted his jacket pocket for a half empty bag of bears.

Jessa wrinkled her nose. "More gummy bears? Isn't this your third bag today?"

"Enough stalling. Read your poem." He chewed a huge gob of them. "I saw you writing it at lunch."

Jessa imagined all the little gummy-bear bodies colliding, all their colors mixing, churning in his teeth. She blinked in the strange light. Tyler picked a green fleck of bear from his teeth. Jessa declined the open bag he held out to her.

"You want me to read it here?" Jessa shivered a bit in her denim jacket, eyeing the spill of tourists from the chapel.

"Why not? You going to offend the pope or something?" Two elderly Italian women passed by in their Good Friday fine dresses, their pinched faces frowning under their kerchiefs. Tyler lowered his voice. "Come on." He shook the bag of bears at her. "Carissa said you would stall. Don't let Carissa be right about anything. You know how she gets."

"OK." Jessa pulled Tyler to a nearby bench, dug through her bag for her journal. She took a breath. "It's called 'Rock, Paper, Scissors.'"

Tyler made a face. "Very funny. But I made you play that game for the audition description, not this one."

"I knew you'd appreciate the reference." Jessa took a breath, then read her poem into the still, rain-scented air:

With you, I am paper, wrapped around, folded, creased,
left cut with your slices. You are rock and scissors—hard
and sharp. You are the metal blades and blue plastic handles
of my childhood craft bin scissors. You are the smooth river rock
I'm collecting and losing in that same sunlit day where the sky split
    open, drenched our towels—and you, your pockets filled with stones,
ankle deep in river water, you smiled at me with rain on your face.
That day—the day after finding the dead dog, the day after my tears
and our fight—that day I filled my pockets with the stones you found me,
the stones you named for me—the black one "night," the quartz-shot
granite "love," and the one I lost, the gray-flecked small one,
you named "George." Now, paper Me is pocked with rainwater,
turning to pulp—and you are nowhere, no one to papier-mâché me
    whole, no one to reconstruct me.

She snapped her journal shut and jammed it back in her bag. Tyler sat silently, his eyes blanketing her, seeking hers out, but she couldn't meet them. She could only wipe at her eyes, unfold Carissa's third instruction, press it into his hand, and say, "Long enough. What it means."

"What does it mean?"

Jessa surveyed the massive walls of St. Peter's Basilica, a church so big, Francesca had told them, that you could fit the Statue of Liberty inside it. Sighing, she closed her eyes against all that ancient stone.

"'Long enough' means that even though I pretty much hate him now, even if he ruined everything, it wasn't long enough. Something about Sean, I don't know what, just something, made me feel whole. Now"—she blinked in the gray light—"now, I just feel like I'm in ripped-up pieces."

#4: valentine's day from hell

Jessa couldn't get off the bus. It sped down the Italian highway, the Tuscan landscape a sepia blur. Sean kept smashing his face all over Natalie's face three seats away, and Jessa couldn't even get off the bus. She had not bought a ticket for this show. Wanting to scream, throw something at them, or better, jump out the window to be swallowed up by the blur, she squeezed her eyes shut. Seriously, if he didn't stop it soon, the girl would have permanent face damage. A smile twitched the corners of Jessa's mouth, her eyes fluttering open. Maybe it wasn't so bad after all. She forced her eyes back to them, her smile slipping, her chest clenching like it had its own gag reflex. No, it was worse than bad.

Blinking tears, she pressed a warm hand to her chest. What was all this muck in her? This shortage of air, this pressure? She had no body memory for it, no tools, no study guide. Like the view outside the window, it was foreign, unknown. Jessa's relatively normal family hadn't prepared her for this brand of heartbreak, if that was in fact what this was—her heart a ceramic dish pitched onto a tile floor. She had nice parents—as far as parents go—who asked her how she felt about things, a basically sweet sister who smelled like strawberry gum and left Jessa little watercolor paper hearts on her pillow. She had friends—Tyler and Carissa, especially. School was a constant, controlled challenge, like running stairs during volleyball practice. There was always an understandable goal—study, get good grades, move forward—checking off the boxes inside her school-supplied day planner with the picture of the Williams Peak jaguar on the front. It wasn't like she was perfect or anything—she wasn't perfect. Things weren't always good, and she had bad days like everyone else, but they didn't feel like this, like being smashed between two huge plates of cold steel.

Of course, she knew what loss was. She'd lost things—spelling bees, parts in plays, volleyball games, Becky from next door, who'd moved to Holland when they were ten. Two of Jessa's grandparents had died. But they had been old—sick. Her parents had spoken to her in soft whispers, their hands warm across hers at both funerals like giant Band-Aids. Everything in the natural order of things, the right kinds of loss, not this inky, evil thing asleep in her.

Before high school, perhaps she'd checked the box next to "Drama I" on the counselor's pink sheet, sought out the theater world simply because she'd lacked so much of her own drama. Maybe that's what had drawn her toward Carissa, who had to put her daily drama into categories the way some people separated their recycling. Carissa never seemed to feel more alive than when she was caught up in a crisis. Or two. Or three. Jessa had been swimming in Carissa's disposable angst since Carissa had plopped down beside her in Ms. Jenkin's third-grade class—her pigtails bouncing, one red ribbon slipping—and told her they had to be friends, because both of their names ended in *ssa*, so it was *destiny*. And Carissa leaned on steady, box-checking Jessa for the right words said in the right order. It's what they did for each other. It was like that biology word—what was it? Symbiosis.

Until now.

Because this break, this ache, this pressure in her chest, it *hurt*—a sticky, ugly stomach-flu type of ache, like a tiny miserable elf had burrowed under her skin and had started pulling apart her nerve endings. No steady Jessa now. No, Jessa couldn't shake it, couldn't seem to stop from wobbling. It wasn't the kind of pain you just popped a couple of Advil for; it wasn't isolated to her ankle or her back—it existed everywhere, even in the balls of her feet, in her cuticles.

Being here wasn't helping. She had thought maybe Italy would make it better, but it seemed like it was having the opposite effect. The dawn light spread across the Italian countryside like syrup; she could almost drown in it. There was too, too much of it, all that yellow light, all the *newness* adding to the death grip on her heart. She needed to do something to release it, to pry open the grip of that miserable elf, kick him to the side of the Italian road, so she could regain her footing. She hated how she felt, didn't want to be one of those annoying, angsty girls who were wrecked by the slight of a boy. Carissa knew that; it's why she sent the instructions. She wanted to help drag Jessa out of the muck, plop her back on steady ground.

Tyler shifted beside her, asleep against the faded bus seat, her iPod blaring into his ears, the rockabilly tap-rattle pulse of the Lee Rocker he had made her download because of the band's kick-ass drummer. Like the way she heard the music, she was feeling things only as echo, her body trying to wall itself off from any more pain. She caught a shuffle out of the corner of her eye, watched Ms. Jackson slip down the bus aisle to the Sean and Natalie make-out accident scene, where they were definitely not coming up for air anytime soon. Ms. Jackson leaned over them, a human jaws of life, and waited until they pried themselves apart, neither of them looking as embarrassed as they both should. Ms. Jackson returned to her seat but not before catching Jessa's eye and making a gag sign with her finger. Jessa nodded, mirrored it back to her.

Tyler stirred again, rubbed his eyes, sat up. "Where are we?"

"Somewhere between Rome and Florence."

"Dubious." He took a long drink of water from the bottle he fished out of his backpack and opened a bag of gummy bears.

"You think maybe you can OD on gummy bears?" Jessa grabbed a handful.

"Some people believe gummy to be a life-extending elixir."

"What people?"

"Me." Tyler chewed. He handed her back the iPod. "Thanks for the loaner."

Jessa tucked it into her backpack. The bus whispered down the highway, full of morning hush, the group quiet. They slept or stared out the window, texted people, listened to music. In the row next to her, Jade was writing postcards, a huge stack of them, her curls bouncing around her face as she wrote. Francesca chatted on her phone at the front of the bus, preparing their day. Jessa tried to push aside the loss that weighted her to the seat, tried to open her glossy blue guidebook to the Florence section, fasten herself to some concrete facts about their next destination.

In Florence, they would see Brunelleschi's dome, the Uffizi and *The Birth of Venus*, and the famed Piazza della Signoria. The pages in her lap, all those black-and-white words, told her that the square held statues humming with political contradictions, each with a different agenda. Contradiction, confusion—she'd feel right at home. Closing the book, she opened the envelope she'd been using as a bookmark.

Reason #4: Valentine's Day from Hell: I don't think I need to remind you, but I'll paint the picture anyway. February 14th. Bright, cold. You waited in the front of school with the soccer jersey we stayed up all hours of the night bidding for on eBay until you got it for him, waiting for his car to pull in by the tree where he always parks. Did I mention how cold it was???? Fast-forward one hour. No car. No Sean. No answer when you call. He is not at school. And when he does finally appear somewhere around four for rehearsal, here is the reality. He has nothing for you. Has forgotten it is Valentine's Day, and (here's the kicker) gets MAD at you for having "commercial expectations for his love" which is some dial-an-excuse-crap for being a lousy boyfriend. Double kicker: You gave him his present anyway when the rest of us thought you should shove it up his pathetic ass. But you said maybe he had a point. Maybe Valentine's Day has too many expectations attached to it.

He *DOESN'T* have a point. He's a lazy, lying jerk cheater who doesn't deserve you.

Jessa frowned at the instruction at the bottom, the un-Jessa-like thing that Carissa seemed to think she needed to do to move this two-thousand-pound weight off of her heart. She read it again. No way. She was *not* going to do that.

With the hum of travel all around her, she studied the arm of the Tim Burton boy from the other school through the slit in the bus seats in front of her. Folding the note back into the envelope, she looked out at Tuscany, the clusters of stone villages and sweeping vineyards, the castles dotting the landscape.

Carissa had lost her mind.

. . .

Tuscany must have its own sun. Jessa squinted into the buttery light of Florence.

Firenze, she mouthed, the word like working taffy around her tongue. The light infused warmth all around, into the creamy stucco of the buildings, into the arch and roll of the hills across the Arno River. She sent a picture of it to Carissa, with a note that read:

Florence. Miss you. Thank you for the envelopes. BTW: NOT doing #4. You're CRAZY! They will send me home! Did I mention how beautiful it is here? p.s. when I read #3 to Tyler, there were two old ladies walking by and a million tourists. That counts.

They followed the frog through the streets, heading to the Galleria dell'Accademia to see *David*, Michelangelo's, not Donatello's. Francesca told them that one of the interesting things about Michelangelo's *David* was that he chose to depict him in anticipation of the battle, whereas Donatello choose victory, with Goliath's head at David's feet. "Anticipation," she had said—the moment before the moment when all of history spilled out in front of him.

Walking around, Jessa felt like a dyslexic David, with all of history spilling out *behind* her instead of in front. The colors, the sweeping churches, the stained-glass widows, even the buzzing scooters and people calling to each other, kissing each other's faces, bursting from the small shops with loaves of fresh bread or cut flowers seemed formed from all their history. Everything was so *old*. Not like California, where old meant "last month."

"Where'd you get that scar?" Tim Burton boy from the other group had fallen in step beside her. He ran a hand through his mop of dyed black hair and studied her with close-set eyes like two smoldering coals. "I'm Dylan, by the way. Dylan Thomas."

"Like the poet?"

He looked impressed. "Yeah. Right. Wow, a girl with a brain in her head. You'll excuse me if I seem a bit shocked considering who I'm here with."

Jessa's eyes swept over the gaggle from the other school, like a pack of designer ducklings all trying to find the water's edge. "Not the sharpest knives in the drawer?"

He laughed, low and soft. "Not as sharp as spoons."

"Why'd you come?" Jessa watched him from the corner of her eye as they walked. "I mean, if you knew you'd hate traveling with them?"

He shrugged. "It was this or my cousin's house in Oregon. My cousin collects bug carcasses and smells like a wet washcloth. At least Italy has gelato."

They walked a bit more. "So, not going to answer me about the scar?" Dylan Thomas asked. "Too personal?"

She held up her wrist. "I used to ice-skate when I was younger. It's from another skater's blade when we crashed."

"Do you still skate?"

Jessa shook her head, fingering the iPod cord curling out of her sweatshirt pocket.

He nodded toward it. "Any good tunes?"

"Oh, I'm sure I don't listen to music you like."

He laughed again and Jessa liked him more, that low, breathy laugh wrapped itself around her insides, swirling like mist. "Assumptions. And what kind of music must I like?" He wrinkled his nose. "Whoa. What's that smell?"

Jessa inhaled a whiff of something stale, something organic and rotting. Jessa imagined piles of it in the darkest corners of Florence, the parts tourists didn't see, imagined tossing Sean and Natalie right into the middle of a big stinking pile of it, covering them with banana peels, coffee grounds, sticky gelato-melted cone wrappers.

"What's funny?" Dylan Thomas asked. Jessa realized she'd laughed out loud at her little fantasy garbage-pile world.

"I was just imagining throwing my ex-boyfriend into a pile of Florence's secret garbage heaps."

She wondered if maybe he would bolt, hurry ahead wondering about the crazy ex-boyfriend-throwing nut from the other group. Instead, he asked, "Can I help?"

They walked a few more minutes in silence, the hum of the city drawing them forward, their eyes on the blur of stones beneath their feet. Even the streets here were prettier, older, more interesting, than the flat concrete back at home.

"I was just listening to *Mamma Mia!* by the way. Stage, not the movie."

To her surprise, he busted out a few lines of "Honey, Honey," dancing a circle around her.

Tyler wandered up alongside them. "Am I missing the show?"

"This is Dylan Thomas from the other school," Jessa told him. "He sings and maybe dances."

Tyler swept some of his own not-dyed black hair from his face, stuck his hands in jean pockets. "Dylan Thomas?"

He took a little bow. "My parents made me a tribute before I could breathe real air."

Jessa watched the two boys appraise each other. Boys were so different from girls. She knew they weren't comparing hair or asses for that matter. They were just circling the outside of a ring, figuring out where each one should stand.

They opted for either side of her.

"So, the *David*, huh?" Tyler broke the silence. "In California, we'd probably have a statue of Will Ferrell." That was Tyler, offering out a peace treaty.

"And he'd be fine with the nudity," Dylan Thomas said, signing and sealing it.

Now Jessa had a posse. This trip was looking up.

• • •

"What is he wearing?" Cruella waved a hand again into the middle of whatever Francesca had been saying. "What's that around his neck? A scarf?"

The group shifted uncomfortably. Cruella's husband, the travel-shirted teacher from their group, buried his head in a Frommer's guide.

"It's a sling." Francesca tucked her curls behind her ear. The frog sagged in the curl of her arm where the stick was tucked.

"Is that a nod to the designers of Florence?" Cruella pushed her husband's hand away from where he had settled it on her arm.

"It's a nod to the Bible." That was Tyler. And he got a full-body glare from Ms. Jackson for it.

Francesca tried again. "He's David. From David and Goliath. Before the battle. He kills Goliath with a slingshot and a rock."

The woman gasped, her hand over her heart. "That's so violent. I'm not sure that's appropriate for a school tour? That kind of violence."

Jessa stared. This woman was like some sort of sociological experiment. Jessa wasn't really religious. She'd been raised in one of those vague northern California quasi-Zen-we-value-everyone-secular-humanist sort of households, but even she knew most of the Bible stories. Someone seriously couldn't be this dim, could they? Even one who clearly worshipped at the altar of Neiman Marcus?

The only other teacher from their group moved himself a bit away from Mr. and Mrs. Cruella until he was standing close to Jessa. He never seemed to say much, mostly just hung out in the background. He was Quiet Guy. Of course, Jessa would be quiet all the time too, if the only people she had to talk to were Cruella and her horse snack–mustache husband.

Finally, Ms. Jackson's hand shot up. "You mentioned we will see the original work inside the gallery?"

Francesca looked like she might jump into the group and kiss Ms. Jackson right on the mouth. "Yes, yes. Inside we will see the original *David* in the Tribuna, which was built to especially house this piece of art. Come on, then."

Jessa hesitated, watching the annoyance wash over Cruella. What brought someone to Cruella's place, to that constant default to snarly irritation, a look that always suggested she was barely stomaching all of this, all of them?

• • •

Waiting in line outside the sweeping columned stone of the Uffizi Gallery, Jessa leaned down and plucked a piece of paper from the ground at her feet. It was a computer printout of a painting, a portrait, maybe Roman or Greek. A funny-looking little man draped in sheets, his head adorned with leaves, holding a glass of red wine. "Room 43" was scrawled across the top in green pen. Underneath the blurry black and white of the photo, someone had written:

Bacchus. (c. 1595) Patron deity of theater. And wine.

Caravaggio. Dark and light. Considered enigmatic.

Humanist.

"Hey! Did someone drop this?" Jessa called up ahead to her group, waving the sheet of paper over her head.

Jade shook her head and went back to her conversation with Christina. Kevin frowned. "Maybe it's Tim's? He went for a gelato."

"Actually, it's mine."

Jessa turned and found Natalie, standing with her hands clasped by her side, looking nervously at the paper, or maybe she was really looking nervously at Jessa but couldn't meet her eyes.

"Oh." Jessa handed it over. Natalie wanted to see a Caravaggio painting? Jessa loved his work, all that dark and dangerous paint, always playing with light. But Natalie? Jessa would have pegged her as a Raphael's-little-angels sort of girl.

Natalie smoothed the paper, folded it once and slid it into her bag.

"Why that painting?" Jessa blurted. "I mean, that one in particular?"

Natalie shuffled her feet a little, cleared her throat. "Just something I want to see here. It's just…" She fiddled with the skin around her nails. "My dad used to have a print of this in his office. Something my mom gave him in college. As a joke. She used to call him Bacchus. They were both theater majors. And, well, sort of partiers, I guess?"

"His work was very controversial."

"Whose?"

Jessa pointed at the paper. "Caravaggio."

"Oh." Natalie shrugged. "I just sort of want to see it in person, that's all."

Sean came up along side her with three cones of what looked like pistachio gelato. "Oh." His eyes darted between the girls. One of the cones dripped a green drop of melty gelato onto his shoe. "Um, here." He handed a cone to Natalie.

"Anyway, thanks." Natalie nodded to Jessa, taking a dainty lick of her ice cream.

With the eyes of a cornered animal, Sean held up a cone. "I'd offer you a bite but you hate pistachio."

"I'm kind of gelatoed out."

Jessa watched them wander away and join Hillary in line, where Sean handed her the third cone. Jessa's eyes strayed again to Natalie, who was laughing at something Hillary had just said to L. E. Wood and taking small bites from her cone.

Natalie seemed like a girl entirely free of angst, as if she didn't have the time for the sort of silly nonsense when there was so much hair product to experiment with. Jessa bit her lip, a distressing thought creeping in, a candle flicker of fear. Maybe Sean just wanted to be with someone who liked pistachio ice cream as much as he did, who would want to share the Junior Mints at the movies, or who when asked didn't really have an opinion about most things.

. . .

Jessa's heart thumped against her chest as she roamed the ornate rooms of the Uffizi, her eyes trying to pull in everything at once. She tried to stay mostly by herself, determined not to let the other groups' stupid questions or the stupid penis jokes of the boys from her own group ruin the gallery for her. The *David* had been a bit of a disaster earlier that day, but Jessa knew that putting that big of a bare butt, even a marble one, in front of a bunch of teenage boys pretty much annihilated any chance of an artistic experience.

But here, this place—this was what she had dreamed of seeing, all these paintings in one spot. When she was a little girl, her family used to visit her grandmother in Arizona. Her grandmother always had a huge glossy *Art of the Renaissance* book on her coffee table. While her parents talked in the other room, Jessa would flip through the pages for hours, her fingers hovering above the paintings—Botticelli, Parmigianino, Raphael, Cosimo— each one a tiny window onto an untouchable world, their rich colors like candy in glass jars. The clock would tick on the wall of the quiet room and Jessa would imagine herself in each painting, floating to the earth on a giant seashell or as one of Raphael's tiny crouching angels, full of secrets. In each painting, she would hold still for that invisible hand of the artist, imagine herself inside the world the artist created.

Now here she was standing in front of *The Birth of Venus*, her favorite painting as a child. A woman brought to earth held in her seashell on the waves, fully formed, blown here by the zephyrs, her body long and odd.

"Ick. Why are they all so fat?"—redheaded Madison from the other group, Madison with her entrepreneurial camera and cracking-glass voice.

"What's beautiful changes throughout generations," Jessa heard herself saying, remembering her mother telling her that as she turned the pages of her grandmother's glossy book.

Madison shrugged, waved to her friend across the gallery. "Um, yeah. They're still fat."

Then Dylan Thomas was at her side. "Madison, I think they sell original thought in the gift shop."

"And imagination," Jessa added helpfully.

Madison rolled her eyes, already texting into her phone as if the press of each small key deleted them from her presence. She vanished into the sea of people all around.

Jessa turned back to the painting. "Why did they even come to Italy?"

Dylan Thomas stuffed his hands into the pockets of his black pants, shook his head a bit. "Their families have buckets of money. They know they *should* go to Italy. My mom says they're the kind of people who know the price of everything and the value of nothing."

Nodding, Jessa studied the faces of the winds, almost bored as they blew their charge to shore. Maybe they were teenage zephyrs.

"You ever think," Dylan Thomas waved a hand toward Venus, "that it would be better if we all just showed up full grown?"

Jessa noticed Mr. Campbell across the room, peering closely at a small painting she couldn't see. A sadness seemed to glow halo-like around him, like one of the many religious paintings here. Shaking her head, she said, "Would it matter?"

• • •

Jessa didn't know who had started it. Probably Tim or Devon. It was right up their alley. And it *was* hilarious. Still, she had never seen Mr. Campbell so mad. He had ushered the whole group right off the bus, which idled softly behind them in the dusty parking lot.

"I don't want this kind of behavior on the trip." Mr. Campbell stared at them, his face red, his eyebrows at war with his forehead. "I don't care if you think she's annoying. I just don't care. You don't act like that." Ms. Jackson stood quietly by him, dragging a toe of her shoe through the dust. She just shook her head in disbelief.

What had happened took all of five seconds.

Cruella had boarded the bus. And someone had whistled the Wicked Witch theme from *The Wizard of Oz*, quietly but loud enough. "Do-do-do-do-do-do. Do-do-do-do-do-do. Do-do-do."

Cruella stopped cold, her sunglasses huge bug eyes surveying the students. Then someone laughed. Just a titter.

Mr. Campbell had been on his feet in seconds. "Williams Peak. Outside. Now."

They'd scurried from the bus like ants.

Outside, Hillary raised her hand. "I think you're assuming it was our school. It could have been one of them too. But if it was one of us, whoever it is should just say. Don't be a coward." Practical, look-at-all-sides Hillary.

Christina whispered, "I think we know it was our group."

"I'm not going to force someone to be a rat," Mr. Campbell said. "But that was just awful. I mean, the woman has feelings."

"You sure about that?" Tim muttered.

Mr. Campbell sighed, ran his fingers through his hair, settled his hands in a clasp atop his head. His face had returned to a normal color. "You know, I have one rule," he said. "What is it?"

Like a Greek chorus, they all singsonged, "Don't be a jerk!"

"Right." He paused, taking the time to settle his eyes on each one of them. "You broke the one rule."

Everyone stared at the ground. Somehow, wrapped up in the bleak air of his disappointment, they had all broken the one rule.

Mr. Campbell sighed again, and this time Jessa thought maybe he was taking the whole dramatic-pause thing a little too far. Finally, he asked, "What do you want to do, guys?"

Devon cleared his throat. "I'm sure that you all think it was me and it wasn't. But think about *why* someone did it. That rule should apply to everyone. We need to request a new group. Seriously, I'd rather travel with a knife-wielding barracuda."

The group, a cup brimming at the edge, spilled over, with everyone talking at once. Ms. Jackson's whistle brought back the silence. "That," she said while looking at Devon, "is not the point."

Sean raised his hand, which was weird, because Sean didn't usually raise his hand, even in class. He was more of a blurter when he had anything to contribute at all. "OK, so it was me."

More murmurs. Another whistle.

Natalie giggled into her hand.

"Natalie," Ms. Jackson frowned. "This isn't funny."

"Sorry." She flicked a strand of hair from her eye and set her jaw defensively at Ms. Jackson. "But we've all had enough. I mean, the woman's a total bitch, excuse my language."

What happened next was a bit like a big garbage dump, a big back-the-truck-up-and-dump-a-bunch-of-crap-right-in-the-middle-of-everything dump. That was all Florence needed, more garbage. Everyone, it seemed, had already had a run-in with Cruella. Jessa wasn't sure how she'd missed it, how she'd been so far sunk in the muck of her own self-pity that she hadn't noticed, but she had missed it.

They had a list of complaints—a long list.

Yesterday, when Jade accidentally sat in her seat on the bus, Cruella had told Jade to move her "hippie ass." At Vatican City, she had told Kevin to get his "K-Mart backpack" out of the way on a bench she wanted to sit on. At dinner, she had asked Maya Rodriguez if she could pass the olive oil, "*Comprende?*" That one almost sent Ms. Jackson onto the bus after the woman, muttering, "Racist cow!" Mr. Campbell had to snatch the back of her jacket, fastening her back to the group.

Yesterday morning at breakfast, over tiny rolls and pots of jam, Cruella had told Blake and Erika that their "gothy *Twilight* vampire crap" was boring and couldn't they just "give it up already?" And she called Tim and Devon "losers" when they were practicing some improv stuff outside the hotel. Apparently, on the bus that morning, she had said that Sean and Natalie made her "want to barf." Jessa actually agreed with her on that last one, but her classmates were making quite a case.

In fact, Jessa was beginning to feel a little left out. Cruella hadn't said anything to her.

Without warning, the frog joined the group. Francesca stood, licking her lips, a finger poised in the air, the frog stick tucked under one arm. She had some serious attachment issues with that frog.

"We have a problem?" She blinked at the circle of students, her eyes slipping back toward the waiting bus.

Mr. Campbell cleared his throat. "It seems…Um, it seems that we have some issue with the other group. Or a member of the other group."

Francesca began nodding much more vigorously than necessary, her curls bouncing. "Yes. Yes. She's quite upset."

Ms. Jackson's eyes widened. "Right. Of course. And we will definitely be apologizing." She looked sharply at Sean. "But this incident isn't without, um, provocation."

The frog twitched in Francesca's arm, continued to twitch as Ms. Jackson relayed each incident like blocks rising into the air, a Cruella-complaint tower. Francesca's curls started to wilt with each block added to the stack. Finally, Ms. Jackson stopped adding them.

Francesca sighed through her nose, pinching her lips together. "I am so sorry. This is hard sometimes on trips with two schools. There is nothing to be done." She looked sadly at them, her eyes large pools. She shrugged. "I could talk to her. Might make things worse. She is not…agreeable. I've seen this before. No good comes from making it worse."

She waited. The frog waited. Williams Peak Drama Academy waited.

"Um…" Mr. Campbell's mouth pulled at the edges, like he was trying to form words for the first time. "Isn't there…someone to call?"

Ms. Jackson placed a hand on his arm. "Maybe we should talk to her. Maybe have the adults meet to discuss this." She spoke quietly, the way she might talk to a student who'd come to her desk to ask a question during a test.

He nodded, and Francesca brightened. "Yes. Very good, then. We go? Dinner now." She kissed the tips of her fingers, then turned on one pointy black-heeled boot and escorted the frog back to the bus.

One by one, with shoulders at varying degrees of defeat, Jessa and her classmates followed the frog onto the bus.

As Jessa passed Cruella, their eyes met briefly, and Jessa's heart sagged.

The woman's eyes were filled with tears.

• • •

The restaurant walls were too close, pressing in at Jessa at odd, fragmented angles. The tables all seemed a bit too snug, the chairs too small, and Jessa felt suddenly like Alice, fumbling her way through Wonderland. She was crammed at a table with Dylan Thomas, Tyler, Erika, and Blake in the middle of the small room. Erika, in between bites of *caprese* salad, argued with Blake about vampires in the 1800s, something about how women vampires had more power then than now, because apparently, vampire rights were going through a rocky phase or something. Bad time to be a girl vampire in Erika's opinion. Blake didn't agree.

Jessa tugged her jacket off and hung it on the back of her chair. The room sweltered; sweat beaded on her upper lip. She nibbled at her salad, but it tasted like paste. At the next table, Sean laughed at something Natalie leaned in to say, brushed a strand of hair from her eyes. She fed him tiny balls of mozzarella with her fingers.

Tyler watched them too. Jessa could see his eyes dart back to them every once in awhile when Erika started repeating herself. He pointed his fork at Jessa. "You want to switch places with Erika?" Erika looked momentarily surprised to hear her name, then dove back into Blake's argument like it was the hazelnut gelato Jessa had devoured after the Uffizi.

Jessa shook her head, tried to focus on Blake's words, but she couldn't quite get them to stay in one place. They'd spill from his mouth and then dissipate before she could put them in her ears, form an opinion about them.

Dylan Thomas lost interest in the vampires. He studied Jessa, drank his soda, studied her some more. His coal-black eyes took on heat, bore into her skull.

"What?" She finally asked him, wanting to hose his face down to extinguish those eyes.

"What's with the PDA at the next table?"

Jessa stabbed at a tomato on her plate.

"Former *amore?* The garbage boy?"

"Garbage boy?" Tyler looked confused. Jessa shrugged and ate the tomato out of her salad.

Tyler cleared his throat, leaned in a bit. "A week ago, he was with Jessa." Erika and Blake stopped talking instantly. Even vampires were no match for Jessa's mangled heart. Tyler filled him in.

"What a wanker!" Dylan Thomas said a little more loudly than Jessa would have liked. Of course, the wanker in question was too involved feeding buxom Barbie to notice.

"Total wanker," Tyler agreed, sipping his Coke.

"Are we even allowed to say 'wanker' if we're not British? You guys sound like posers." Erika fiddled with one of the million safety pins on her jacket.

"Right," Tyler drawled. "*We're* the posers."

Erika flipped him off.

"Can we talk about vampires again?" Jessa leaned back as the waiter set the pasta she had ordered in front of her. The slender noodles twisted through a sea of red sauce, her heart on a plate.

"You should slap him right in his face," Erika suggested, tucking into her lasagna with meat sauce. She wiped some red sauce from her lips, looking more like a vampire than ever before.

Dylan Thomas's eyes widened. "Excellent. Yes. You need your moment."

She arched an eyebrow at him. "My moment?"

Dylan Thomas nodded, curling his arms in front of him on the table, his pasta untouched. "Sure. When you found him—did you give him a good smack? Did you scream at him? Did you break something of his that was especially important? A favorite CD? An arm?"

Tyler laughed and slurped some pasta into his mouth. "Jessa would never do that."

Jessa frowned. What had she done? When Carissa split up with John Marshall, she'd papered his locker with magazine ads about erectile dysfunction. And with Tom Levy, she'd swiped his phone and set the ringtone so that it played Beck's "Loser" over and over, knowing that he had no clue how to reset his ringtone. Seriously, he'd had that ringtone for a week before he could convince anyone to change it for him. But what had Jessa done? The door of the costume barn had swung open. She saw them there, all blurry and kissing and tangled in the red dress she'd worn to play Kate. Kate would have broken his arm. Mr. Campbell had said something about giving it a rest. Said something to stop them, but he'd swept her away into the theater. Sat her there on the metal chair. She'd stared at the smooth cement of the floor, at a smash of gum like a tiny handprint there next to a crack. She hadn't screamed or slapped or broken anything at all.

"I didn't do anything."

Dylan Thomas shook his head. "To quote our friend here," he pointed at Tyler, "dubious." Tyler slurped some more pasta and wiggled his eyebrows at Jessa.

Reaching into her pocket, Jessa ran her finger over the velvet edge of Carissa's note. "Excuse me," she said to the waiter as he passed with a tray of steaming rolls in a basket. "Can I get a drink? An orange soda?"

"What are you doing?" Tyler asked, his forkful of pasta halfway to his mouth, his face suddenly flushed.

"Buying myself a very belated Valentine. Carissa's orders."

Tyler set his fork down.

The table watched silently as she waited for her drink. Watched as the waiter set the clear glass of toxic orange liquid down in front of her. Their eyes grew wider as she took a sip, then stood, squeezed through the chairs between their tables, and without preamble, threw the entirety of the glass into Sean's shocked face.

#5: quicksand

"What happened back there?" Mr. Campbell placed his hands on the curve of stone next to Jessa and tipped his face toward the cool wind coming off the water.

She leaned on the stone bridge railing, looking out on the darkening waters of the Arno River. The dusky evening light was turning the water pink and yellow and blue. "I was having my moment." She sighed, the colors all around pressing against her, her ears buzzing with distant scooters, the murmur of restaurants, somewhere a woman's laughter ringing out.

"Feel better?"

"Actually I do." Only she didn't. The orange soda had soaked his white T-shirt, flattened his hair. That look of complete shock, the way his face had cracked like an egg into surprise, then understanding, that must have been how she'd looked last Monday framed in the doorway of the costume barn; he'd mirrored it right back to her.

"That boy's going to need a shower." Was it her imagination

or was Mr. Campbell smiling a little, just at the corners of his mouth. "But for the record, I'm officially against you throwing drinks in people's faces."

"I broke the rule."

"Little bit, yeah."

He stayed there next to her, leaned his body against the edge of bridge. Jessa liked the way the stone curved with her body, as if the designers of the bridge knew how many people would lay against it, stare out at the water, wonder where it had all gone wrong.

"The light is different here." She glanced sideways at her teacher.

"Not hard to see how Michelangelo got his palette." His eyes searched the water, and the hills glazed with twilight.

"I'm sorry about all that. I actually thought it might make me feel better." Jessa wiped at her eyes. Seriously, how much more would she cry about it? Ridiculous. She tried to laugh, but it came out a hiccup. "No more drinks. I promise. Are you guys going to send me home?"

"What? No. Of course not. You need to apologize, but no, we're not going to send you home." His hands found the pockets of his jacket. "Besides, it's not exactly the best landscape for a broken heart."

The city spread out around Brunelleschi's burgundy dome standing majestically over the brick-colored rooftops. Jessa turned at the clop-clop-clop of a horse and carriage along the cobbled streets near the bridge. A man and woman clung to each other, eyes wide with each other. Mr. Campbell wiggled his eyebrows up and down at her. She burst out laughing. "Seriously, right?" he said. "You don't stand a chance here. It's like we're extras on a set for a musical called *Love Me!*"

She watched a bird glide out over the water. "Well, I'm happy to play Rosalind, the scorned lover."

"Are you?" His smile vanished.

Jessa sighed. "Sure. I mean, it's a more interesting part right?"

"Maybe in theory." He pressed his palms into the stone, his fingers arching up with the strain.

"Do you miss her?" she asked.

He let his breath out, sending it over the shifting water. "Very much."

"Maybe you should throw a drink at her."

"Not my style."

She leaned into the stone, welcoming the solid feel of it against her. "That's what Carissa thought would help me. But it didn't. Not really."

He nodded. "Didn't think so."

"So what should I do? Why doesn't this get easier? Each day, I think I'll wake up and hate him. I'll be so mad at him that I just won't care."

"It hasn't even been a week, Jess. You need time to grieve."

"But why? He's a jerk. He cheated on me. I should just be done. Over him."

"He's not a paint color. You don't just swipe on Sunset Red over the Meadow Green you've had for a year and be done with it." The wind caught Mr. Campbell's hair, fluttered it, and his hand instinctively smoothed it down. "A friend of mine gave me a quote from John Updike about death, but she meant it more for the death of a relationship. Updike said death is a 'ceasing of your own brand of magic.' What's painful is that what you had together, all your inside jokes and favorite restaurants and that movie you both loved but everyone else hated—that's gone, and there's no replacement for it, you never replicate it, never get to have it ever again…" His voice trailed off. He shuffled his feet a little, cleared his throat.

Something dark and shadowed filled Jessa's belly, made her light, feel like she would float away. Grief. Because there *had* been a special brand of magic with Sean, their own brand. She wanted to ask Mr. Campbell why he and Katie broke up. Did she cheat? Jessa studied his veiled expression. Had he cried into the night like she had with only the shadows for company? Maybe it didn't even matter why they broke up, maybe that wasn't the point. Because you can't have what's already gone. You can only grieve for it, walk around with a huge hole in your gut knowing you will never be the same again.

Standing there on the bridge, his body warm next to her, he somehow melted from her teacher to just a guy. Not standing on stage directing them. Just a guy nursing a broken heart like she was. He must know her better than anyone else on this trip, know the deep, hollow shadow of her heart.

"Why do people leave people when nothing's wrong? It doesn't make any sense." She searched Mr. Campbell's eyes, thought of the way he laughed at their stupid improv games, the way he got there early every day so they'd have somewhere to go before the first bell, how he listened with his whole body when they came to him with their problems. Why had Katie given that up? Why had Sean kissed Natalie?

Finally, he shook his head, his eyes slipping to her face. "I wish I could answer that. Maybe human beings search for what is wrong, pick through what is right until they find the scrap of wrong and then blow it up to life size. It's all part of this dark nature of ours. Unanswerable questions. Why do we betray someone? Why do we love at all? It's the mystery of the ages, isn't it? It's why we have music and art and theater—it's all about love, about losing it, finding it, wanting it, betraying it. We love. We cause pain to the ones who love us. It doesn't get easier—you start playing the game differently maybe. Each time, maybe, you take a tiny piece of your heart and you save it for yourself just in case. So you always have something left."

"OK, that is like the most horrible thing you could tell me right now."

Mr. Campbell's laugh was a bird suddenly released from a cage. "Yeah." He seemed surprised by his outburst but lighter somehow. "Sorry. But I mean, here we are in Florence—the heart of the Renaissance. All these paintings, all these buildings— there's so much love and betrayal here. As humans, we haven't figured much out, have we?"

"Doesn't seem like it." Jessa studied the great dome, such a feat of engineering, especially at the time it was built. "For how smart humans can be, we're a remarkably stupid species."

Mr. Campbell closed his eyes against the cool wind. "But we keep choosing love. Over and over. Across time. You'll love someone else. Someone who isn't Sean."

Jessa closed her eyes too, tried to imagine the ache in her chest gone. "My dad told me that the heart regenerates. Like a lizard that's lost its tail—it grows back. But I've never had to grow mine back before." Monday night, she had curled her body in on itself, rocking through her tears on their deck, the stars splattered out above her, had cried into her father's shoulder while her mom made tea and her favorite butter cookies inside, the ones rolled in powdered sugar she usually made only at Christmas. Under that dark sky, her dad had told her it would grow back. He'd promised.

"The first time's the worst. Your heart doesn't know, doesn't have the muscle memory of it." Mr. Campbell put his hand on her shoulder, held it there, warm and reassuring. "But your dad's right. It'll grow back. Some people think it's stronger in the broken places." She felt Mr. Campbell's hand through her thin shirt, its heat spreading through her. His face was a blur of concern.

Before she knew what she was doing, she leaned forward, kissed his mouth. Soft. Warm. For a second, it seemed he kissed her back, then, like ice, he cracked, pulled back, wiping his mouth as if the kiss could be given away to the air. Disintegrated. Untraceable.

"Oh, Jessa. I…" He put actual distance between them, stepped backward a few steps. "I didn't mean to…"

Her face must have pulled in all the colors of the sunset at once. "Oh my God, Mr. Campbell. I don't…" Her head whirled, her heart pounding. "I'm sorry. That was my fault. I don't know what I was thinking."

He shook his head, his eyes darting about, his face flushed. "No, Jessa. I'm sorry. Damn." He had made it most of the way off the bridge now, backing up, turning around, a strange choreography of uncertainty, like a fumbling toy soldier who'd lost his way.

She watched him stop abruptly, study her for a moment, then turn and hurry back toward the restaurant, and in that moment, Jessa wondered how many people had thrown themselves off this bridge.

• • •

"That," Tyler told her, sitting cross-legged across from her on the bed, "is one hundred percent jacked up."

"I know." Jessa dipped her hand into his gummy bears, chewed a huge wad of them in her mouth. "He was so nice, you know. Totally trying to help me. All philosophical and open."

"So you kissed him. Good form!"

"Yeah, right? Not crossing any lines there. I'm such a mess. I should give seminars. How to screw up your life in one week or less." She smoothed out a wrinkle in the quilt on the bed and glanced around the small room. The shower was at least in a bathroom this time. When they got home from the quiet bus ride back to the hotel, she'd stood under the hot spray until it had run cold. Through the bus window, she'd watched the lights blink on across Florence and tried not to notice people whispering, staring in her direction. Mostly, people tried not to gawk at her, the girl who threw an orange soda at her ex-boyfriend. Cruella had even smiled at her a bit, given her a thumbs-up when she'd gotten off the bus. Great.

Jessa began to braid her damp hair, smiling wryly at her friend. Tyler wore black sweats and a T-shirt that said "Genius by Birth, Slacker by Choice."

"Wow," Tyler whistled softly. "Even Carissa wouldn't have told you to kiss your teacher." He shook his head. "What's gotten into you? I thought, 'No way is she going to do that drink thing.'"

Jessa stopped braiding. "I don't remember showing you that instruction?"

Tyler hesitated. "What? Oh. No. But of all the things so far, it's the most un-Jessa-like thing to do. It had to be one of your instructions." He tugged at a loose string on the hem of his sweats.

"Are you talking to Carissa about me? What is she saying?"

"I'm not, actually. You're doing the instructions. My job was to make sure you're following them. For the most part."

Jessa held his gaze for a minute. "I'm doing them."

He held up his hands. "Don't get defensive."

She wrapped a hair band around the end of her braid. "OK, sorry. I've just had a really weird day."

"Speaking of weird." Tyler held up Carissa's Reason #5 with a poem taped to it. "A quote from a Dylan Thomas poem?" Tyler started to read the note out loud.

Reason #5: Quicksand—

"The force that drives the water through the rocks/Drives my red blood…The hand that whirls the water in the pool/Stirs the quicksand…"—Dylan Thomas

"The hand that whirls the water in the pool stirs the quicksand." Sean is your quicksand. You lost yourself in him.

3 Examples:

1. Office Fest. You bailed on me the second he called. You bailed on Casino Night.

"Casino Night?"

Jessa plucked the letter from his hand, scanned the reason. OK, that was true. She had bailed. Jessa and Carissa had this huge crush on Jim from *The Office*. The American one. They had decided to spend a whole Friday night watching key Jim episodes, especially the one where he first tells Pam he loves her after Casino Night. "Sean called," she explained to Tyler. "Wanted me to come over. Huge fight with his stepmom or something. And I just left."

Tyler nodded, but quietly he said, "How many times has Carissa bailed on us for a guy?"

"Number two is not fair at all." She passed the letter back to Tyler.

2. Santa Cruz!!

"I didn't go to Santa Cruz because I knew we'd get busted, which she did, and now she's baby-sitting to pay her parents back instead of here with us in Italy."

"I don't think she was ever planning on going to Italy." Tyler frowned at the letter. "I'm not sure I really get this Dylan Thomas quote?"

"Carissa wanted to talk about quicksand so she probably Googled 'poems with quicksand' and got this one."

Tyler squinted at the quote. "Or maybe she feels like Sean sucked you in."

Jessa shrugged. "Whatever. Santa Cruz was not about getting

lost in Sean. Santa Cruz was Carissa pissed at me because I didn't want to hop on her little train of bad behavior."

"At least you were invited." Tyler set the letter on the bed. "What about number three. His band *is* lame."

3. Dracula. You chose his lame-ass band. That SUCKED!

Jessa let out a whoosh of air. "They're not lame."

Still, *Dracula* had been a serious bone of contention between her and Carissa since last summer. Instead of auditioning for the SummerArts! production of *Dracula* with Carissa, she'd spent any time she wasn't working that summer holed up in Sean's garage listening to him, Kevin Jones, and Hunter Parks cover a random mash of old Green Day, Radiohead, and other bands—and rereading all of the Harry Potter books. Carissa spent much of that summer in her Lustra costume, a permanent scowl on her face, even though she'd hooked up with the college guy directing and spent any time they weren't rehearsing with him at the river. So Jessa didn't really know what she was so pissed off about.

"I needed to work. Not be an undead sister." Jessa stretched out across the bed on her belly. "What's the instruction?"

Instruction: Water is the shifting of the elements, it is always moving and changing. You are water. Be water. Water heals itself.

Tyler handed the paper back to her. "Be water? What—is she Zen now or something?"

"Carissa is whatever she is that day." She pulled a pillow from behind her onto her lap, leaned into it. A breeze rustled the linen curtains at the window. She welcomed it on her face; it was cool and slightly wet. Outside, clouds gathered in the dark sky, blanketed the moon. Tomorrow, she would spend her last day in Florence, with its stone streets, its wide river, its buildings stuffed so full of art that even after so many hours she hadn't even started to see it.

Someone knocked on the door.

"Come in."

Ms. Jackson peeked her head in. "Lights out. Tyler, back to your room now, OK? Where's Erika?"

"Mine and Blake's room." Tyler hopped off the bed. "I'll get her."

"Thanks." Ms. Jackson opened the door a bit wider to let him by. She licked her lips, leaned her head against the doorway. Jessa picked lint from her pajamas.

"Mr. Campbell told me what happened."

"He's probably worried I'll throw a drink in his face tomorrow." Jessa felt a tear slip down her face, saw it fall on the letter in her lap, blurring two of the words.

Ms. Jackson sat on the bed next to her. "He's worried about you. So am I."

"It wasn't his fault, Ms. Jackson. If you're wondering. I don't want to get him in trouble." She folded the note quietly, concentrating on smoothing each bended edge with a slow pinch of her fingers.

"Well, it's not good that it happened. But he told me. You've told me. There's nothing else we can do. It would be best if you two weren't alone together." Ms. Jackson pushed her glasses on top of her head, rubbed her eyes. "And you really need to start reeling in your behavior."

The sob started low in Jessa's gut, rattled around there, pushing and plying at the confines of her body, checking for weak points, for a place to break through. It prickled underneath her eyelids and skin, bubbled to the surface like sulfur.

"Oh, honey…" Ms. Jackson held her, her arms around her, rubbing her back the way her own mother did the night before she left when she had told her, "You don't have to go. You don't have to go. You don't have to go," in the glow of the small table lamp Jessa had had since she was five, the one shaped like a milkmaid carrying water for her cows.

Jessa melted into her teacher, who smelled of pastries and a little like cut flowers.

Carissa knew. *She knew*, Jessa thought. This was mostly what her friend meant by the Dylan Thomas quote, not just the stuck-in-quicksand part. She knew Jessa needed to cry as much as she possibly could, to get him out through her tear ducts, until she couldn't cry anymore. *The force that drives the water through the rocks, drives my red blood...* But maybe she didn't know that the tears rolling down her face, water changing her, cleansing her, shifting, were just the start of something else—a river carrying her somewhere else. She didn't fight it, just leaned into her teacher, whose arms around her became the only solid thing in the room; everything else was water. Jessa was her tears—her whole body washing away, washing into nothingness, forever changed, heading somewhere completely unknown.

#6: the chicken and the eggs: an easter limerick

Of course, Carissa also had another side to her. It's why Jessa loved her so much. She could be super intense and deep and dark and then turn around and write something like Reason #6:

> There was a stupid boy from our town
> Who decided to start messing around
> He found that he cared
> Not about what was upstairs
> But the eggs in the front of her gown.

The bus had let them off at the Palazzo Pitti, a sprawling Renaissance palace. After a quick tour, they had an hour to roam, armed with the boxed lunches Francesca had passed out to them. Jessa, Tyler, and Dylan Thomas wandered through the Boboli Gardens, pointing out statues and funny tourists—what was *with* the guy in the leg warmers?—until they found themselves at the upper, southern edge of the gardens.

Jessa read the note again, shaking her head, still exhausted after the outpouring last night. She had avoided Ms. Jackson's gaze at breakfast, could still feel the weight of her arms around her body, a body still partly liquid. But now there was this poem of a different sort. Jessa had to laugh even though the limerick was totally stupid. She handed it to Tyler.

"Frankly, you need no other reason than this." Tyler gave it back. "He's a big coward who opted for boobs over brain. Not only is that generic, hers are too big anyway. I mean, that just has to get in the way."

"Seriously," Dylan Thomas agreed. "More than a mouthful's a waste of space."

"That's lovely. Charming. Both of you." Jessa tipped her head toward the sun, watching the bustle of the Easter picnics all around them. The view of the palace and countryside stretched out in front of them. Jessa's dad always told her a view was as good an education as anything, so they decided to sprawl out and soak up the lazy, Easter Sunday sky, the sounds of laughing families and lilting Italian all around.

"Maybe someone should tell Carissa that a limerick might be more appropriate for St. Patrick's Day, not Easter." Tyler opened his lunch box.

Dylan Thomas stretched out on his back. "I think I'm a little in love with this envelope girl."

Tyler shook his head. "Oh, friend, that's a whole bucket of

mess you do not want to dig into." He kicked his legs out in front of him and munched an apple. "You're supposed to read it out loud where the chicken can hear it."

Jessa opened her boxed lunch. "What is with Carissa's obsession with me publicly denouncing him?"

"She's trying to take you out of your nice, orderly little shell," Tyler said through apple bites.

Jessa frowned. "Well, I'm not doing it."

"You weren't about to throw a drink in someone's face either."

Jessa peeled open her baguette sandwich, peered in at the fatty meat. "I can't get on board with this salami." She picked off each piece and handed them to Tyler.

Dylan Thomas made a face. "Now it's just a mustard sandwich."

"And cheese. There's cheese." She held up the bread for inspection.

Tyler chewed the salami and stared out over the Tuscan countryside. "I could live here."

Nodding, Jessa bit into her sandwich, then took a sip from her bottle of water. The breeze tingled her face—it was both warm and cool and the air was rose scented. A perfect day. She closed her eyes.

A shadow fell across her face. A cloud across the sun?

In a matter of speaking. Sean stood above her. No sign of Natalie. She felt Tyler stiffen next to her. Dylan Thomas sat up, intrigued.

"Um, Jessa?"

"What do you want, Sean?" Jessa took another bite of her sandwich, hoping she looked casual, like she couldn't care less. "I'm eating."

"Yeah. I'm sorry to bother you. Could I talk to you for a minute?" Sean cracked his knuckles and waited, an annoying habit Jessa had always hated. She could add "cracks his knuckles" to the growing list.

She set her sandwich back into the little brown paper box. Tyler looked like he might say something, but instead he ate his own sandwich slowly, not taking his eyes off Sean.

"Here." Dylan Thomas offered her his soda. "You might need this."

Smiling, she walked away with Sean, aware of the space of their bodies, the prickly sizzle of his nearness. What was it about this boy that made her skin feel drizzled with something electric, something alive?

They found a bench several yards away and out of sight of her friends. When he didn't say anything, just picked at a hangnail, she finally asked again, "What do you want?"

He sighed, his face dark. She could see a piece of lint in one of his lashes. A week ago, she'd have picked it off so it wouldn't get into his contact lenses. "I deserved the orange soda."

"Yeah. You did." She crossed her ankles, swung her feet a bit under the bench.

"I can't believe you threw it at me, but I deserved it." He glanced sideways at her. "Carissa tell you to do that?"

"No."

Sean shrugged. He wore the blue long-sleeved shirt she had bought him for his birthday at a ski shop near her house. She remembered holding it up against the boy working there to make sure it would fit him. She tried not to notice how good it looked on Sean, how the slim bones of his wrists peeked out beneath the cuffs.

He leaned in to her a bit, his shoulder brushing hers. She could smell his shampoo, spice and citrus. He said softly, "It was actually kind of hot."

At first she thought he meant the shirt, that it was too warm here in the sun-drenched gardens for long sleeves. Then she realized he meant her. The drink in his face. Jerk.

"Where's the Boob Job?"

He sat up straighter. "You know you and Carissa really shouldn't call her that. She didn't have a boob job. It hurts her feelings." His words forced sudden distance between them, a brick wall of Easter air. No more brushing shoulders.

"I wasn't aware androids had feelings. She must be a hybrid." Jessa kicked her legs a bit harder, imagined kicking Sean, hard, in the shins and running away, the way she did to her cousin Warren at Easter when she was six and he took her red egg. Another Easter kick for good measure, ten years later.

Sean planted his hands on either side of his legs on the bench. "You know, she's actually going through a really tough time right now. Her parents are blasting each other in their divorce. Her dad took off and she doesn't know where he is and she hasn't seen him for more than five minutes in months." He stopped, catching his breath. "Forget it. This isn't about Natalie."

Jessa hated the way her name sounded in his mouth. The way he almost breathed it, like it was something gossamer, something with wings. "What's it about then?"

He put his hand on her leg, just a little higher than her knee, and she knew her jeans must be singed, that a big black burn mark must be appearing beneath him. "I miss you, Jess."

Using what must only be superhuman strength, some sort of superhero power deep inside in her cells from a former cape-wearing life, she stood up, knocking his hand from her leg. Her jeans were fine. No burns.

"You don't get to miss me. Besides," she pointed across the gardens to where Natalie stood in a white tank top talking to a boy from the other group, the boy who had kissed Madison inside the Pantheon. Jamal, his name was—a basketball player with the easy charm of a movie star. The blonde girl from the Pantheon whose name had turned out to be Cheyla, sauntered up, whispered something in his ear, then wandered away.

"Isn't your girlfriend waiting for you?" Jessa spit the word *girlfriend*. She knew it sounded petty and mean, knew her eyes were shooting microscopic knives into Natalie from afar, but she didn't really care.

Sean looked like a four-day-old balloon deflating there on the bench. "I just thought...forget it." He shook his head, turned, and walked away.

She watched him go to Natalie, wrap his arm around her waist. Natalie laughed at something Jamal said but turned and kissed Sean, was still kissing him when Jessa turned and walked slowly back to her friends.

• • •

That night, Jessa leaned on the sill of her hotel window and gazed out at the lights of Florence. Tomorrow, they would leave this place and travel to Venice. She'd miss this city with its rich frescoed walls and cobbled streets, with its fat, churning river. She watched a couple walking on the street below her. Something in the way the woman held the man made Jessa think of the painting she'd seen earlier in the palace, a Rubens painting *The Consequences of War*. Venus trying to stop Mars from going to war as a Fate pulled him closer, the pull of destiny. The man and woman rounded the corner of a building, pulled toward their own fate.

Fate. What if Sean was supposed to kiss Natalie? What if Fate pulled him into the costume barn, pulled Jessa toward the door, opened it right at that moment? What if she was supposed to be in Italy alone watching the night sky through a hotel window?

Down on the street corner a figure emerged from the hotel, talking quickly, heatedly into a cell phone. The glow of a streetlamp cast her suddenly into a yellow-white light, and Jessa saw it was Natalie, gesturing wildly with her free hand.

Abruptly, the call seemed to end. Natalie sat down on the dark curb, back into shadow, and buried her face in her knees.

"Jessa?" Erika stood in the doorway behind her. "Ms. Jackson wants us all to come to the creativity salon now. She says we have to hurry while the other group's out dancing so they don't try to crash it." She crossed the room and leaned onto the sill with Jessa. "Wow. It's beautiful here, isn't it?"

Jessa pulled her eyes from Natalie's dark shape. She had never heard Erika call anything beautiful, had never heard much positive energy escape her black-lipstick mouth.

Erika tucked a lock of purple-black hair behind her ear. "It's hard to believe that a place so beautiful could have such a dark history. I read somewhere that in the fourteen hundreds the Italians would publicly kill homosexuals." Classic Erika. "They were drawn and quartered or burned at the stake. Right in the square for everyone to see." She shook her head. "Actually, it was Florence that was lenient for a while, I read. But then they had to start doing it too. For political reasons."

"Where do you get all this stuff?"

Erika smiled at her. "Gotta love the Internet." She pointed at Jessa's wrist. "Cool scar. Where'd you get that?"

"Oh, this." Jessa considered the girl next to her, all that black and dark makeup, all that talk of vampires and burning at the stake and blood. "Just stupid seventh grade. Bad year. I'm fine now."

Erika nodded, lifted a section of her sleeve. A thin, spidery line was etched there in her right forearm. "Sixth grade. Still not fine." She smiled wryly, pushed away from the window. "See you down there?"

Jessa frowned but found her journal with the poem she'd written there in case Ms. Jackson got the crazy idea to start calling on people to read at the salon.

When she looked to the street again, Natalie was gone.

• • •

Jade was playing one of her original songs, "She's Not Me." Jessa had heard it before, but suddenly it had a very different effect on her. Funny how music did that—changed on you. She would've actually thought Jade's song was a play-by-play of Jessa's love life, except she knew Jade wrote it last year—before costume barns and overzealous bra sizes.

> Baby, she's not me. With her hair cut short,
> Standing by your car last night in the moonlight.
> Baby, she's not me, she's just your last resort.
> Why'd you tell everyone that we were through?
> Why'd you drive her home, why weren't you true?

Jessa pressed herself back against the base of the couch, where she sat against Tyler's legs. Ms. Jackson sat across the room cross-legged on a blue ottoman, her head bobbing along with Jade's rich alto. The creativity salon had been Ms. Jackson's idea, to get them all together to share some of their creative work. It sounded kind of fun when she'd told Jessa on the plane. But now it was really more of a train wreck.

Ms. Jackson had ushered them into a little room off the lobby of the hotel, where they sat mostly on the floor, propped up against couches and chairs. It had started off OK. Lizzie and Maya had each read a poem, Lizzie's a funny pigeon's-eye view of Italy, Maya's filled with symbol and color. Devon and Tim had done one of their comedy sketches they'd been practicing in the hallway earlier. Something about a soccer player with no feet, which wasn't actually very funny, but they thought they were hilarious, so everyone else thought they were hilarious. Those two could really commit to a scene. Jessa tried to laugh, but she couldn't help feeling more like she wanted to run for the nearest exit.

Mr. Campbell seemed to be trying to look everywhere but at her. She'd been trying to talk to him all day, but he was like some sort of magician, always stepping from her presence into some unseen hidden paneling.

And now Jade had come up with that guitar of hers and picked that song:

When you kissed her in the rain,
Could you feel the pain drip down my face?
Disgrace…ooohhhhh…

Jessa leaned against Tyler's legs, lacing her finger through the fringe of one of the woven rugs. He squeezed her shoulder. Across the room, Sean and Natalie were practically plastic-wrapped together on a totally cliché pink love seat. He rubbed her back in slow, steady circles. Her face seemed pinched, but she kept rubbing Sean's leg, kept leaning back to give him tiny kisses, each one a dart on Jessa's target body. Jessa's chest strained, and she shifted beneath Tyler's hand, her head starting to pound.

It's like you didn't blink.

You didn't pause to think.

And now I'm crying…

"Whoa, Jade. Enough already. You're killing us over here."

Jessa's eyes shot up to Tyler, who seemed just as surprised as the rest of the room at the words that had just tumbled out of his mouth. Seventeen sets of eyes swiveled his way.

Jade's guitar stopped, her hand dropping away from the strings in the same slow fall as her jaw. "Tyler?" She ran a hand through her curls, fumbled with the woven headband pushing them back away from her wide face.

"Look…" Tyler's hand went up like a flag. "Sorry."

Across the room, Ms. Jackson went suddenly still, upright, like one of those prairie dogs that pop up out of a hole on the Discovery Channel, a prairie dog with Tina Fey glasses.

"Oh, this should be good…" Devon started.

"Shut it," Mr. Campbell told him, and he did.

Sean and Natalie moved as far away from each other as possible on the couch. Jessa could practically hear the plastic wrap unsticking. Nobody looked at Jessa.

"I'm sorry." Tyler made a move to get off the couch, then sat back down, his hand coming to rest again on Jessa's shoulder. "But, Jade, I mean, come on. Your audience." He made a motion toward Jessa, another one toward the pink couch.

All the blood escaped Jessa's body. She was floating, bloodless, her hand still caught up in the carpet fringe. No one moved in the warm air of the hotel. Outside, the night sky seemed to grow darker. In the patch of night at the top of a window, Jessa could just make out the blur of a star.

Jade's sweet orb of a face crumbled. "Oh, Jess. I…I…I'm sorry." Her gaze slipped from Jessa to Sean. "I didn't even think about…"

"OK, OK," Mr. Campbell said, keeping an eye on Ms. Jackson, who still seemed frozen to her blue ottoman. "OK, we should just move on."

"It's fine, Mr. Campbell." Jessa's voice echoed in her own ears, like she was talking underwater. "We all know what happened. I mean, I threw a drink in his face." Devon and Tim cracked up, and their laughter was a buoy under her in a rough sea. She turned her eyes to Jade. "It's really pretty, Jade. You know I love your voice. And I'm totally fine. Totally. Fine. I am." And then, without any explanation, she just blurted out Carissa's limerick into the room. Her instruction. Quick, staccato words, like bullets:

There was a stupid boy from our town

Who decided to start messing around

He found that he cared

Not about what was upstairs

But the eggs in the front of her gown.

A tiny bubble of quiet, then—pop!—everyone started talking at once.

Jessa listened as her friends argued her life in front of her. Had she really just spat out that limerick into the air? Had she really just done that?

The weirdest thing, though, was watching Sean and Natalie listen, watching their faces transform as thirteen of their classmates aired their interpretations of their stupid little love triangle, realize how much they all *knew* about them—or thought they knew. Even Kevin Jones, a junior who was always reading Shakespeare or a spy novel the size of a small car and who was in Sean's band, even Kevin thought Sean was an "insensitive prick." But they weren't all defending her. Like depositing rocks in her belly one after the other, she heard Hillary wonder aloud whether Jessa hadn't "been too busy to be a girlfriend," had perhaps "brought it on herself," only to have Rachel agree with

her, referring to Natalie as some sort of by-product. Brought it on
herself? By-product! Biohazard was more like it.

A whistle cut through the air. Ms. Jackson, having unglued
herself from the ottoman, had her fingers in her mouth, had
climbed on top of a chair. "Hey, hey, hey!" she shouted. "That's
enough. This show is over."

Natalie burst into loud, hiccupping sobs.

Quietly, eyes downcast, the students filed out of the room,
leaving Jessa still sitting pressed against the couch. L. E. Wood,
the pretty, soft-spoken sophomore, hovered for a minute next to
her. "You know, Jessa. I'm going running in the morning. You can
come if you want. A good run always helps me sort things out."

Jessa thanked her, watching her petite, lithe form leave
the room.

Mr. Campbell was in a corner talking to Sean and Natalie,
who had turned the volume down on her sob but the speed up
on her tears. Sean was trying to mop her face off with his T-shirt.

Jessa felt a warm hand on her back. "So, that's not exactly
what I had in mind when I asked you to reel in your behavior."
Ms. Jackson squatted down next to her, her eyes searching Jessa's
face. "Do you want to talk?"

Jessa shook her head.

Ms. Jackson sighed. "I know you're hurting right now, Jess.
But I'm done with you making it a public part of this trip. What
you just did right there—that's not OK."

"I know." Jessa wouldn't look at her teacher, her eyes dry, something icy-dark settling in the pit of her. "I can't even believe I did that."

Ms. Jackson watched Sean walk a now-under-control Natalie from the room, then turned back to Jessa. "I know you're confused, I really, really do. But let me tell you something for sure. You're not going to find any of your answers in Carissa's little instructions. In case you hadn't noticed, they don't seem to be doing much good."

#7: blank

"*Actually*, I love to eat hot dogs with mustard," Mr. Campbell announced, standing up in his bus seat, the heavy emphasis on the *actually*. A few groans from Williams Peak students. A few whistles.

"*But* I really love ketchup on my hot dogs." Devon caught on to the game right away, calling out from his seat up front.

"*Certainly*, you would also eat them with relish?" Tim said, turning around in his seat, holding onto the back with both hands.

Jessa grinned. The ABC game. The point of the game was to make a conversation that took you as far into the alphabet as possible using each letter of the alphabet to start the next sentence.

"Do you think you guys could not play this stupid game?" Lizzie spoke up, her eyes never leaving the book in her lap.

"Even though you think it's stupid," Blake called out, "the rest of us are bored and this helps!"

"Forget it," Lizzie countered.

"God only knows," continued Mr. Campbell, "that there's no such thing as boredom, only boring people."

A few more whistles as Tyler high-fived Mr. Campbell. Blake turned, bowed, and said, "Honestly, touché, Campbell."

"I didn't mean it personally, of course." Mr. Campbell's eyes sparkled.

"Just about me as a person is all," Blake shot back.

"What are they doing?" Madison, flipping through a *Vogue*, squinted out from her seat a few rows ahead of Jessa.

"Some drama thing," Cheyla said, sniffing, her face buried in her BlackBerry, her thumbs whirling. Jessa had never seen anyone text as fast as Cheyla.

"They're doing the alphabet," Jamal said, then called out. "Klondike bars are my personal favorite, not hot dogs!"

Williams Peak cheered, and Jamal's face broke into a bright smile.

They narrowly avoided the dreaded *X* as the bus pulled to a stop in a small parking lot in the town of Bologna, where they would eat lunch before heading the rest of the way to Venice. Everyone stood, stretched, pressed fingertips to the bus windows, pulled backpacks from the overhead storage.

The energy of the alphabet game dwindled, and the whole bus seemed to sag a bit, everyone looking tired, like they were starting to feel the trip in their bones. Jessa felt like her body's seams were pulling slightly, splitting tiny threads around her joints, the skin around her eyes dry and tight. She sniffed, hoping she wasn't getting a cold. Tipping one of the vitamin packs her mom sent with her into a water bottle, she watched the now-yellow liquid fizz and shift, then switched off her iPod, cutting off the strains of "Sun and Moon" from *Miss Saigon* in mid-wail.

Francesca clapped her hands at the front of the bus. "Today is National Picnic Day, Easter Monday, so Bologna's market will be closed. But we have almost two hours here. Meet your teachers outside." She went down the steps and off the bus. Francesca seemed agitated this morning, robotic, and Jessa could hear strain in the clipped edges of her voice.

Jessa pulled her bag over her shoulder, slipped on a pair of sunglasses, and made her way down the bus aisle. She tucked Carissa's Reason #7 into her pocket. She hadn't opened it last night, Ms. Jackson's warning ringing in her ears as she fell asleep.

"What are you drinking? Pee?" Tyler waited for her outside the bus.

"Yeah. I'm drinking pee. It's vitamins."

"It looks like pee." Tyler headed with her toward the tree where the other students from their group were waiting. "Are you hungry?"

"Sure."

Dylan Thomas fell into step beside him. "What…?"

"It's vitamins," Jessa told him, tucking the bottle into her bag. "And your group is over there."

"OK, grumpy." He didn't make a move to join them.

A gorgeous Italian woman passed in front of them. She wore a tight white dress with huge black sunglasses and pin-thin heels that click-click-clicked on the cobblestone. Her dark hair gleamed. "Wow." Dylan Thomas let out a whistle. "My Bologna has a first name. It's F-I-N-E fine."

Tyler followed his stare, jaw literally dropping.

Jessa rolled her eyes. "You are both revolting."

"I'm just admiring all the beauty Italy has to offer." Dylan Thomas finally tore his eyes away as the woman disappeared around a corner.

"Yeah, well, be careful not to slip in your drool."

The Williams Peak group gathered in the shade of a tree. Jessa studied her friends as they stood, waiting in the dappled light. Mr. Campbell counted heads. Then counted again. "Are we...?"

"Permission to come aboard, Captain," Dylan Thomas clarified. "It's like an IQ suck over there." He motioned to where his group still stood by the bus.

Mr. Campbell had that eating sour soup look he got when he was trying not to laugh. "Go check in with Bob. He needs to know you're jumping ship."

Dylan Thomas gave a little salute. Jessa watched him stroll over to where Cruella's husband and Quiet Guy were chatting near the bus. Jessa had been right with her initial history teacher impression. Mr. Cruella taught, as Dylan Thomas said, "the world's most boring world history class." He said he would rather rub sand under his eyelids than listen to one of his lectures on the First World War. The other chaperone wasn't so bad, though. Quiet Guy taught art, kept to himself. Dylan Thomas took clay for his visual art so he'd never actually had Quiet Guy as a teacher, but he seemed nice enough. At least he didn't offend people and ask a zillion stupid questions.

"OK, one hour, you guys, and then we'll meet back at this tree." Ms. Jackson waved them off.

Jessa noticed most of the other group heading straight for the McDonald's. She followed Tyler and Dylan Thomas toward one of the little side streets, winding their way around a crowd of parked Vespas.

All she wanted was cheese, bread, and a small table in some shade.

• • •

Zero for three.

Somehow, they'd ended up at a tiny café table in a blinding spill of suddenly too-hot sunlight. For National Picnic Day, the café was sure busy. Shouldn't more people be picnicking? Dylan Thomas nabbed one of the two tables left, then begged Jessa to hold down the fort while he and Tyler went in search of bathrooms.

Jessa didn't even have time to blink before a couple sat at the other empty table next to her. It took her a second to realize it was

Cruella and Bob, the world's most boring world history teacher. At first, she couldn't see Cruella under a ridiculous hat that made her look like the man with the yellow hat in the Curious George books her sister used to make her read endlessly. Fidgeting in her seat, Jessa wondered three things simultaneously. One: who would buy a hat like that? Two: who would pack it all the way to Italy? Three: would the woman be snatching any monkeys out of their natural African habitat and then passing them off as pesky but well-intentioned pets?

Cruella noticed her staring. "Well, hello." She slapped her husband's bare arm to get his attention. Rubbing it, he nodded in Jessa's direction. "That's the girl who threw the drink," Cruella hissed.

"Yes, yes, I know." He smiled, almost apologetically, though he could just be squinting into all that sun.

"Hi." Jessa scanned the café for her friends, sweat dripping down her back.

"You're a fidgety little thing aren't you?" Cruella snapped her fingers at the waiter walking past her who pretended not to notice, holding his black tray like a shield.

Jessa stopped fidgeting.

Bob scanned the menu. "Why is everything here so expensive? What they charge for a Coke? Criminal."

"So did he deserve it?" Cruella flipped the menu onto the stone table. "That boy."

"Not sure anyone deserves an orange soda in their face." Bob's eyes never left the menu. His voice had a way of dipping under the air, as if he could make it inaudible at a moment's notice.

Jessa licked her dry lips, saw Tyler starting back toward them, a look of alarm crossing his face when he saw the couple at the next table. Jessa stood up. "No. He did."

"Well, good for you." Cruella pursed her lips, then went back to studying the menu.

Spotting Dylan Thomas, Jessa jumped to her feet, hooked Tyler by the sleeve, and led them both out of the café.

• • •

Jessa found her shade, under the tree they had first gathered by with the group. She studied the slip of white paper in her lap. With Reason #7, Carissa had written only one word:

Blank

No reason with this one. And no instruction.

Tyler bit off a chunk of the cheese they had bought at a small market.

"Gross," Jessa told him. "At least break it off."

"It doesn't break." He studied Carissa's page. "She probably wants you to do one of your own."

"I figured." Jessa took her pen out of her backpack. She crossed out "Blank" and wrote:

What we deserved

"What are you writing?" Dylan Thomas chewed a piece of baguette and sipped from his soda.

"My reason is: I didn't deserve this. And I'm writing a list for my instruction." Jessa made a line down the center of the paper, then titled each column.

What I deserved

What Sean deserved

A breeze skittered across them and it ruffled the paper a bit. She held her face up to it for a minute, let it soak her skin. Around them, the sun stippled the ground through the trees, the tiny diamonds of light shifting and changing.

She noticed their bus waiting for them in the lot across the way, the driver leaning against it, smoking a cigarette. Francesca sat in the first seat. Jessa could see her through the window talking on her phone, gesturing wildly.

Under her column she wrote:

honesty

time

a key to Frodo

Sunday mornings

friendship

love

your soccer jersey to sleep in

answers!

Under Sean's column she wrote:

love

dreams

my locker combination

attention

friendship

gas money for Frodo

She hesitated for a moment, remembering what she'd told him at the Palazzo Pitti, that he didn't get to miss her, then wrote:

to miss me

She stood up.

"Where are you going?" Tyler bit off another hunk of cheese.

"I'm giving him the list."

• • •

Jessa lugged her bags up the narrow stairs of the hotel. She pushed open the door of her room and crossed the small space to the window. They were staying a bit outside of Venice, across from a beach and a wide blue stretch of the Adriatic Sea. Jessa took a deep breath of sea air. It felt good to be out of a city.

Before third grade, Jessa's parents moved them out of San Francisco and into the small foothill town of Williams Peak. Jessa sometimes missed the buzz of the city streets, the whirl of lives. As a child, she would often stare out at the street of their first floor window at the passing shoes. All those shoes hurrying by, year after year. Her mother would bake cookies in the small kitchen behind her, slipping chips into Jessa's waiting mouth. But she wouldn't take her eyes off the shoes: red heels, sneakers, flip-flops, glossy black business shoes.

In Williams Peak, they bought two acres, rescued a puppy named Taco from the local shelter, trimmed their apple trees. Jessa made forts out of twisting manzanita bushes and helped her dad string twinkle lights from their outdoor gazebo each spring. But she always felt straddled between those two worlds, that hurried city life and the taffy-stretched days of her life in Williams Peak. Something about Italy cinched those worlds together inside her like the strings of a purse. Her breath came more easily here, her senses more into focus as if even the colors here were more defined, the world suddenly drawn straight and right.

"Hey, Jessa." Hillary stood in the doorway behind her. "Guess I'm your roomie for this stretch." She wheeled in a green bag behind her. "Can I have this one?" She motioned toward the bed closest to the door.

"Sure." Jessa turned and hefted her own bag onto her bed, the soft mattress giving slightly. Hillary flopped onto the bed with her iPod and closed her eyes. She must have sensed Jessa staring because she opened an eye. Jessa never understood that one-eye instinct. It actually seemed harder to open one and not the other.

"What's on your mind, Jess?"

Jessa shrugged, kicked her shoes onto the ceramic tile, and sat cross-legged on the bed. "Nothing."

"Liar." Hillary sat up, pulling her knees into her chest, tossing her iPod aside on the bed. "Spill it."

Hillary had one of those big-sister things going for her even if she was actually the youngest of four, the only girl. The roles she got were always the best friend, the comic relief, or the old man whenever they needed an old man. She'd been Polonius in *Hamlet*, the mother in *Brighton Beach Memoirs*, the janitor in *The Breakfast Club*, a role that seemed larger and more important because Hillary played it that way.

It had been Hillary's words at the salon that had stuck to Jessa like gum on her shoe, that she'd been trying for the past day to scrape off against the stone streets of Italy. She told Hillary that—not the gum part. That would be weird. Just the part about her words, how they'd hurt her.

"You said I brought this on myself."

"I said *maybe* you brought this on yourself."

Jessa failed to see the difference. "What did you mean by that?"

Hillary ran her fingers through her short, blonde hair. "Look, Jessa." The way she said her name, the breathy patience of it, annoyed Jessa. That big-sister thing had its drawbacks. Jessa made a mental note never to talk to Maisy like that. Finally, Hillary said, "Look, Sean's not a jerk."

"I think he's a jerk."

"Right. OK. But he's not. Not empirically." Hillary and her SAT words and her whole I-just-found-out-I'm-going-to-Cal-next-year superiority. Jessa was starting to wish she could just sleep in the hall. No more roommates. "Look, he's not going to end up one of those guys who beats his wife and hangs out at Lit Lantern after work instead of going home to his three kids."

"Well, I'm sorry, Hil, if I think there are a few more levels of jerk above that particular scenario."

"You're a busy girl, Jessa. Your drama stuff, your honors stuff, your sports stuff, your choir stuff." Hillary stretched her arms above her and yawned. "A bunch of us have always wondered how you even had time for a boyfriend, you know?"

No, she did not know. What did that mean? A *bunch* of them wondered? And who was Hillary to judge anyway? She could medal at the Olympics in over-achieving. Jessa's stomach turned, like when she ate one finger dip too much of Tyler's magic cookie dough, the one with the M&Ms, the marshmallows, and the gummy bears.

"Don't get mad." Hillary watched her closely, her liquid eyes filled with what seemed like genuine concern. "I say more power to you, Jess. I think you're fantastic. You're a girl who's going places. You've got a future ahead of you. I get that. I just think Sean got tired of always being last on your things-to-do list. No offense."

Jessa frowned. Hillary dropped back again on the bed, her iPod spinning, closing her eyes, and for a tiny, delicious moment, Jessa imagined tossing her and the whole bed out the window.

#8: something real

In honor of National Picnic Day, Ms. Jackson suggested dinner on the beach that night, although Jessa wondered if it was just a sly way for Ms. Jackson to get a break from the other group. Francesca found blankets for them to use and managed to have their whole meal packed up into baskets that they carried across the busy road to the beach.

Jessa sat on the cold sand, watching water that churned like melted pewter. Storm clouds gathered. The game of Frisbee playing out in front of her at the water's edge was turning rapidly into contact Frisbee as Tim and Tyler dove at the same time, colliding into one another. Of course, to boys, this collision was something like gossiping. They seemed energized by it. Sean snatched a high toss from Mr. Campbell out of the air, whirled, and soon the Frisbee was out against the sky again, a spinning red saucer.

So athletic. The whole length of Sean's body leaned into his throw, then unwound from it, his eyes searching out where it landed, skittering into the water. He still hadn't said anything to Jessa about the list she'd handed him that morning outside the bus, his hair dipping into his eyes as he took the folded note.

Natalie had stayed back at the hotel, claiming a migraine. Probably a reaction to the implants. Only even now as she thought it, Jessa felt a tiny stab of guilt. Natalie had seemed really pale on the bus, sullen. Still, it was nice to have a break from having to watch her maul Sean. Sitting here on the beach, Jessa got to imagine the trip through the eyes of what might have been—her boyfriend playing on the sand with his buddies, her journal and a half-read novel nestled at her feet. No pesky boobs in the way, obstructing everyone's view.

But Carissa's envelope reminded her. No easy lean into the evening here, no pretending for a minute that the boy with the long, lean body in his jeans and hooded sweatshirt would throw one more toss, head over, and kiss the top of her head.

As if nothing had happened.

As if he hadn't shredded her heart with the thin, metal blades of his lies.

Reason #8: I HAD seen something real. He was showing signs well before the costume barn.

Carissa had seen it coming. Or so she said. Had seen him with Natalie once before, tucked into the shadows of the little alley out behind the gym after an assembly two Fridays before. Had seen him run his hand over the curve of her forearm, wondered if she'd seen something real—or imagined.

She apologized in the letter.

I'm sorry. I didn't tell you about Sean and the Boob Job—I just wasn't sure, wasn't sure I'd really seen anything. AND I had just had a conversation with him after class the day before I saw them where he said how there was just "something real" about you. How much he loved that about you. How "real" you two were.

Why had Carissa been talking to Sean about her anyway? Something real. Her new instruction. Do something real. Whatever that meant.

Instruction: Do something real—something that makes you feel like you've done something you can actually see, something you can touch.

She saw Dylan Thomas walking alone along the shore, his pants rolled to his knees. His hands were in his pockets and his head was tilted out toward the water, a stray ribbon of sun falling across his face. Dylan Thomas always seemed a little lost in his mind, a little pensive. Jessa started to gather her things. Maybe he'd like some company.

It started to rain.

The drops hit her face slow at first, then faster and faster. The Frisbee game disbanded. Mr. Campbell started folding up blankets. Hillary and Christina tucked unfinished food back into baskets. Jade picked up a few windblown pieces of trash. Ms. Jackson whistled, and like puppies, they followed her back across the empty street, now dark and spotted with rain.

• • •

The disco throbbed with techno music, mostly hits from the early nineties, tinny and hollow in the way that kind of techno pop could give the brain its own pulse. Tyler handed her a lukewarm soda, his head bobbing. They surveyed the room. The kids from the other group were decked out in full glamour gear. They gyrated and writhed on the dance floor, their bodies sending up a steamy haze in the smoky room. Most of the girls wore tight jeans or short skirts and halter tops, revealing bare midriffs, and heels.

Jessa didn't even own a pair of heels. She had been planning to buy a pair for junior prom, though now she probably wouldn't even go. She would stay home and have a *Bourne* marathon with Tyler, or maybe *Freaks and Geeks*. Make Ben and Jerry's Cherry Garcia and 7-Up shakes. She studied her jeans, her black ballet flats, the gray long-sleeve shirt that had seemed cute standing in front of the mirror in the hotel room. She must look like a Gap ad for the nerd girl—the one who might let down her hair and be sexy—only her hair was already down and she wasn't sexy, not even close.

"I'm going to dance," Tyler told her, handing her his drink. He disappeared into the fray, reappearing minutes later, stuck to some girl from the other group whose name was something that rhymed with Sam—Cam? She was cute, like a little imp. White-blonde hair. Black pants, a tank that said "Rock Me" in tiny rhinestones. Sexy. Go Tyler!

Jessa pushed through the doors out into the street, her senses slipping into recovery mode, her eyes squeezing the smoke from them, her ears ringing. It took her a minute to register Mr. Campbell standing there, looking out into the dark of the narrow street. She saw him before he saw her and she almost dipped back inside. Almost.

Then he noticed her. "Oh, hey, Jessa. Having a good time?"

"No."

He laughed, tucking his hands in his pockets. She noticed how far he stayed from her, the distance he put there. "Not your scene?"

"I hate these kinds of places." She didn't really hate them, that was too strong a word. But they weren't for her. Something about dances, parties, clubs, always made her feel like an imposter, like she had been taking voice lessons when all the other kids her age met for their learn-how-to-act-at-parties classes. They graduated, got their membership cards. She got piano lessons.

"At least there's no smoking in there. The only thing I've never liked about Europe. All the cigarettes." He watched a couple zip by on a Vespa and moved closer in toward the building. Good instinct. Jessa had learned pretty quickly that Italians will drive on the sidewalk. For no apparent reason. Tyler was almost road-kill in Rome. Or sidewalk kill.

"You've been to other parts of Europe?"

He nodded. "France. Switzerland. Germany. I actually taught summer school in Switzerland in college. For two months."

"I love it here." Jessa surprised herself, tossing around all her hate and love that evening. Words she didn't even actually like to use very often. Too extreme.

He started to say something, then seemed to rethink it. Turned instead again to the street. The rain had stopped, but there were tiny pools in the grooves and gullies of the cobblestone. They reflected the lights from the disco and the other buildings all around.

"I'm sorry about what happened, Mr. Campbell." And she was. She flushed, though, remembering how soft his mouth had been.

It was dark but she saw his face flush too.

"You're hurting. People do stupid things when they're hurting." He cleared his throat but didn't say anymore.

"What stupid things have you done?" The rain started again, just a light mist. It coated her face like dust. "You know what—you don't have to tell me that." She listened to the hush the rain brought, the way it seemed to use up the air, pack it with cotton. What was he thinking about, her teacher? Standing there in the rain.

"You're easy to talk to," he said, so quietly Jessa was surprised she had heard it, as if it had been brought to her on rain fingers, pressed word by word into her ears. She didn't speak, barely breathed. "And I wish I could talk to you, but it's sort of…I just don't want to give you the wrong idea."

"I'm not going to jump you or something." Jessa let out a strained laugh, tried to get him to meet her gaze. "I know about the whole teacher-student boundary thing. I mean, contrary to past displays of inappropriateness."

He ran his hands through his hair, still avoiding her eyes. "Yeah, I know."

"OK," she said brightly, "so, I guess I probably shouldn't ask you for a letter of recommendation, huh?" She broke into a formal voice, "Jessa Gardner's a great kid, very studious, hard-working. But don't let her near the new chemistry professor!"

Mr. Campbell's face broke into a smile. "I will, of course, write you a letter of recommendation. And I'll save the warnings for the last paragraph."

Jessa felt the ice thaw. "Thanks."

After a moment, he said, "You know, I've only seen her once since."

"Katie?"

"Yeah. At Whole Foods. Buying milk. She was wearing my old Sharks jersey from college. The one she always borrowed to wear to yoga."

Jessa remembered her list: Sean's soccer jersey he never let her borrow. She cleared her throat. "Did she see you?" Jessa imagined little Katie in that huge jersey, buying milk. Maybe for a new boyfriend who drank lattes and liked to eat Applejacks in the morning.

"No." For a moment, it seemed he might turn away, step off the curb into the street, but then he took a step toward her. "Thing is, I've only seen her that one time and it was the worst. And here you are, seeing him twenty-four seven. I don't know, Jessa. I think you're holding up pretty well."

Jessa shrugged. "It's like that kind of therapy where you overcome your fear of spiders by being stuck in a room crawling with spiders. It's kind of like that."

That fractured smile again and the silence of the wet, Italian night.

Finally, Jessa said, "Sean keeps wearing a shirt I bought him for his birthday. That blue one he wears all the time here. That was from me."

Mr. Campbell sighed. "They shouldn't be able to do that, huh? There should be some sort of clothing law against it. The Laundry Act of 2011. No more wearing of clothes bought or given by the one you betrayed."

"I'd sign it."

Carissa's note had said, "Something Real. Do something real."
Something she could touch. Her mind was spinning off into
the future. Tonight, she'd take that shirt off his back. Her own
Laundry Act of 2011. Throw it into the sea.

That would be something real, right?

She caught Mr. Campbell's eye and smiled what she hoped
was a smile filled with all that she was filled with: understanding,
hope, doubt. But really, maybe, it didn't say anything at all.

Maybe this was as real as it got.

#9: it's just
a reflection
(aka mr. narcissus)

"Has anyone seen my blue shirt?" Sean asked the whole group. They stood in Piazza San Marco, the central square of Venice, stealing some much needed time away from the other group after a morning of touring Basilica di San Marco. Jessa averted her eyes, studying a huge pack of pigeons that seemed to be winning the fight with the tourists for domination of the square.

Ms. Jackson squinted at him, confused. "Actually, Sean, I was wondering if anyone had any questions about the next couple of hours."

"Oh." He stuffed his hands in his pockets, kicking his foot slightly at a pigeon who was getting a bit too friendly. "I thought you meant in general. Any questions in general." He surveyed the group. No one had seen his shirt.

Well, no one admitted anything. Jessa remembered the way it had just bobbed there in the dark water, then washed up onto the shore, a wet mess, like a clump of seaweed. She had taken it easily.

Gone into his room, pulled it from the chair he had slung it over, walked across the road, and thrown it into the night sea. Totally anticlimactic, not real at all. Actually, she had just felt stupid, standing there with the wind in her face, with the clump of blue shirt washing up on the shore. She had waited, willing a shark or something to snatch it in its jaws and swim it furiously away. No shark—just a waterlogged clump under a cloudy night sky.

Maybe she needed to be officially done throwing things—drinks, shirts. It wasn't really working out for her.

Mr. Campbell pushed his sunglasses onto the top of his head, snuck a quick look at Jessa, then returned to some notes on his clipboard. The light kept shifting behind a cloud, the world alternating stripes of light and dark. "The key thing to remember, you guys, is that we want you to just write without editing yourselves. Venice is a place of so much water, and water brings reflection. It brings clarity. This has been a busy trip so far, and we just want you to have some time to process it all."

"You didn't tell us we'd be getting writing assignments." Devon pulled his eyes away from the mime entertaining a group of tourists sitting at one of the café tables in the plaza. The tables were eight deep at least. Jessa itched to find somewhere at bit more remote, the tables not so stuffed together. And maybe with not so many pigeons.

Mr. Campbell frowned. "You know what, Dev? Think of it as a time to jot down some ideas for sketches."

"Bonus." He whispered something to Tim, who smiled and nodded vigorously.

"We have our phones." Ms. Jackson held hers up as if they had somehow forgotten what a phone was. "Call us if you need to."

They splintered. Jessa noticed that for the first time Sean moved off by himself, away from Natalie, headed back toward St. Mark's, a small notebook tucked beneath one arm.

• • •

As Jessa wrote in her journal, a cool rush of air hit her in the face, lifting the strands of hair from her forehead. She sat at a small café table just off the Grand Canal, the sound of gondolas shushing by, the lapping of water all around. She checked her watch. She still had an hour before the group would meet up again.

She sipped from her hot chocolate, long grown cold in the little ceramic mug. She watched a gondolier in his black-and-white striped shirt maneuver through the canal with an older couple snapping pictures below him in their seats. "Glorified bus drivers," Dylan Thomas had called them that morning before their Basilica tour, "with a better outfit." Jessa had wanted to push Dylan Thomas overboard into the green water. She had liked her gondolier.

Closing her eyes now, she just listened. Her ears had tuned themselves to Venice, no cars anywhere—just people moving by feet or water. Peaceful. She had started writing immediately, channeling the rush of this place onto the lined paper beneath her pen, pressing its movement, its green water, its sea wind onto the white of paper with her black pen. Black and white, like the gondoliers.

If only everything could be black and white, right and wrong, yes and no. Then Sean could just be wrong, and she wouldn't have to think about how she missed the way he said her name, the way he used to laugh at her jokes, how she wished she could just kiss him again.

She didn't want to think about what Hillary had said about how maybe she brought it on herself. Her busy life, no real room for Sean. Where had it gone off track? One minute, a quick kiss before he drove Frodo into a pale twilight, and the next day, the red dress. She wanted to rip open the rest of Carissa's envelopes and find her answers before she was supposed to. But she didn't. She followed rules. Stupidly. Blindly?

This morning's reason:

Reason #9: It's Just a Reflection (aka Mr. Narcissus)

The myth of Narcissus. Ring any bells? It's why I call him Mr. Narcissus. The lovely youth is so captured by the image of himself in the pool that he DIES there. Hey, dummy! It's just a reflection! But no, he DIES because he is so in love with himself. I'm surprised Sean hasn't died yet—a tragic by-product of his love affair with himself.

Carissa had plastered a square of mirrored paper onto the page and beneath that:

> Instruction (I know you hate this kind of stuff but…!):
> Look at yourself. Do you like what you see?
> Start by writing a list of everything you do.
> What does it say about who you are?
> Don't freak out. It's just a reflection. You won't die.

Now Mr. Campbell and Ms. Jackson had them writing a whole reflection exercise, writing about what you feel, your dreams, your hopes—taking time to reflect.

It was a conspiracy.

Jessa opened her eyes. Reflection. Like the mirrored paper, Jessa's reflection was rippled, distorted. She tried to write about what she was feeling, what she thought all of this travel brought out of her, but mostly she could just describe it all, the crumbled bottoms of the water-lined buildings, the hot chocolate grown cold, the bright metal gray of the sky here. Black and white. And gray.

As much as she wanted to, Jessa didn't always like gray. She liked things to make sense. Have reasons, closure. It's why she loved musicals, well, at least the older ones. She knew stuff was darker now, but she liked her musicals hopeful. In her favorites, even with all the conflict, all the pain, she was always left with hope at the end. Always left reaching for something. She could count on that. That hopeful future. Hillary's words scratched at her brain, batted the word *future* like a cat with a ball of yarn, rolling it to the front of her mind.

Carissa wanted a list? Fine.

Quickly, Jessa wrote out a list of all her activities including hard classes. Twenty-one things. Could that be right? She counted again. Twenty-one things: Three sports, drama, choir, three AP classes, piano, voice, honors English, four clubs, two volunteer assignments, Little Pals tutoring, baby-sitting, and two other little jobs. That didn't even include friends, daughter, sister, girlfriend, or reading for fun, which she almost never did, which used to be her favorite thing.

She tapped her pencil against the paper, wondering what she could give up, but she couldn't bring herself to draw a line through any of them. She needed them all. She needed them all to get into the right college. She needed them for her future.

When she was seven, a friend of her father, another lawyer, had told her: "You'll make a great lawyer, just like your dad." Had that been it, then? She'd just fastened her future to those words, heading out across her childhood in the direction of Lawyerland. Easy answer, no gray. Did she even want to be a lawyer, or go to the right university? She'd been set on it for so long, was it possible that, somewhere along the line, she'd lost sight of what it was exactly she was working for? Would she get to the big bronze door of that land and wonder why she'd been traveling so far only to find herself not even wanting to knock? Wanting instead to settle in the patch of grass by the door, watching clouds move across a darkening sky, gray clouds?

Her iPod switched to a new track, her ears filling with "The Song of the Jellicles" from *Cats*. She thought of Alonzo, the tomcat—black and white. Her mom had taken her to see *Cats* when she was ten. Sitting there in the dark, she had watched all the cats emerging onto the stage, the Alonzo cat so confident, taking the stage by storm. All puffed up with feline confidence and grace. Each cat had a place, each cat a purpose. Even sad, messed-up Grizabella got to go away at the end, whirled away to a better life.

Jessa clicked ahead to "The Naming of Cats." She had always loved this poem best of all, had it plastered inside her English binder, highlighting the line:

You may think at first I'm as mad as a hatter when I tell you, a cat must have THREE DIFFERENT NAMES.

Three different names.

Nothing black and white about that. She wrote the line into her journal under her activity list. Then wrote, "How many names do I have? How many people do I try to be?" Jessa the choir girl. Jessa the drama girl. Jessa the track girl. Jessa the smart girl. Jessa with the super résumé. Where *did* she make time for a boyfriend? She drew a line through Jessa the girlfriend. Was it possible to have too many names?

She picked up her cup, staring out over the Venice landscape, her head pounding. Her teachers had mentioned going to Harry's Bar, and Jessa was tempted to seek them out, sit where Hemingway had sat, soak in the history of writers and artists who sat within its walls. At least she wouldn't have to think about this stupid writing assignment anymore or future lawyer Jessa or the little mirrored paper in Carissa's note. Too much gray.

Her eyes snagged on a couple on a nearby bridge. A blonde ponytail dangled down a narrow back, with strong arms around her. It took her a moment to realize that the ponytail belonged to Natalie, and another moment to realize those arms were not Sean's.

She saw Jamal's face when he pulled away, smiled down at Natalie, grabbed her hand, and pulled her across the bridge and out of sight. Jessa placed the cup slowly back onto the little table, her hand shaking slightly. She closed her journal.

Right answer: Tell Sean. Wrong answer: Sean had this coming.

Jessa's stomach treaded somewhere in between, into that spinning gray pool of uncertainty she seemed to be swimming deeper and deeper into each day. She folded Carissa's note back into its envelope and stuffed it inside her journal next to the list of activities, the list of names. She studied the place on the bridge where Natalie and Jamal had been kissing

Imagined Sean watching them too.

Thing was, Carissa forgot to mention the end of the Narcissus myth. From the place Narcissus died grew a beautiful flower. Somehow, that seemed like the most important part of the story.

#10: the night les mis came to dinner

They weren't sitting together at dinner. Jessa noticed that right away. Sean was sitting with Devon and Tim, his face blank, and Natalie sat between Christina and Maya. Jessa wanted to talk with Tyler, ask if he knew anything, but no one was really paying any attention to the others.

They were too busy noticing the new boy. New man? He was somewhere between a boy and a man. A sudden addition to the group sitting across from Francesca in the hotel restaurant. The whole group just stared, and for good reason. He was beautiful, like some sort of Michelangelo statue free of its marble casing, emerging into flesh and blood and bone, into dark curls and liquid eyes and a jaw chiseled and smooth. Come to think of it, that jaw could still be made of marble.

He drank a glass of dark wine and leaned in to hear what Francesca was saying to him. After several minutes, he shrugged and pushed his chair back away from the table as if he'd had enough of her words. He picked up the frog from where it leaned against her seat, spun it like a baton.

Francesca snatched it away, settled it on her own lap, her eyes narrowed.

Jade was the first to talk. "Yum." She motioned toward the new arrival. "Let me be more specific: Yum!"

Erika actually giggled, something Jessa had never heard her do. "I know, seriously," she breathed as if Jade had said something profound.

Dylan Thomas swallowed half his water in one gulp. "Not really my type."

Commotion at the door. Cruella bustled in, her face red. "Here you are!" She plunked her huge blood-colored bag onto a nearby table and pushed hair out of her face.

"We were looking *everywhere* for you." She glared down at Francesca, then noticed the brought-to-life David sitting across from her. "Who are you?"

He pulled out a pair of aviator glasses and squinted at them, pulled his shirt up to clean them, exposing a smooth, tan stomach. Jessa was pretty sure she heard several intakes of breath at that tan stomach. Then he examined Cruella, his syrup eyes clearly asking her back, "wouldn't you like to know?" before he slipped on the glasses.

When he didn't answer, Cruella rolled her eyes, moved her bag to another table near the back and plunked herself down in a chair. She snapped her fingers at the waiter. "A vodka tonic?" She caught the look from Ms. Jackson. "Oh, please. If I'm going to be marooned in this water-locked hellhole of a city, I'm going to have a vodka tonic." She pulled off a designer flat and started massaging her insole.

Jessa took a long drink of mineral water, feeling a bit like she was at sea, like the time her dad took her sailing out past the Golden Gate Bridge with all those inky, rolling waves. Something about Venice, about all the water and no cars, all that sky, made her wobbly at her center. On the ride back to the hotel, she'd flipped through her journal, read over what she'd written.

She definitely didn't like what she saw.

In her even black lettering emerged a girl who didn't really know who she was, why she chose things, what she even wanted. She was a laundry list of activities and triumphs, of awards and summer programs and parts in plays and job experience. She was a college application with all the little categories neatly filled in. Academics—check. Volunteer service—check. Extracurriculars—check. Clear career goal. All-fields-covered Jessa. But there was no category for just Jessa, nowhere to check that box off the list.

And what made Jessa, *Jessa?* Something about Venice had made her ask that question, made her, for the first time in her life, fail to answer it, fail to check the right box. Just because she *could* do all those things, be all those different Jessa girls, *should* she? Did all those little pieces of Jessa add up to one complete girl?

Tyler pushed Carissa's envelope across the table at her. "I think Carissa's running out of ideas."

The next reason read:

The Night *Les Mis* Came to Dinner.

Carissa's birthday last November. They told Dylan Thomas about the night *Les Mis* came to dinner. They had reserved the back room at Village Pizza, where they could get Carissa her favorite pepperoni and pineapple pizza and they had decided to do a dinner theater for her, a reenactment of *Les Misérables*. Only they didn't have a Javert. Sean wouldn't play Javert because he wanted to play Jean Valjean, which was totally Sean, because he always had to be the hero.

"The hero is the only character big enough for his ego," Tyler said, winding pasta around his fork.

"He was a good Valjean," Jessa mumbled.

Tyler snorted. Jessa was pretty sure, somewhere, an ocean away, that Carissa would be rolling her eyes.

"Who did you play?" Dylan Thomas asked Jessa.

"Éponine."

"Of course." Dylan Thomas reached over and stabbed the mushrooms she had pushed aside on her plate.

"This is why the other group doesn't like you." Jessa pulled her plate toward her, not that she would have eaten those mushrooms in a million years, even if they were the last food on the earth and someone had coated them in dark chocolate.

"Why didn't you play Javert?" Dylan Thomas asked Tyler.

"Because I played, like, every other guy character in the whole play." He leaned back to let the waiter set a bowl of steaming soup in front of him.

"What does this have to do with anything anyway?" Dylan Thomas motioned toward the envelope. "Why is she bringing it up? Sounds to me like these envelopes are becoming a little more about Carissa than they're supposed to be."

Something snagged in Jessa's chest. Had she been feeling that too, staring down at Carissa's insistent handwriting? "It's not a reason."

"It *is* a reason." Tyler swirled his soup with his spoon. "Carissa is addressing the very relevant fact that Sean is a self-absorbed jackass." He glanced at Dylan Thomas. "Judge's ruling?"

Elbow on the table, Dylan Thomas propped his chin on his hand. "I'll allow it."

"Good man!" His eyes were back on Jessa, who was rolling hers at Dylan Thomas. Tyler continued, "The guy who ended up playing Javert got the chicken pox the night before the birthday party."

"Does anyone even still get the chicken pox?" Dylan Thomas interrupted.

"Not the point." Tyler jabbed his spoon in the air. The point was, he told him, that Jessa stepped in at the last minute and played both parts, that she sang "Stars" in the back room of Village Pizza and other diners came in from other rooms to hear her. She made people cry, it was so beautiful. She made everyone cry.

"It's a really beautiful song," Jessa whispered.

"I always thought it was kind of judgmental," Dylan Thomas said, wiping some stray soup from his face with a napkin. "With all its 'you're wrong and I'm right and I have God on my side blah blah blah and when I find you you'll be sorry...'"

"Point is," Tyler said, interrupting, holding up the envelope. "She wants you to sing it somewhere where Sean can hear it. To remind him."

Jessa peered at the paper. "Where does it say that?"

Tyler paused. "It says."

Jessa checked again, turning the note over. "No, it doesn't. It says to sing it. It doesn't say anything about singing it where Sean can hear it. It doesn't say anything about reminding him." She held out the note for inspection.

Sing the song again, Jessa!
A grand symbol of why you're you and he's, well, him.

"Oh." Tyler fiddled nervously with his napkin, pretended to look for something under the table, like suddenly there was some sort of government summit going on right under the table that Tyler really needed to witness.

"Tyler?"

"What?"

"What exactly did Carissa say to you about this reason? Since you two have obviously been on the Batphone about this."

He emerged from under the table. "Nothing."

"Just tell me." A dull ache started creeping behind her eyes.

Instead of answering, he pushed back his chair, mumbled something about getting his water bottle—apparently it had been his water bottle he'd been conveniently rummaging for under the table—and left the room.

• • •

Jessa followed Tyler out to the hotel courtyard. "Why are you acting all weird?" The courtyard echoed with the sound of her voice, muffled only slightly by the drone of the ocean across the street.

Tyler turned around, his features shadowed in the feathery evening light. "I'm not."

"Tyler, you're obviously talking to her or you wouldn't have known that thing about reminding Sean." He was lucky she'd adopted a no-throwing policy because she seriously wanted to hurl something at him right now. Maybe that water bottle he'd gone looking for? He didn't answer her. "You know what? Forget it. If you're going to lie to me, you can just climb into one of those envelopes right there alongside of Sean. I'm used to it!" Jessa hurried out of the courtyard toward the beach, the sea air stinging her eyes.

"Jessa!" Tyler's footsteps behind her. "Wait…would you just wait!"

Looking both ways, she crossed the street toward the little strip of beach where they'd eaten the night before.

"I got my own envelopes!" he shouted behind her.

Jessa stopped but didn't turn around. In a minute, he was beside her, the buckles on his jacket ringing like tiny bells in her ears as he removed the stapled index cards from his inside jacket pocket.

"Well, not envelopes exactly."

He showed her the cover.

INSTRUCTION MANUAL TO MISS JESSA GARDNER

For Tyler, in case of emergencies

and cases where Jessa will be prone to act like, well, Jessa

"Instruction manual?" Jessa's head started to spin. "What? Like I'm a lawn mower? Some predictable machine?" She reached out to take the papers from Tyler.

He pulled them back. "She really, really didn't want you to see this."

"Too late." She reached for the manual.

Again, he pulled it away.

Head throbbing, Jessa felt the wind come off the water cold and quickly, and she shivered. "This isn't some reality TV show you guys get to have a good laugh at. I'm your friend."

Tyler was shaking his head before she'd finished talking. "No one's laughing. We're trying to help. And Carissa's not here. She just wants to help. We've never seen you like this before."

"Well, guess what? This isn't about Carissa for once. Or you. I don't need you stage managing my life, OK? Both of you are officially off Jessa watch!" Without waiting for his reply, she turned and ran toward the silver strip of beach.

• • •

A soccer tournament had come to Venice, or at least to the outskirts of Venice. To their hotel, to be precise. And the place crawled with boys in soccer jerseys—cute boys in soccer jerseys.

Later that night, Jessa found one of those boys dangling from a sheet out her hotel window.

She had walked the beach until about an hour before curfew, her mind spinning with Carissa's manual. Staring out at the churning water, she had tried to focus on what Carissa must have meant, that she must be thinking in some sort of twisted-Carissa-universe sort of way that she *was* helping or that she and Tyler *were* being funny, but Jessa's whole body kept settling on a feeling that was some sort of mashed up version of anger and bruised feelings and betrayal, that clenched-up gut feeling she got before she puked. She wanted to trust her friend, wanted to appreciate her trying to help, but mostly she just wanted everyone to leave her alone. She could find her own way without notes, without some stupid instruction manual, without Tyler's manic, stage-managery control issues.

Staring out at the sharp, churning water, she'd never felt so far from the worn quilt on her bed, the feel of her favorite blue mug in her hand, the view of pine trees out her own window.

Exhausted and cold, she'd headed back to the hotel to take a shower in the shared bathroom at the end of the hall. She had expected to come back from the shower, crawl into bed, and sleep. Instead, she found her bed jammed up against the window, its sheet and the one from Hillary's bed tied together, wound around a bedpost, and draped outside—and their room was on the fourth floor of the hotel.

"What are you doing?" She stared down at the dangling boy, puzzled, as he tried to gain some footing on the slick side of the building.

"Hillary," he managed in a thick Italian accent, clearly holding on for dear life, his feet gaining and losing ground.

Jessa pulled him into the room.

He tumbled in, gasping for breath, "Grazie."

They blinked at each other.

"Wait here," Jessa told him.

• • •

Hillary had been waylaid at the roadblock that Mr. Campbell and Ms. Jackson had set up at the entrance to their floor sometime after Jessa had come home to take a shower. Hillary stood under the arched doorway, arms crossed, glaring at the floor. Ms. Jackson waved a bottle of some sort of clear alcohol at her.

"What were you thinking, Hillary? I mean, really—what were you thinking?"

Jessa noticed the pile of alcohol bottles at their feet, some empty, some still capped. For a horrified moment, she thought they were all Hillary's until she realized that her teachers must have been collecting them from all the students as they came back in for curfew. Ms. Jackson added Hillary's to the pile with a dangerous clink of glass.

"Um, Hil?" Jessa started when Hillary looked up and caught her eye. "Um…"

"Oh, damn it! Bruno!" She raced toward their room.

"Bruno?" Ms. Jackson followed her down the hall.

Mr. Campbell raised weary eyebrows at Jessa. "Who's Bruno?"

"We didn't have much chance for introduction."

He groaned, sinking down against the hotel doorway. "This is going to be a long night."

• • •

Jessa peeked at her watch—4 a.m. So much for going to bed early. She leaned on the wide windowsill, the curtains billowing behind her, the sea air cool on her face. No one had really slept yet. After hours of tears, of doors slamming, of urgent texting, Mr. Campbell and Ms. Jackson had almost everyone accounted for. Then came all the phone calls home to parents. Jessa was pretty sure they were all being sent home—Mr. Campbell had suggested as much when she passed him in the hallway.

Somewhere around two, she and Hillary had finally untangled the sheets, scooted the beds back into their rightful positions, and Hillary had gone to sleep wrapped in Bruno's jacket.

An hour ago, she'd heard Ms. Jackson's door across the hall click shut after rounding up the last of their group—L. E., who'd been taking a moonlit run on the beach with a tall midfielder from one of southern Italy's premier teams. At least that's what she told Ms. Jackson (and her mom via cell phone) in heated whispers in the hall. Hillary and Jessa had pressed down on the floor to listen through the crack under the door. Jessa believed L. E. She'd seen them come in through the courtyard, walking hand in hand, two sets of running shoes side by side. She probably was taking a run, knowing L. E., and it seemed like Ms. Jackson believed her too. But she'd been chasing them into their rooms all night, sorting through lies and truth like mismatched socks.

Technically, most of the group had broken the behavior contracts they'd signed before leaving. Still, Jessa didn't believe her teachers would send the whole bunch of them home. Besides, the other group was in more trouble than Williams Peak. Two of them had even come back to the hotel in Italian police cars. Those two were *definitely* going home. Quiet Guy had stood in the courtyard nodding along to whatever the officer told him, his jacket over a pair of red plaid pajamas. When Jessa passed Bob-the-world's-most-boring-world-history-teacher in the hall, she thought he looked so worried he might throw up, called to the lobby in his robe, face green as an alien, Francesca hurrying behind him, spouting Italian into her phone. For once, there was no sign of the frog.

Jessa watched most of it unfold from her window. Madison, Cheyla, and a few other girls laughed their high hyena laughs with a pack of soccer players, passing a glinting bottle back and forth. Kevin and Rachel wandered through the courtyard, his arm around her shoulders. When had that happened? Even Cruella wobbled in alone around 3 a.m. on spaghetti legs, her sunglasses still perched atop her head, looking thin, worn.

Now it was quiet. A hush had settled over the hotel, a cloak of sleep around its stone shoulders. Jessa could see the ocean from her window, a dark, moving thing. The sky was choked with stars, the storm clouds having passed through. She thought of Carissa's instructions. She had told Tyler to make Jessa sing where Sean could hear her. A ribbon of anger fluttered through her stomach, then settled like a feather. As much as she hated to admit it, Carissa did know what made her feel better. And singing always made her feel better, replenished something in her, her own little electrolyte tonic. Even if she didn't need him to hear, she needed to sing.

Quietly, like mist, she started to sing "Stars."

There was movement behind her. Hillary pulled the curtain aside and leaned next to her against the window. "Pretty," she murmured, rubbing her eyes.

"Did I wake you up?"

She shook her head. "I couldn't really sleep."

Jessa started from the beginning, Javert's song about chasing his fugitive, the despair of his failure, because really, it was less about judgment and more about being a slave to his own dogma that sent Javert leaping to his death. Her voice picked up, sent the song up and out, and she heard a movement at the window of the next room. Suddenly, Jade's voice joined hers, floating out, then falling into the courtyard below. Jade shifted the words around, catching onto the underbelly of Jessa's voice, adding dimension to her song.

They sang through to the end, their voices widening, entwining, and Jessa watched a few lights click on around the hotel, people leaning out, blinking from their windows below, looking up. Somewhere, Jessa was sure Sean was listening.

Several rooms over, Devon shouted out. "What do you think this is—*West Side Story*? Go to sleep, you idiots!"

#11: café dumbass

No one from Williams Peak was being sent home, but Mr. Campbell and Ms. Jackson let them know at breakfast that they were on very short leashes—collars, really. And they were leaving Venice early, losing the opportunity to take the cool boat ride that had been planned for the morning.

They left Venice with the dawn just a peeking glowing band on the horizon, the night above still spattered with stars. Francesca sat in the first seat, rubbing her temples, the man-boy whose name Jessa still didn't know asleep next to her, the side of his face pressed against the window.

Rachel slid into the seat next to her. "His name's Giacomo," she whispered, offering Jessa a wafer cookie from a bag.

"Who?" Jessa took a cookie, popped it in her mouth where it melted almost instantly. Yum. She grabbed another.

Rachel motioned to the front of the bus. "Adonis up there."

"Who is he?" Jessa helped herself to yet another cookie.

Rachel shook her head. "We're working on that. But he's definitely with Francesca. Lizzie heard them fighting last night."

"What about?" Jessa studied the back of Giacomo's head.

"Who knows? It was all Italian. But she said it was *heated*. Can I sit here?" Rachel tucked her knees up against the back of the bus seat in front of her and flipped open a *Tennis* magazine.

Jessa's eyes searched the bus. Tyler sat up close to the front with his sweatshirt pulled over his eyes. She nodded at Rachel. "Sure. You playing first singles this year?"

"Hope so. Kelly Stahl is hitting really well. She'll give me a run for my money."

"Not a chance. You're more consistent than Kelly."

Rachel seemed surprised. "Thanks. Do you still play?"

Jessa sighed. "Not really. Volleyball kind of took over. Can't do it all." She cleared her throat, averted her eyes out the window. She and Rachel had gone to the same summer camp for tennis all through middle school, and she'd played a bunch when they lived in the city. But volleyball and tennis were the same seasons at Williams Peak. Jessa couldn't remember the last time she picked up her racquet. Maybe she'd dig it out of her closet when she got home.

She could feel Rachel studying her. "Well, if anyone can do it all, it's you. We should hit sometime. For fun," Rachel added.

Jessa fiddled with her iPod. "I'd like that. You'll obliterate me, but I'd like that."

Popping her mint gum, Rachel went back to her magazine, winding a piece of honey-colored hair around her finger.

Jessa clicked to *Evita* on her iPod and let the music wash over her. She pressed her palm against the cool glass of the bus window and bid farewell to Venice, its green canals still snaking through her veins. Maybe once you drifted through the water world of Venice, it never really left—your body was somehow forever tied to the floating island city.

Jessa shut off her music, fidgeting in the seat. She couldn't get comfortable. Something was wrong. She knew it, felt it in the pit of her belly. In some sort of mid-trip fractured way, she knew that something had broken for her. Not just her fight with Tyler or Carissa's stupid manual or the chaos of last night. Not even Sean, who sat three seats away, reading his *National Geographic*—was he fifty? He loved that magazine. No, it was something bigger than that.

But Sean and Natalie, who now snuggled up front with Jamal, were definitely over. Somewhere between Florence and Venice, she had switched boys the way Jessa might change her shirt at the last minute before running out the door. Red shirt, blue shirt. Sean shirt, Jamal shirt. Sean must have felt her watching him. He turned, the magazine slipping slightly against where he had it propped on his knee. He gave a quick, practice wave, like he was auditioning to wave to her. Jessa pretended to be searching her iPod. No, this feeling wasn't about Sean. What had shifted? Something had split off, was left bobbing there in the Venice canals.

"Jessa?"

Mr. Campbell stood in the bus aisle. He slid into the now-empty seat beside her. At some point, Rachel had moved up a few seats and was snuggling with Kevin, their voices low purrs. Jessa pulled her earbuds out and tucked them into her sweatshirt pocket.

Mr. Campbell seemed like he'd aged four years, his eyes all dark circles and his skin red splotched.

"Rough night?" she asked.

"You could say that." He held a book out to her. An old paperback with a black-and-white cover. *A Portrait of the Artist as a Young Man*, well read and dog eared.

She took the book, smoothed her hand over the cover, looked at him expectantly.

"You gave me a book for the trip. I figured I could return the favor." He folded his hands in his lap, leaned into the seat.

"James Joyce?" She had seen Hillary reading it for AP English during rehearsals last month. She said it was confusing—beautiful, but confusing.

"Kind of changed my life." Mr. Campbell smiled a sad, half smile at her. "In the way that some books can change what you know about yourself. For better or worse, when you look at the world through an artist's eyes, it's nice to know you aren't alone."

She thanked him, flipped it open. He had marked some of the pages with a black ink pen, little flecks in the margins.

"Ignore the marks. I wrote a paper on it in college. You'll find your own marks."

"What's it about?" She read the small description on the back. A boy "choosing between a religious vocation and an artistic one." Her stomach fluttered. A boy finding his way.

"Just read it. We'll talk." He moved back to his place near the back of the bus with Ms. Jackson who quickly, but long enough for Jessa to see, squeezed Mr. Campbell's hand as he slid into the seat beside her.

• • •

Time travel. That was really the only explanation for it. Umbria. Castles and fortresses standing out against the sky, the hills all layered like waves, dotted with terra-cotta towns and row upon row of olive trees.

They waited for the frog to point them in the right direction.

Here, though, sitting on a smooth stone bench in the center of the Piazza del Comune, Jessa wasn't sure there was a right direction at all.

Assisi—even the word took time to say. Time didn't seem at all in a hurry here, not the busy buzz of Florence and Rome, or even the drifting, dreamy haze of time in Venice. Here, time took a long lunch, planting itself firmly on a blanket in a fat beam of sun. Was it the twenty-first century or the nineteenth? Did it matter? Not really.

Well, that's not totally true. It seemed to matter to her friends.

And to the other group. Everyone, it seemed, was in full-force fidget mode. Squirmy, like ants on a banana peel—ants with iPods, and phones, and PlayStations, and Nintendos.

The frog wanted their attention. Francesca waved it in three, quick flaps over her head. "Who has heard of St. Francis?" She waited. A man buzzed by on a Vespa. St. Francis—Jessa had *heard* of him, but she wasn't sure where or why.

"The nature monk?" Dylan Thomas called from a bench where he and Tyler had been lounging in the sun. He blinked and looked around the group. "Oh, come on, people. He was like Dr. Doolittle or something." He shook his head, apparently disgusted either with their lack of knowledge on St. Francis or perhaps with Dr. Doolittle, Jessa wasn't sure. He collapsed back on the bench and closed his eyes.

"Um, the Eddie Murphy movie?" Cheyla volunteered without missing a moment on her phone, texting someone furiously, her fingers flurried bees. Could someone get carpal tunnel in their thumbs?

Francesca looked skyward. Perhaps the frog would have a reason for their tragically incomplete educations?

Mr. Campbell cleared his throat. "You guys will like this one. Rich kid who denounces his dad to live in poverty, to seek out the quiet life, the virtuous life tied to nature."

Devon frowned. "No offense, Mr. C, but what about that story did you think we would like?"

Tim nodded. "Yeah, no offense, but he sounds like kind of a tool."

Francesca leveled her gaze at them. "He was buried on Hell Hill with convicts and outcasts."

Erika and Blake stopped whispering, their heads swiveling to attention. A hush blanketed the group. Cruella clucked her tongue disapprovingly.

Francesca had them at "Hell Hill."

• • •

"Are you talking to me yet?" Tyler offered her a gummy bear, staring down at where she sat on the steps outside the Basilica di San Francesco.

Jessa shook her head, returned her gaze to the book in her lap.

"What if I do a dance?"

She squinted up at him, the sun against his back making him glow with the warmth of Umbrian sun. "No dancing."

"What if I promise *not* to dance?" He put on his sweet, please-forgive-me-puppy-dog-who-ate-your-shoe face.

She took the bag of gummy bears, folded them up, and put them in her bag. "I'm officially cutting you off."

He sat down next to her, pulled out another bag of gummy bears from his bag, and ate a handful. "OK, I have an idea."

"What idea?"

"I know Carissa can be a real pain. She can be a spoiled, selfish drama queen."

"I'll tell her you said so."

"Let me finish." Tyler held up his hand. "You know what she loves more than anything?" Jessa held his gaze. "You," he finished. "She put a lot of time into these envelopes, and believe it or not, they're helping. I mean, you don't have that beat-puppy face twenty-four seven like you did when we first started." He twisted his face into a replica of the aforementioned puppy.

"I don't make that face." Jessa returned her eyes to her book, but she wasn't really reading.

"You know what I think?"

"Enlighten me."

"I think we finish. We've come this far. You finish the instructions. I finish the manual. If for no other reason than I'm getting really tired of looking at churches."

Jessa pushed her sunglasses on top of her head and rubbed her eyes. Something in the air here seemed to slow the world around her, disperse time like dandelion fluff left suspended in the cool, sun-spilt air. Her eyelids drooped. She thought of her sister, Maisy, when she was barely two—how her eyes would give up before she would for a nap. Her mom would drive around and around to get Maisy to sleep, her eyelids thick as her head bobbed and fought in her car seat. Jessa would ride next to her, watching, waiting for that exact moment they'd close for good and they were safe to go to the drive-through coffee place, latte for Mom, mango smoothie for Jessa.

Finally, she said, "OK."

They watched everyone regroup, wander back to the steps from the little shops they had been perusing. Mr. Campbell stood a few feet away, checking his watch every few minutes.

Tyler motioned toward the note tucked into her book:

Reason #11: Café Dumbass.

"But in the spirit of full disclosure as you now *know* that I know what's coming next, I always thought this one was Carissa at her bitchiest."

"Me too." And it was. Usually after a show, they all went to Tony's, an old diner out on Highway 174, mostly because it was open late and also because Tony Stevens, the owner, gave them free French fries and acted like they were some kind of celebrities because they were in the high school show. But during the *Hamlet* run, they had wanted to find a café for after the Sunday matinees. So L. E. had suggested Café Dumas, a new one that had opened downtown that was supposed to have really yummy muffins and play good music on Sundays. Another kid who worked there had been passing out little glossy cards after the show that day.

Sean got lost finding it, so they were already fighting, but when they walked in, he said, "What kind of place calls itself Café Dumbass?" and he wasn't trying to be funny. Jessa tried to make it seem like he was joking, like he didn't just totally mispronounce it and look like an idiot announcing it to the room. But Carissa knew better, eyed Sean with icy eyes from her perch next to Aaron Wright, who played Laertes and was too cute for his own sweet nature. Carissa had taken to flirting with him like she might qualify for an Olympic trial in toying with nice guys' feelings.

"It's *Doom-ah*, moron," she had drawled. "But we could call you Café Dumbass if you'd like."

And even though most of them meant it in fun, Jessa still watched Sean prickle anytime he walked into a room and someone yelled out, "Café Dumbass!"

Jessa pulled out her phone.

"What are you doing?" Tyler peered over her shoulder, watched her text.

"Telling Carissa that I'm not doing it. She should've come up with some other ideas than having me shout things at him, throw things at him. Her need to have things hurled in his general direction is getting a little generic."

"But don't tell her you know about the manual!"

"I won't! Shut up for a second."

She was halfway through the text when she realized the group had fallen silent. Jessa paused, her thumbs hovering over the tiny keys.

Mr. Campbell was boring a hole into her head with his eyes. Not a happy hole. A dark, smoldering hole.

"What?" Her question was barely a breath.

"See," Mr. Campbell addressed the group. "This is what I mean. This is what I'm talking about. Here we are. In Italy. Halfway around the world, walking through ancient ruins and buildings with ancient stories. And all you guys can do is bury your heads in your machines." He threw up his hands. Ms. Jackson stood next to him, her face unreadable.

The group was silent, their phones, iPods, cameras, PSPs, Nintendos drooping like overripe fruit at the end of their arms. What had she missed? Had he been talking? Her face went hot. She jammed the phone into her bag. The other group hurried away as if avoiding a sudden rainstorm and reconvened on the other side of the courtyard.

Francesca leaned into Mr. Campbell, whispered something. He waved her off. "No, really. It's ridiculous. You're trying to talk to them and they're so plugged in they can't even hear you. It's embarrassing. You've got all this reality around you, all this history and you're too busy…" At this point, Mr. Campbell did something that could be described only as performance art—sort of a mime mixed with bleeps and clicks that was surely meant to be them texting, talking on phones, listening to iPods, but it made him look like Pinocchio on speed.

Clearly, he'd lost his mind.

"Put them away," he finished, his face beading with sweat. "Away. Text your parents, friends, whatever. And tell them you're offline, unplugged, deactivated—for the next twenty-four hours. You're done."

"Ben…" Ms. Jackson started, quietly, her eyes down.

"No way, Amy. No way. We're done. Turn them in." He zipped open his backpack, held it open.

One by one, they each dropped their electronics into Mr. Campbell's bag. Hillary went three rounds with him over whether her Kindle really counted since all she did on it was read books and was he taking books away? With a sigh, he let her keep the Kindle.

Soon, though, his bag was bulging, so Ms. Jackson bit her lip, unsnapped her bag, and held it out away from her as if someone might puke in it.

Jessa sent a text to her parents:

Doing experiment. Offline 24 hours. No worry. Fun. Talk tomorrow.
Luv U. Text Mr. C if you need me.

She dropped her phone and iPod into Ms. Jackson's bag, who sighed and widened her eyes a bit at Jessa. "You'll get them back tomorrow. Or when Ralph Waldo Emerson over there cools off a bit."

Mr. Campbell stood in a clench, arms knotted across his chest. When all devices had been surrendered, he took a long, steady breath. "You have one hour. I don't want you with anyone or talking to anyone. Just walk around. Listen to this place. Smell it. Hear it. Then we'll meet back at the bus."

• • •

This part of the world had been quilted, patchworked in swatches of olive trees and stone, green and earth and sky knitted together. The layers of hills, the bleached pastels of the little houses. The world smelling of sunlight, Jessa found a shady hollow of ground beneath a tree and instinctively reached for her iPod.

Maybe Mr. Campbell had a point.

She rubbed her eyes, leaned her head against the tree trunk, felt her body settle into the air. "Listen," he had told them. Nothing. So quiet she could hear the air dreaming through the leaves above her.

Jessa took stock of her body, something the yoga teacher made them do when she and her mom went to class on Wednesdays together. Aware of feet, of legs, of stomach, of shoulders—aware of the tight skin around her eyes, aware of the way her eyes felt slightly dusted with sand.

Aware that here it was earth that flooded her veins, not water, like in Venice. Earth. Sky. Clouds. She opened *Portrait* and started to read where she left off last night, when her eyes where too blurry to read the already shifting and looping words of Joyce. Talk about Café Dumbass. She could open a cafe of her own right here in Assisi. She was pretty sure she didn't understand the book at all, so much of it blurred on the page before her eyes.

Still, something about his language, something about the way he
put words next to each other, made her breath catch, made her
feel like Joyce could see deep into the dark parts of her. Even if
she didn't know what the hell he was talking about.

She sighed.

"Such a sad sound."

She started, sat up. Francesca's mystery companion, Giacomo,
stood a few feet away, dressed in denim, a snug black T-shirt,
those funny shoes all the Italian men seemed to wear, his
sunglasses fixed into the curls atop his head. Edged in sky, the
Assisi landscape behind him, all castles and towers and stone, he
was a god—or a prince. He should have a white horse. Maybe a
cape of some sort. Jessa laughed out loud.

"What is funny?" He squinted his dark eyes at her, tipped his
head the way her dog Taco would while she watched Jessa do
her homework.

"I'm sorry. I'm sorry. I just…you standing there. You look a
bit like something out of a fairy tale." Juvenile! She could *not*
believe she had just said that to him. She blamed Joyce, all that
language on the page.

It was his turn to laugh. "Why do you sit here? All alone?"

"Our teacher kind of freaked out. Sort of gave us a teenage
time-out."

"What is this 'time-out'?"

"Like a break. Time to ourselves." She wished she were

standing, not slumped up against a tree. But her legs didn't seem to be working.

He sat down next to her. "Sounds like a nice thing—this time-out."

Up close, his beauty was even more disarming, the olive smoothness of his skin, the dark eyes flecked with a deep green. Jessa's whole body shivered, like being close to a famous piece of art. He was one big, walking, talking Italian cliché—the dashing, handsome stranger with an accent like rich, dark chocolate. She would have rolled her eyes if they were working. Which they weren't. They couldn't seem to focus on anything but his face.

He leaned over and Jessa thought for a fluttery moment he might kiss her, but he was offering his hand. "Giacomo."

"Jessa," she said, shaking it, and realizing she was, ridiculously, disappointed.

He kept her hand in his, turned her arm, took in her scar. He traced a finger along it.

Jessa thought she might faint, which would be super embarrassing, so she really, really willed herself to not. *No fainting. No fainting*, she repeated over and over in her head. So far so good.

"What is this?"

She cleared her throat. "Oh, that? I was in a Sea-Doo accident. When I was eight."

"Sea-Doo?" He laughed again, the funny American word like rocks in his mouth.

"A thing you ride across water. Like a jet-ski. Like a little motorized boat that you sit on." Jessa swallowed, her throat full of what felt like sponges. Wet ones. He was still holding her hand, his finger still resting on her scar.

"I know jet-ski." He let go, sat back, and rested his arms on his bent knees. His eyes swept over the groove of trees they were sitting in. "Assisi hasn't changed so much in a hundred years. It is nice here, no?"

"I love it here." Jessa blinked into the yellow light. Somehow, even the light here seemed settled, slower. "Being here makes me feel like my whole life somewhere else is just a huge fraud."

His smile let her know that she hadn't said something stupid, and Jessa noticed something almost sad in the curve of it. There seemed a weight on his body, the way his shoulders sagged at the edges—and it wasn't from wearing a cape.

Without thinking, Jessa rushed on, "I feel like crying here. All the time."

He stretched out on his back, lying flat on the ground, his hands tucked under his head like a pillow, and closed his eyes. "That is Italia."

#12: dictionary definition

Outside the church entrance, Jessa could still see the muzzle of the sleeping dog lying in the pool of late afternoon sun. She had stepped over him to get into the church, and he hadn't blinked. Two women called to each other, one from the street, one from a high, out-of-sight window. The Spoleto streets hummed with Italian, with machines rebuilding, reconstructing all the beauty of this terra-cotta town, competing with the birds in trees twittering, rustling their wings.

Jessa lit a candle and gazed at the Virgin Mary. The virgin gazed back. The church was both warm and cool, the air smelling of ancient dust, of candles. Her body seemed to drain of all its tension, becoming part of the flickering light, the primordial air. It struck her that this feeling was a lot like she felt in the costume barn, the peaceful emptying of her mind, or at least the way she *used* to feel in the costume barn—before. Jessa was starting to separate her life in this way: B.C.B. (before costume barn) and A.C.B. (after costume barn). Never before had her life been so cleanly divided into a before and after, not even when she moved out of the city. For better or worse, that day she threw open the door of the costume barn, she found herself on a distinctly different path, without a map.

Here, in the matte light of the church, it seemed for the better. In the candlelight, she traced the scar along her arm, the ghost line of Giacomo's fingers. Smiling, she checked her watch. Ten minutes until she needed to be back for dinner.

After their time-out, they'd boarded the bus in silence, penitent, under Mr. Campbell's watchful eye. She'd watched the landscape slide past the bus windows, the olive trees, the watercolor sky, on the short drive from Assisi to Spoleto, where they would spend the night in a converted church.

"That is Italia," Giacomo had said.

She sat on a little wood bench in the church and peeled open Carissa's latest envelope. She hadn't done the last one, hadn't shouted "Hey, Café Dumbass" into the still air of the bus. Mostly, it just seemed really, really stupid. Not to mention that none of Carissa's other shouting instructions had done much to help with anything. And Sean's phantom smile when she walked past his seat had been too sad. Maybe Italy had gotten to him too. All that air and sky, that melted-candy palette.

Or maybe it was just that Natalie and Jamal had taken their two-act show on the road. Act 1: break hearts. Act 2: make out. No intermission.

The paper crinkled, echoed in the dim of the church. Her

candle flickered and shifted next to the others, casting the room in dappled yellow light.

Dictionary Definition—they'd been playing the game since sixth grade. Well, forcing people to play it. No one liked it quite as much as Carissa and Jessa did. She'd been waiting for Carissa to bring it up as a reason Sean's a jerk, was actually kind of surprised it hadn't come up until Reason #12.

One of her most uncomfortable moments with Sean had been during a game of Dictionary Definition. They'd been backstage at the end of the *Hamlet* run, their relationship not even fully formed, like a bubble emerging from a wand, not even caught on the air yet. The word had been *amorous*, and they were playing in teams. Jessa had defined the word as "feelings of love," and it was Sean's turn to use it in a sentence. Without pause, he'd said, "Jade makes me feel amorous."

Jerk. Carissa had thought that Jessa should break up with Sean then and there, but he'd said he was sorry, just blurted it out, didn't mean it. Jessa hadn't much wanted to play team DD since.

But Carissa's instruction wasn't for a team game. It was the individual rules.

OK, you have three definitions to write:

Boyfriend

Love

Jessa

For individual DD, the game worked like this. You made up a fake definition and a real definition. The other person playing had to guess which one was fake and which one was real. Usually the words were a little harder, like *contrition* or *aromatic*: SAT words.

Or maybe these words were harder.

Tyler slid into the seat next to her, smelling of perfume. "Holy candles, Batman."

Jessa passed him the envelope. "You smell like a girl."

He flushed, a totally un-Tyler thing to do. "Yeah, I was hanging out with Cameron." The girl from the disco in Venice.

Jessa shot him an amused look. "Hanging out?"

"She's really cool actually. She totally hates her school. How all those girls are so materialistic. And she can't help it that she's super rich or whatever." He cleared his throat, kicked a black shoe onto his knee, motioned to the envelope. "So, Dictionary Definition."

"Yeah, no surprises for you, I guess." Jessa gathered up her things, trying to keep the knife edge out of her voice.

Tyler ducked under its blade. "For the record, I think it's one worth doing." He stood up, dug his hands into his pockets. His hair seemed especially shiny and black in all the candlelight, his dark skin warm.

"Thanks for not pushing the last one." Jessa slung her bag over her shoulder.

He shrugged. "Hey, didn't want to *manage* you and all that."

"Even if sometimes I really, really need it?"

"No comment."

Jessa looped her arm through his, and, with the candles dying behind them, they exited the church into the pink Spoleto evening, the air smelling of roses.

• • •

Ms. Jackson collected them after dinner for an attempt at another creativity salon. She looked at little skeptical, considering the disaster of the last one, but there they were, all huddled into a nook of the converted church they were sleeping in that night. They sat on wooden benches, the walls lined with candles. At least it gave them a break from the other group.

Jade took her guitar to the front of the room, hooked the braided strap across her back. She sang in that coffee-ice-cream voice of hers, a sweet song she had written on the bus:

> Why can't Pluto be a planet anymore
> If he's still up there in the stars?
> Why can't Pluto be a planet anymore
> While Neptune parties with Venus and Mars?

Jessa closed her eyes, her body rocking back and forth.

Someone was staring at her.

Her eyes blinked open. Giacomo stood in the doorway, his

eyes on her. When he saw her see him, he smiled. Jessa nodded and fixed her eyes on Jade.

> Pluto, you were promised an atmosphere,
>
> You circled the sun, a rogue moon masquerade,
>
> Pluto, we're all promised constellations,
>
> We're all orbiting alone, don't trade
>
> Your planet dreams…you'll always be a planet
>
> To me. You'll always be a planet to me.

Jade finished singing, nodding to the applause and whistles.

"Fabulous, Jade." Ms. Jackson beamed. Her eyes searched the room. "Who's next?"

"I'll go." Jessa surprised herself, her body standing before she'd registered it. She knew the room was nervous. What nut-bar thing would crazy-heartbreak-drink-throwing-limerick-spewing girl do this time? "I promise I won't be a jerk this time."

"OK." Ms. Jackson motioned toward the seat Jade had just left.

Jessa unfolded the sheet of paper from her pocket, her instruction from Carissa written on the back of the note itself. "So you guys know about that game Carissa and I play, Dictionary Definition?"

Nods all around. They'd been going to school together for a while. Jessa was pretty sure she'd made them all play it at some point or another.

Tim raised his hand. "Will this make me feel amorous?" Sean flipped him off.

"OK, so Carissa's making me give the definition of my name." Jessa licked her lips, focused on her own handwriting. "So I wrote this. It's called 'Middle Name.'"

It might help to start with my middle name. Ray. Not the girl way of spelling it. The boy way. R-A-Y. It was my grandfather's name. He lived in San Diego where my mom grew up—out in El Cajon which means "the box," which is a little like what you feel pressed into when you're there in the summer but where I used to swim in this huge blue pool and so it will always feel like water—that place. Like floating.

When I was four, my grandpa would play Scrabble with me on the little balcony of his mobile home which always felt like walking on the moon, all foamy and flexible. Of course, I couldn't really spell very well. I was four. But he'd let me make words up with my jumbled string of letters. Then he'd pronounce them to me and declare the points. KLQGT—fifty points! RUSBD—thirty-five points! And he'd tell me, his calloused hand like a butterfly on my arm, when maybe I accidentally put them into some sort of order that actually made sense.

Once, I spelled *slick*—and he brought out a shiny piece of white paper from his pocket, a receipt or something, and smoothed my little finger along it. "Slick," he told me, the skin wrinkling like tissue around his eyes the way it always did when he smiled at me. A real word entirely by chance. Each tile clicked up against each other, unknowingly making sense. At least to my grandpa.

That's Italy so far. To me. All those tiles suddenly making sense.

Folding the paper into tiny squares, Jessa sat down again next to Dylan Thomas, who had come in from the meeting with his group and sat on the end of a wooden bench. The clapping happened slowly, then some whistles. She tried not to notice Sean's face, the way he watched her like he smelled roses all around, like the candles weren't the only light in the room.

• • •

The girls all had to sleep in one big room. It was sort of like that *Madeline* book Maisy had been obsessed with when she was four and made Jessa read about five thousand times a week. Sleeping in *two straight lines*…Which meant she had to sleep in the same room as Natalie, watch her shimmy out of a pink shirt over a black-lace bra, slip into silky red pajamas Jessa's mom would never in a million years let her try on much less own. Watch her brush her white-blonde hair with a glossy pink brush over and over and over as if the brush transferred shimmering rays into that hair with each stroke. No one's hair should be that shiny when it wasn't under hot stage lights. Seriously, there should be some sort of law.

Maybe she could get appendicitis just like Madeline did in

Maisy's book. Men in white shirts would wheel her away to a hospital bed lined with flowers and a dreamy rabbit picture on the ceiling and a distant papa would buy her a dollhouse. It would be so great to get appendicitis right now.

Jessa pulled on her own cotton pajamas that made her look five. Natalie was applying some sort of mint-scented lotion to her feet and it wafted across the room. She caught Jessa staring, held out the green tube. "Want some?"

Jessa shook her head, made a big show of tugging on some socks. She had to get out of this room.

• • •

After a maze of hallways, Jessa found a courtyard outside lit with small torches. Ms. Jackson had said to take twenty minutes, get some air. She curled up against a stone wall of the church in her sock feet and a jacket over her pajamas. The air had turned cool, coppery, like pennies tinged faintly with smoke.

Someone was playing the guitar. It drifted like snow across the courtyard, a low tune she didn't recognize—a sad, gorgeous melody that made Jessa think of blank, starless skies over a dark sea. It made her want to swim in that sea, let it cover her.

Then she saw her. Red-haired Madison from the other group, caught up in shadow only a couple of yards from where Jessa sat, a guitar across her lap.

Madison played the guitar—like that?

Madison's hands fell away and her face tipped toward the

torch light, clouded, tired. Scrubbed clean of makeup. She wore a pair of jeans, the knees ripped out, and a black hoodie. Her feet were bare, the nails manicured a deep shade of purple.

She noticed Jessa and stubbed out a cigarette that was burning in a little dish next to her. "Hey." Setting the guitar to the side, she tucked her legs up close to her chest. "I didn't know anyone was out here."

Jessa inched toward her. "That was beautiful."

Madison shrugged. "For a hundred bucks an hour, the guy better teach me how to play." She ran her hands through her hair, the red like blood in the torchlight. Her gaze fell on Jessa. Her eyes widened. "You OK?"

The question caught Jessa off guard, realizing that it must visibly show that she wasn't—OK. "Not really."

"Tell me about it." Madison traced a groove in the stone court-yard with her finger. "This vacation blows. I should have gone to Vail with my parents."

Nodding, Jessa breathed in the clean, wet air. Had it rained? Lights dotted the layered, charcoal line of hills all around, all the small houses, hundreds of small lives gathering their night together.

"But I don't need to tell you that, huh? I heard she got to your guy first." Madison laughed a little, a real laugh—no glass cracking, just dry and low and sad.

Jessa flashed to the image of Madison kissing Jamal in the Pantheon, on tiptoe, laughing. She realized Madison had been crying just now. "I'm sorry about Jamal."

Shrugging, Madison ran her hand over the strings of the guitar emitting a sound like a ghost. "Guess I should return this to the guy I borrowed her from." But she didn't make a move to leave.

Madison didn't say anything for a long time, and Jessa thought that was it for their conversation. What else could she possibly say to this girl? Not much in common but Natalie's taste in boys. But then Madison said, "I guess I should have just done it. He wanted to. People think I'm such a slut but I'm not." She strummed another ghost note. "What's the big deal, right? You do it sometime or another. So he found option two."

Jessa's whole body grew warm. She and Sean hadn't done it either. Had talked endlessly about it. She had wanted to wait— had felt like she *should* wait, even when being pressed against his warm skin made her skin feel like it was taking root there, finding its home. Actually, she had been planning Italy in her brain. Had thought that maybe Italy would be the right place. She caught Madison's eye then. The girl held her gaze.

"I don't ever want to be just an option," Jessa told her.

• • •

The next morning on the bus, Mr. Campbell passed back their stuff. "Here's your virtual brains," he said. But his smile had returned and he laughed at Devon's dramatic display of reuniting with his PSP. "Nelda! Oh, my soul! Wherefore hast thou traveled, my love? We shall never part again!"

They were heading back to Rome for a lighted tour of the city at night, and the rhythm of the bus was familiar now, the movement from one place to another lulling Jessa into a trance. Earlier, as she'd settled into her seat, Madison had passed her on the way to the back of the bus, had given her a sweet, knowing smile.

As the bus left Spoleto behind, Jessa curled into a seat with her iPod and *Portrait of the Artist*, and just melted into the words, letting Stephen's world become her world, his heartbreak and confusion her own.

An hour or so later, a passage in the book made her pause. She clicked off the Sarah Brightman humming low on her iPod and scanned the beautiful lines in the novel again, her eyes resting on the line:

A day of dappled seaborne clouds.

In the book, Stephen had realized that words, the sheer beauty of them, could alter the *glowing sensible world*, turn it into a *prism of language*. She read the passage again, its taste sugary in her mind. Words—and, for her, music. The way she could wash herself with sound, with words, with the luscious order of them—so free, but put there on purpose, in a journal, in a song. Her Harry Potter invisibility cloak from the real world. She preferred the words, the music, to dust-covered reality. She saw the world the way Stephen did—in all its crazy, beautiful disorder.

Love—her dictionary definition. This was love.

Not everyone saw life the way she saw it, not everyone stared out a moving bus window and saw the world's sherbet colors, its gauzy, shifting clouds like wraiths, full of beauty and sadness. An eternal, tumbling world. But she did. She saw the world this way, read its pain between the beautiful lines.

She pulled out her phone and texted Carissa:

Love is the beauty of this world pressed nose to nose with all its pain.

She had tears in her eyes—tears. And they weren't about Sean. They weren't about her loss of him or even the beauty of olive groves slipping by outside. They were just tears, for all of it and none of it; for being so very, very small in a world so very, very big. For *noticing*. When most of the bus around her was probably just blissfully wondering what they would have for lunch. Sean always told her she was too sensitive, an "overthinker," but she realized this was just the start of it. She was an overnoticer, an overfeeler. She walked around like an exposed nerve, her skin alive with millions of tiny little antennae, when he just walked around, fully armored, ensconced in his own singular world.

She added another line to her text and hit send.

Boyfriend: someone who gets that I see the world in this ridiculous,
beautiful overfelt way, knows how necessary it is to me. Who maybe,
just maybe, feels it too.

She rattled a sigh out of her closed throat, blinked into the dry air of the moving bus. Mr. Campbell glanced up at her over his *New Yorker* and he knew. Somehow, he *knew*. She held up the book. He nodded, his smile barely there, just enough to tell her he knew.

#13: backstage

"Sean kissed Carissa!" Jessa shoved the envelope into Tyler's face, which wasn't very nice considering that he'd been three inches from a lip lock with Cameron. Still, he could come up for air to spare a minute for her. He'd been MIA since Spoleto. He and his little instruction manual.

She tapped her foot impatiently. The bus idled in the parking lot, waiting for them all to pee and choose whatever sugar or salt they needed for the rest of the trip back to Rome. Tyler and Cameron cuddled on a crumbling stone wall next to the gas station or rest stop or whatever they called these things in Italian. Or at least they had been cuddling, before Jessa stuck Reason #13 in Tyler's face.

"Um, what?" Tyler plucked the paper from her hands.

"Sorry to interrupt," Jessa said to Cameron. To Tyler, she said, "He *kissed* her. During *Hamlet*. Backstage. But I guess you already knew that. So what does her little instruction manual say about how to handle me for this juicy piece of information?"

Tyler sighed, rubbed his temples. "OK, I knew. I mean, even before the manual."

"What!"

Cameron grabbed her handbag. "I'll save your seat." She kissed two fingers, then pressed the kissed fingertips to his nose. It would have taken some pliers and a court order to pull his eyes from her retreating back.

Jessa waited. "Um, Romeo? Do you mind explaining that you knew my boyfriend kissed my best friend and then, oh, forgot for, like, *eleven months*, to tell me?"

"I didn't forget to tell you." Tyler stood up and walked toward the store. "I'm getting some gummy bears."

"Tyler!" Jessa followed him through the swinging doors. Jade and Christina passed them, giggling. Jade had a handful of little silver-wrapped chocolates, and Christina had an orange soda. Jessa couldn't even look at orange soda anymore. She waited while Tyler pulled the three remaining sacks of gummy bears from the rack.

"Tyler Ramón Santos."

"Ouch, the middle name? You need to calm down."

Outside, she grabbed his arm and made him face her. "What don't I know?"

He shifted his weight around, the gummy-bear bags crinkling against each other. "Yeah, OK—he kissed her. It was opening night..."

"We were together opening night!"

"Telling a story here!"

Jessa pinned her lips together with some undisclosed stash of willpower.

"You know how it goes," Tyler told her, an edge of what must be annoyance in his voice. "We were all jumping around, congratulating each other, over-the-top opening night buzz, and they ended up backstage and they kissed. Probably a little longer than they should have. It wasn't a big deal, really. Usual backstage stuff." Tyler's eyes drifted over Jessa's shoulder, and she turned to see Cameron waving at him through the bus window. "We decided not to tell you. We didn't want you freaking out over nothing."

Jessa's heart stilled a little. *Everyone* acted like puppies on speed backstage on opening night. It really wasn't a big deal. She had actually planted a pretty big kiss on Kevin that night. On the cheek, but still, it bothered her that she was just finding out about it now. "I wouldn't have freaked out." Jessa waved back to Francesca, who was brandishing the frog at them spastically as she walked toward the bus. "I wouldn't have freaked out."

"Yeah." Tyler steered her toward the bus. "No chance of that."

• • •

Outside the hotel in Rome, Jessa sat cross-legged in the small rose garden, watching Dylan Thomas read over Reason #13. She sipped an espresso he had ordered for her from the little

193

restaurant in the hotel lobby. The coffee tasted thick and bitter on her tongue, even with the milk she had added.

"I think she's mostly just saying that she had an instinct she should have trusted. To tell you."

"Tyler told her not to. That I would have freaked out." Jessa held her head up to catch the slight wind that lifted her hair from around her face and cooled her neck.

"And would you have freaked out?" Dylan Thomas sipped his own coffee, eyes still on the letter.

"No. Everyone acts like idiots backstage after a show." She sipped her coffee.

Dylan Thomas stared at her over the paper. "It really wouldn't have bothered you?"

Jessa dropped her voice. "OK, yeah it would have."

Over the lip of his cup, Dylan Thomas said, "So, there's something to Carissa's trusting-an-instinct theory."

Jessa ran her finger around the ceramic edge of her coffee. "Um, I was wondering if you could have found a smaller coffee cup?"

"It's a demitasse, you heathen." He snapped off a piece of biscotti, dunked it, then popped it in his mouth, chewing thoughtfully. "OK, we have a half hour before we have to go stare at another church or something. What do you want me to say?"

"Tell me what you think." She nibbled her own almond biscotti.

"I think they were right to not tell you."

"Traitor." Jessa slumped into the stone of the garden wall.

He shook his head, his black hair falling a bit in his eyes.

Was it just her imagination or had his hair grown a bunch over the trip? She liked it a little longer, in his eyes a little. "Your hair looks good today."

His dark eyes narrowed. "You're changing the subject."

She sat up. "I'm not."

"Then why does it matter?"

"Your hair or changing the subject?" Jessa watched a butterfly settle on a nearby rose the color of cotton candy. She shivered, her bare arms suddenly cold.

"Their kissing." Dylan Thomas tossed her his black sweatshirt.

"Because he isn't supposed to kiss other girls when he's supposed to be only kissing me. Sorry, I'm old fashioned that way." She pulled the sweatshirt around her shoulders. It smelled like pastries, like the bakery they'd eaten breakfast in back in Spoleto.

Dylan Thomas handed the letter back. "I think there is a better question to be asking." He finished his coffee and sat the cup and saucer on the low wall of the garden.

"What?"

"Why is she telling you now?"

Jessa shrugged. "Maybe there's no point. Maybe I should just throw the rest of these in an Italian sewer or something." Jessa stuffed the letter back into the envelope, the inked purple Reason #13 too bright against the white envelope.

"Now that would be trusting your instincts."

• • •

Instruction: Trust Your Instincts!

Jessa didn't throw the envelopes in an Italian sewer. She thought about it, but somehow that would only be giving Carissa her way, following her instruction, and she didn't feel much like doing anything Carissa wanted from her right now.

Instead, she headed back to the room she was sharing with Lizzie Jenkins, a junior with a sense of humor so dry Jessa was pretty sure she was really a sixty-year-old masquerading as a teen-ager. When Jessa got back there, Lizzie was reading a David Sedaris book stretched out on her stomach on the bed by the window.

"I'm taking a quick nap," Jessa told her.

"Not the nap police." Lizzie didn't look up from her book. "No need to register."

Watching her, Jessa's mind flooded with an image of Lizzie at the fifth-grade end-of-the-year barbecue before they all went on to Five Hills Middle School. Lizzie, her brown hair pulled back in a ponytail, on her belly by the little stream that ran through the park, picking stones out one by one, stacking them in a little pile by the water's edge, the sunlight dappling her back through the thick oaks that lined the streambed. Rock monsters, she'd called them, when Paige Ryan asked her what on earth she was doing and said she better watch out because she was going to ruin her shirt.

"Do you remember your rock monsters?" Jessa sat on the edge of her bed.

Lizzie looked up, a smile pulling at her mouth. "Oh my god, rock monsters! How do you even remember that?"

"I just thought about our fifth-grade barbecue where you made them all along the stream at Memorial Park." Jessa watched Lizzie remember, her face lighting like a designer had finally flipped the right switch, hit the right spot on stage.

"My brother and dad used to make them for me when I was little." Lizzie sat up on the bed, flipped the book shut. "I was so afraid of water as a kid, afraid it would just swallow me up. So they'd line them up along rivers, next to lakes. To protect me. It's sort of dumb."

"It's not."

"It's wild you remember that."

"Sometimes I wonder how we're not ten anymore." Jessa suddenly wanted to lay herself next to that streambed, stack rocks and rocks until there were rock monsters all around her. She'd make some for Maisy when she got home.

"Well, I, for one, plan on always being ten." Lizzie fished around in her backpack and pulled out a bottle of water and a bag of almonds. "Want some?"

Jessa chewed an almond, savoring the salt on her tongue.

"I remember something about you," Lizzie said, then took a sip of her water. "That scar on your arm."

Jessa grew warm. It *had* been Lizzie with her, that day in fourth grade on the field when she tried to sneak under the curl of chain link fence to get a red ball she'd lost. Snagged her arm on a jagged piece of fence. How had she forgotten it had been Lizzie? Lizzie had given her one of her socks to wrap around her arm to stop the bleeding.

"It's kind of a boring story," Jessa said, digging through her bag, avoiding Lizzie's eyes.

Lizzie flipped her book open, sprawled back out on the bed. "Maybe."

#14: competition piece

Somehow, once again, Jessa had underdressed. Both schools stood in the courtyard of the hotel, waiting for the bus to pick them up for Rome by Night, though she heard Rachel whisper to Kevin that it should actually be called Slut Fest by Night, with all the cleavage showing.

The other school was sporting a vast array of halter tops (which Jessa could never pull off; she would need an actual chest), tight denim, short skirts, and glossy makeup (again, never pull that off—she'd look like a rejected extra from *Starlight Express*). Jessa sighed. Her jeans were cute enough, but her shirt bagged in the wrong places. Not a good Rome by Night look. She eyed Tyler, all black leather and dark denim, his arm around petite Cameron who could wear a brown lunch bag and look cute but who wasn't wearing a brown lunch bag. She was wearing a silver, gauzy tank that looked spun by fairies and some skinny black jeans.

"You look good," Tyler told Jessa. "Are you wearing eyeliner?"

"Yes. Jessa own eyeliner," she quipped in her best caveman

voice, aware it came out bitchier than she meant it to. She should try to tone it down. Tyler was just being nice. But Cameron gleamed like a goddess in that silver tank top and Jessa didn't feel like apologizing for her tone.

"OK, then." Tyler widened his eyes. "We'll save you a seat." They moved away, Cameron looking like she'd rather get dental reconstruction than save Jessa a seat.

• • •

Suddenly, Rome became a jeweled city, something from *The Wizard of Oz*. The light seemed to disappear all at once, night replacing day in a blink. Jessa felt it in her chest, squeezing the little pillow of flesh around her heart. As the bus whirled them toward the Trevi Square, dozens of fountains lit the way, the ice-blue water against the marble figures becoming otherworldly, floating ghosts. Tall, stone buildings that would seem dirty in the daytime were suddenly magical palaces arching into the black sky, their windows swollen with yellow light.

The bus pulled to a stop in a wide parking lot, and after Francesca's quick set of instructions and a nod from the frog, the students spilled out of the bus into the dewy haze of Rome at night. Jessa had noticed Giacomo slip off the bus well before Francesca stopped talking, noticed the slight skip of Francesca's eyes toward his exit, the way her face seemed to tighten.

The square was alive with laughter and music. Couples strolled by with arms wound round each other, Vespas beeped their friendly horns, groups of Italian teenagers called loudly, their Italian thick and full. Tyler and Cameron disappeared almost instantly. She searched the group for Dylan Thomas. He'd been on the bus, up near the front, chatting with Mr. Campbell during the ride. Back at the hotel, he had mentioned getting gelato, finding a quiet place to hang out together.

"Hey." Sean appeared next to her, hands in his pockets.

Jessa's skin spread with warmth the way it always did when he was close, like he had some sort of radioactive ability to up her internal thermostat by a couple of degrees.

"You hanging by yourself?" He pulled on his jacket, and Jessa tried not to watch the long sweep of his arms into the sleeves, tried not to think about the way it used to feel to be wrapped up inside of them. She tried, and failed—miserably.

"I think I got kind of ditched." She flipped open her bag and dug through it to have something to do. She didn't even need anything out of it. She found a stray lip balm, uncapped it, pressed it to her lips.

"Where's that Dylan kid you're always with?"

She had not imagined the scissor edge to his voice. She popped the cap back on the Burt's Bees. "Not sure."

"Are you guys, like, together now or something?" He grabbed the Burt's Bees and helped himself.

She snatched it back. "No. I mean, Dylan Thomas is the greatest. But, no, we're not together..." She let her voice trail off. Let him think that she was adding "for now" on the end of that statement even if it was ridiculous to think of herself with Dylan Thomas. Dylan Thomas had an ex-girlfriend named Link who moved to Japan. For him to even notice Jessa she'd have to pierce her nose and add about twenty black long-sleeve shirts to her wardrobe.

"Right, right," Sean said, his eyes scanning the square. The Trevi Fountain was breathtaking, striking—the horses charging out and away, lit up, emerging from the eerie blue of the water. "Sure. You want to go eat or something? The pizza here is really good. Even if it's flat."

"Isn't all pizza flat?"

"You know, like almost no crust or whatever." His eyes locked on to something over her shoulder and she turned, following his gaze. Natalie and Jamal were locked in an embrace next to the fountain, an embrace playing on the passion the fountain exuded, like they were performing a live, non-marble interpretation. Her hair looked white in the ghost light of the fountain, striking in its spill against the dark skin of Jamal's arm.

"I saw them in Venice," she said, her eyes on Sean's face.

He swallowed hard. "Yeah. She broke up with me that first night there."

"At least she broke up with you first."

His eyes fell back on her, his shoulders sagging. He rocked back and forth over the cobblestones under his shoes.

"Do you think…" Jessa trailed off, her voice feeling like it was made of feathers. "Were you ever going to talk to me about that?"

"I'm talking to you."

"About that?"

"I tried."

"What?" Jessa pulled her own coat tighter into her, crossed her arms across her chest. "When?"

"In Florence. In the gardens. At that palace."

Jessa dug through her memory. Had he tried to talk to her about it? She mostly remembered wanting to kick him in the shins. She shook her head to clear it, but he mistook it for disagreement.

"I did. I tried. You didn't listen."

"Um, that was a few days late. Generally, you talk to your girl-friend before mauling another girl in the costume barn."

"OK, yeah. But I did try. And you just used it as an opportunity to attack Natalie."

Jessa felt her body start to tremble, start to fill with tiny bubbles on the surface of her skin. "I think if anyone has a right to attack her, it's me."

He sighed. And for some reason, Jessa got the impression he was thinking about pizza.

"I'm sorry," she said. "Am I boring you? Is smashing my heart into a million pieces and humiliating me in front of all my friends not so much worth an explanation?" She knew what was happening to her voice. She was going to the banshee place, the nether world of screechdom, as her dad would say. She put a lid on the banshee.

"You know what, Jessa?" Sean went to his quiet, zombie, blank place, a perfect mini-replica of all their past fights. Her screaming, him silent. Quietly, he said, "Maybe for once you could learn that the whole world isn't here to owe you an explanation."

"How about just you?" She could feel the tears, hated them, wanted to erase each single tear as they bulged in her eyes, but she couldn't stop them.

"You know what? It just always seems like when girls say they want to have a conversation, they just really want to do all the talking." Sean sighed again, ran his hands through his hair—his great hair.

For a minute, she imagined shaving it with one of those sheep-shear things she'd seen at the farm they visited with the environmental club last month. It helped, a little. "I want to have a conversation," she whispered. "I want to know what happened with you and me. One minute we're about to go on a romantic Italian trip and then the next minute I've got standing room only to your romantic vacation with another girl, which, by the way, has been just a rocking great time for me—not that you'd notice."

"Yeah, really romantic." His eyes over her shoulder again.

"It was a horrible thing to do to me."

"Jess…" Every once in awhile, Sean looked at her as if she were the only person in the world, the rest of the world falling away around her like a dark stage, leaving her flush in the middle of a circle drenched with spotlight. Now was one of those times. "Jess," he repeated, leaning in toward her a little. "It's like you're in a race. You're always in a race."

"What do you mean?" Her stomach prickled with his words. Always racing—after that elusive future.

He dropped his hands, his face going slack. "I just…I wanted things to be easier. You're…not easy."

"No," she said, her voice hiccupping, fighting the tears back down to her belly. "No. I'm not."

"I do miss you. You said in your note. What I deserve. I deserve to miss you, you said." His eyes searched her face. "But, it's just…" his voice trailed off, his eyes on something over her shoulder. Maybe Natalie and Jamal had invited a mime to participate in their little show?

"Jessa, *bella*." The voice caught her from the side, like a sudden wind.

She turned as Giacomo moved in next to her, his arm coming around her shoulder in one clean move and settling there, warm.

"You are crying." His eyes darted to Sean, who, Jessa smugly noted, looked guilty.

"I'm fine." She wiped at the skin beneath her eyes. It felt papery, like tissue.

"We get something to eat?" Giacomo motioned toward the busy square behind him. "We drink something?"

"We were kind of talking," Sean said. He stood up a little straighter, folded his arms across his chest.

Jessa leaned into Giacomo. "I'd love to get something to eat." She caught Sean's eye. "That way your evening can be *easier*."

Giacomo whisked her away into the blurry, busy Rome night.

• • •

Giacomo wiped his mouth with a napkin and pulled the letter closer to him. "So she writes you these reasons. With these instructions. And you forget this Sean?" She thought he might be making fun of her. His eyes glinted, crinkled at the corners.

"It's not going so well." Jessa read the note upside down.

Competition Piece.

Carissa had reminded her of their festival piece they had taken to competition that winter. About Sean's sulking that he didn't make it in.

No one wants a big baby for a boyfriend!

But apparently, Jessa glowered, it was fine to kiss the big baby backstage when he was already your best friend's boyfriend.

"Why the lemon face?" Giacomo sipped his wine. "You don't enjoy the wine?"

Shaking her head, Jessa took another small drink of her own

dark red wine. "No, that's not it. I was just thinking about something." She tried to clear her thoughts, focus on the fact that she was sitting in the shadowed courtyard of a Roman restaurant, sipping red wine with an Italian man. She tried really hard not to slouch.

Giacomo pointed to Carissa's instruction. "What is word for word?"

"It's a type of theater." Jessa finished chewing her bite of *caprese* salad. "You perform a piece of prose, like a novel, word for word. We did Dr. Seuss's *The Lorax*."

The waiter set down two plates of pasta and the smell of garlic and herbs permeated their table. Jessa took a deep breath. Giacomo said something quickly in Italian to the waiter, laughed, then refocused his gaze on her.

"What did you guys say?" Maybe they were laughing at her. The American kid with the stupid notes. She took another quick sip of wine.

Giacomo checked his BlackBerry, stuck it back in his pocket. "What we? The waiter?" He picked up his fork and spoon, swirled the noodles with his fork into the belly of the spoon before taking a quick bite, setting the utensils down again. "I told him that Roberto must love his garlic."

Jessa didn't know who Roberto was. Maybe the chef? She just nodded.

Giacomo studied her from over his wineglass. "So this Carissa says you should pick a word-for-word piece for Sean. One that says something about him."

She swirled her noodles, feeling very sloppy and young—no spoon, noodles everywhere. "Yep," she slurped.

"And what would you choose?"

She set her fork down, resting it on the plate at an angle, the way Giacomo had his. "Who knows? Is there a book about a boy who doesn't know what he wants?" As the words tumbled out, Jessa realized she was currently reading that very novel.

"I think that's what most novels are about." He ate another bite of pasta. "Unless the book is about a girl."

She laughed, folded the letter up, and stuck it back in the envelope. Giacomo's eyes glinted in the candlelight.

He smoothed the tablecloth, then set down his wineglass. "You don't want to do her instructions? Don't want to read her reasons?" He took a sip of wine.

"Not really." She paused, realizing she had grown completely tired of Carissa's little game, her know-it-all instructions to Tyler. But there were envelopes left—unopened—and she had already gone this far. She had promised Tyler she'd finish, not that he seemed that interested anymore.

"So don't." Giacomo waved to the waiter, who filled his wineglass.

"There are still six envelopes."

He laughed. "You Americans. So many rules. Always having to finish things. So…what is the word? Productive?"—said as if he might have uttered the word *toilet* or *congested*.

Jessa flushed. "'You Americans.' That's a bit of a generalization."

"What is this 'generalization'?" The word rolled in his mouth like working it around a triple wad of gum.

Jessa thought about it for a second. "When you state something about a whole group. Like Italians care too much about shoes."

"Italians do care about shoes. Too much? I don't know." He smiled, seemingly enjoying Jessa's annoyance.

She stabbed at her pasta. "Why are you suddenly here?" She snatched the small dish of cheese and dumped a spoonful over her pasta.

"I asked you to have dinner. And we are here." He sat back in his chair, his palms up in defense.

"No, not here, the restaurant. Here on this trip."

His face darkened. "I was asked to leave school."

Jessa set her fork down. "Why?"

He waved his hand in dismissal. "Narrow minds." He leaned on the table. "My mother locked the house and left no key. So here I am."

"Your mother?"

He mimed the frog bobbing along, a big goofy smile on his face.

"Francesca's your mom!"

He nodded, returning to his pasta.

Jessa took another small sip of wine, a smile pulling at her mouth. "OK. Interesting. But she doesn't look like that. At least not the smiling part."

"Yes. My mother could smile more."

His smile was like something in one of the fountains, lit and otherworldly and maybe, at the edges, a little sad.

• • •

Rome buzzed with the night, something alive and electric as she walked with Giacomo back toward the bus. She had never had dinner for three hours before—pasta and lamb, gelato drizzled with strawberry sauce, a sweet dessert wine in tiny, smoky glasses. Jessa wasn't much of a drinker. Was always happy to be designated driver at her friend's parties. As they walked, the wine whirled about her head, drawing a dreamy cloak behind her eyes. And she had never eaten lamb before, was actually fundamentally against lamb. A baby sheep—who ate that? But it had been seasoned with what could only be herbs grown in heaven and marinated in something smoky and dark.

She felt a little criminal eating it.

On their way out of the restaurant, she realized she had left Carissa's envelope on the table. She didn't go back for it. Didn't care if it ended up in the bottom of a garbage can filled with congealing noodles and leftover salad.

She laced her arm through Giacomo's, the sounds of water from the fountains filling her ears, and tried to watch him without him noticing. Giacomo was eighteen. Amazing. He could pass for his early twenties. Jessa had always been jealous of her friends who could pass for older. Last summer, she had been carded for a PG-13 movie, which made her want to rip off the ticket-window glass and strangle the little idiot selling tickets who was like fifty years old. PG-13? Sean had not stopped laughing through the entire previews. "Why don't you call Maisy and see if she can come down and get you into the movie," he'd said, slurping his soda. She'd thrown most of her popcorn at him and moved three seats away. Not funny. OK, sort of funny, but the worst thing was she'd had to use her school ID card to prove she was in high school. Idiot troll working at the movie theater when he was fifty. But Jessa knew she looked young. Something her mother always told her she'd be grateful for when she was thirty. Whatever.

Giacomo didn't seem to find her young.

"Oh, I want to show you this." He unwound his arm, grabbed her hand, and pulled her toward a side street.

Her heart began to pound. Was he going to kiss her? He would, right? She licked her dry lips, brushed at some strands of hair that had fallen from her ponytail. She really, really wished her hair wasn't in a ponytail. She probably did look thirteen.

The side street was suddenly quiet, the air still and shadowed.

Her heart skipped. Maybe she shouldn't be heading down this street with a total stranger—an Italian stranger, who had been kicked out of school. Why had he said he'd been kicked out of school? Narrow minds. What did that mean? What if people were narrow minded about him killing people?

He led her down the little street, the buildings pressed a bit too snug next to each other. Jessa eyed the balconies overhead, the hanging plants and pots of flowers, their petals velvet with night. From one of the windows, an opera played and its steady, lilting sound made her think of the Sarah Brightman she'd been listening to earlier that day, the way her voice always made Jessa feel like nothing in the world could go truly wrong, not when a voice like that existed.

"Here." Giacomo motioned to the outside of a small café, closed for the night, tables and chairs pulled inside and stacked. "What do you think?"

"Um…" Jessa hesitated, not quite sure what she was being asked to look at.

"The mural." He gestured to the wide, modern fresco on the café wall. In the painting, the earth seemed to split behind a shadow of cloud, spilling curls of color in a sunburst, almost a spiral toward a black, starry background.

"It's beautiful." Jessa stepped back, trying to take it all in, but the narrow space didn't allow her to look at the whole thing at once.

"Yes," he said. "It's not the best space. You should stand back farther. Yes." He shook his head, bit his lip.

"It's yours?" Jessa watched him study the wall.

"Yes. Mine. And my friend, Aaron. He does most of the original design and I'm the color, the brush." He squinted, frowned at a small patch of graffiti on one side of the mural, said something in Italian Jessa was pretty sure she wouldn't find in her guidebook.

"It's wonderful." Jessa felt the color escaping from the wall even in the darkness, the passion in the brushstrokes. "It has amazing energy."

He snapped his fingers, smiling at her widely. "Yes, energy! That is what we wanted. I knew you would see it."

She grew warm, his compliment like a towel just out of the dryer wrapped around bare skin. She took his hand again. "You're very talented."

He flushed. "Grazie."

Jessa checked her watch. "The bus!" She dropped Giacomo's hand.

She was more than twenty minutes late.

• • •

"Nice of you to join us."

Jessa slid into the seat next to Dylan Thomas, pausing at the snip in his words. "I lost track of time." She settled her bag on her lap.

His eyes strayed to where Giacomo was in a heated whispery discussion with Francesca at the front of the bus.

"We didn't do anything," she added, feeling oddly self-conscious.

Dylan Thomas plugged up his ears with his iPod and stared out the window as the bus began to pull away into the night.

"Hey…" she started, reaching out to touch his arm, but he didn't notice, or pretended not to notice, and she decided not to indulge it. She rested her head against the back of the seat, her body light and floaty. Several seats away, Sean turned and studied her, then folded his arms across his chest, slumping into his own seat. Even with two mad boys, Jessa could only smile into the warm glow of Rome.

#15: *friendship*

Jessa woke suddenly—breaking glass, shouting. She sat up, rubbed her eyes. In the bed next to her, Lizzie fumbled for her glasses on the side table, knocking them to the ground. Jessa slipped out of bed, picked them up, and handed them back.

"Shanks," Lizzie said, her voice thick with sleep, and mumbled something that sounded like, "Blind shout shasses toncats," which Jessa assumed had something to do with being blind without her glasses or contacts. Jessa's mom was the same way.

Another shattering of glass. The shouting seemed clearer, as if the voices were coming down the hall.

Jessa, with Lizzie on her heels, cracked the door open an inch and stared into the dim light of the hallway.

Cruella stood in a glittering ring of glass, like some sort of witch in a trance. Her husband, looking rumpled and small in striped pajamas, was pleading with her. "Please just come back to the room…"

"I hate it here!" she howled, and Jessa realized she would have to concede screechdom to this woman. Her pitch must be what broke all that glass.

Lizzie, attempting to get a better look over Jessa's shoulders, leaned into her, but not before Jessa could get her footing and the two of them toppled into the hallway.

Cruella and the world's most boring world history teacher suddenly took in their audience. "Go back to bed, girls…It's fine," Bob started. Cruella held a crumpled tissue to her face.

"Um," Lizzie said fully awake now, her voice small and airy. "Do you need something…Can we get you something?"

Cruella's eyes fell like embers on them. "You and your horrible friends have done enough, thank you very much." She reached for her husband, who took her arm, and started to step carefully over the glass—a water glass from the looks of it. Jessa and Lizzie both had one by their bedsides.

Jessa studied Cruella—the mascara-streaked face, the deep orange silk of her kimono robe, the pale, thin legs. A rotting pumpkin of a woman.

"Why do you think that is?" Jessa heard herself asking, felt Lizzie's wide eyes on her.

Cruella turned. "Excuse me?" She drew herself up tall, the way some women could, made herself a few inches taller as if her skin expanded like a cobra's.

"Why do you think they're hard on you?" Jessa swallowed, her heart racing.

"Hard on me?" Cruella took a step toward her, and Jessa's feet cemented themselves to the floor. She was not afraid. OK, yes she was. She couldn't move out of fear. But Cruella didn't need to know that. "Those children aren't hard on me. They are vicious. They've ruined my Italian experience. My whole life I've dreamed of Rome and now…I am going to demand a full refund."

She was very close to Jessa now. Only a few feet away. Bob stood behind her, his eyes on the floor. Jessa could feel Lizzie behind her, hear her breathing, low and steady.

Jessa locked eyes with Cruella. "My grandmother would say you're the kind of person who can't find something sweet in a candy store."

Lizzie let out a surprised laugh.

Cruella's eyes narrowed to slits.

"In fact," Jessa continued, her voice taking on the edge of the glass on the floor. "If I were you, I would start to wonder, Why do all the bad things keep happening to me all the time? Why is everything so awful? Everything. Think about it. I mean, you know what flies are attracted to?" And then Jessa answered her own question.

Lizzie gasped.

Cruella's face drained of color. Jessa had heard about that happening, had seen people go pale before, but she had never seen a face drain of color the way Cruella's just had, like the last bit of water before the tub sucked it down.

Cruella's skin expanded again and she took a darting step forward, a white striking snake, and for a sliver of a second Jessa thought Cruella might hit her.

But then something weirder happened.

Cruella smiled at her. Not a creepy Joker-from-*Batman* sort of smile, not Wicked Witchy at all. Something else, something like water. Too sweet, too sad—laced with something distant, something that must be memory. The whole of it made Jessa wish Cruella had just hit her.

"You're young," Cruella whispered, smoothing the kimono over her stomach, studying the diamond on her finger. "You still get to throw drinks at boys and have your whole life ahead of you. Just wait."

Bob knelt down and started to collect the glass, using the front of his pajamas like a little basket.

Cruella took careful steps around the glass, around him, and disappeared down the hall.

Jessa and Lizzie both bent to help him, the clear shards like ice.

"Don't, girls." He didn't lift his gaze to them. "Please. Just go back to bed."

• • •

Mr. Campbell asked Lizzie if he could switch places with her for a minute. She nodded, gathered up the novel she was reading, and let him sit down next to Jessa on the bus.

Jessa pulled her eyes from the view, the pasture land washed clean with last night's rain, the chocolate-brown horses dotted against the deep green of their fields, the small houses creamy in the morning light. They headed toward Pompeii, had left the hotel at five-thirty that morning, half asleep and gauzy eyed.

She stopped the *Rent* on her iPod, waiting for her teacher to say something.

"You finish Joyce?" He nodded toward the closed novel on her lap.

"Almost. His language is so incredible. I love it." She ran her hand over the cover of the book.

"I knew you would." He rubbed his hands on his jeans, staring at the seat back. "OK, so we have a situation."

Jessa nodded. She felt the pull of the bus beneath her, the ebb and shift of its wheels over the black highway.

"Gwen, Bob's wife, from the other group, said you swore at her last night. Said you said some pretty awful stuff. I told her she must have that wrong." Mr. Campbell looked sideways at her. "Does she have that wrong?"

Jessa turned in her seat so she could look at him directly. "No."

He gave a low whistle through his teeth. "Well, Ms. Gardner, you're having quite a trip. You want to tell me what happened?"

She told him, noticing the slow rub of his temples after the last part.

"I'm sorry," she whispered, her eyes studying the silhouette of Stephen on the cover of the novel in her lap. Sometimes, she felt like she existed as shadow, as if the world could only really see a chalk outline of her, couldn't see anything real.

"Well," Mr. Campbell sighed after a moment. "She's gone back home. To California. Taking a flight from Rome later today. She won't be on the trip anymore. All I can say is, thank God for Jason."

"Who's Jason?"

"The other teacher in their group." Mr. Campbell motioned toward Quiet Guy, squinting at Jessa that way her mom did when Jessa had a fever. "He's pretty much their lone adult on the trip. Anyway, Francesca said that Gwen's claiming emotional distress. Not just you. The whole group. But we'll have to document her actions, report to the guys who run this tour." He paused, then said quietly. "I'll be saying that you two exchanged words in the hall after she broke a glass and screamed at her husband, woke you guys in the middle of the night, but I'll leave out what you said. It was late. People are tired. Lizzie will confirm that."

Jessa's face went hot. "It's OK. I know what I said. I can take responsibility for it."

"Jess," Mr. Campbell said, his voice sounding tired. "I talked to Francesca. She feels like you guys have taken on enough already with this woman. It's just a report."

"But her husband was there…"

Mr. Campbell interrupted her. "Here's the thing: he's not saying anything one way or the other. Said he doesn't really remember what was said. Said you girls were 'within your rights of self-expression.' Those exact words."

"He said that?"

Mr. Campbell nodded. "Gwen's apparently had problems on other tours. Francesca talked to some friends of hers in England who had her on a trip last fall. She has a history."

"Poor Bob." Jessa let her gaze slip to the front of the bus where Bob sat, shoulders sagging, his eyes ahead on the road. Then she remembered Cruella's sad, distant face. "I feel sorry for both of them."

Mr. Campbell shrugged. "Everyone has to make their own choices." But she could tell he felt sorry for them too. It was hard not to heap pity on people who just kept electing to be miserable.

Jessa watched her teacher move back to his seat, letting Lizzie out first. Lizzie plopped into the seat next to her and flipped open her novel. "You OK?"

"Yeah, thanks." Jessa plugged herself back into *Rent*. Outside, the landscape shifted, the sky lit in places, dark in others, a glow coming from some hidden sun.

She studied Sean asleep several rows ahead, head back, mouth slightly open, face slack. For the first time since landing in Italy, she didn't really miss him at all.

• • •

"Where have you been?" Jessa found Tyler leaving the little store with two panini wrapped in white paper. They'd stopped in a tree-dotted town to stretch their legs and get some snacks, and they had five more minutes before they had to be back on the bus and on their way. Jessa had been looking all over for Tyler.

He closed the door behind him. "Cameron and I went for a quick walk."

"I need to talk to you." She could see Cameron waiting by the bus, sipping from her water bottle.

"OK," he said distractedly, his eyes smiling at Cameron.

"Are you paying attention?" Jessa heard the creak of irritation in her voice.

His eyes slipped back to her, shadowing. "OK, that's a tone I don't love."

"Sorry, but you've been completely MIA." Suddenly warm, Jessa swept her hair off her neck, fastened it back into a ponytail.

"MIA? Are you serious?"

She had his full attention now but couldn't remember exactly what it was she was going to tell him. Something about Sean? It had seemed urgent. "Um, it's just…you've been kind of distant with me lately."

Clearly the wrong thing to say. Tyler's eyebrows shot up. "Distant?"

"Forget it." She turned and started to head back toward the bus.

"You know what? No." Tyler was suddenly standing in front of her, all black jacketed and eyes flaring. "You're telling me *I've* been distant."

Cameron perked up, took a couple of steps toward them, then stopped.

Heart pounding, Jessa shook her head. What just happened? "Tyler, I just meant that…"

"Have you noticed for one second that I have a girlfriend now?" His voice arched, and Jessa could see Tim and Jade stop their conversation several yards away, their heads swiveling to watch them.

"OK, sorry…" Jessa inched her way toward the bus, her eyes on the dusty ground.

His face flushed red. "You know why you haven't said anything to me about it? Because it has nothing to do with you. Because this whole trip has to be about you, right? *Brokenhearted in Italy*, starring Jessa Gardner? Who cares about Tyler? He's just the stage manager! I know you're upset about Sean. I know you're frustrated, but could you maybe just take a time-out to be even remotely happy for me? To let me star in my own little show for a bit. I mean, I was taking all sorts of time to help you out. To do the envelopes with you."

Jessa swallowed, her throat full of straw. She couldn't move, could barely blink. She couldn't remember Tyler ever getting mad at her, not like this. Not shouting at her. "I'm sorry," she whispered to the dust.

She heard him take a shaky breath and brought her eyes to his. He was done, it seemed. Tyler could be a bit like a summer rainstorm, a flash of thunder and lightning, driving rain, then skies clearing. Of course, she'd never felt his deluge, never had it empty on her. His eyes darted about. Tim and Jade jumped back into their conversation, pretending they hadn't been listening, but three girls from the other school openly stared. Finally, Cameron came quietly up alongside of him, took his hand, and led him onto the bus.

Back in her seat, against the faint rumble of the engine, Jessa plugged her ears up with "Anthem" from *Chess*. Her stomach clenched, she stared at the back of Tyler's head, willing him to turn, to see her, to give a nod—anything to show the storm had passed, but he didn't turn around, didn't feel her eyes on him or, worse, didn't care.

. . .

Even the other group was quiet for once.

The bodies were just casts, just models made of where the archeologists found the pockets of earth where people had been encased, voids in the ash where the bodies decayed, where the frightened villagers cowered as their lives blinked away. In August of A.D. 79, Mount Vesuvius, so long thought dormant, erupted and a city was gone, frozen. Jessa blinked tears from her eyes. Just imagine. You're walking downtown, you've got your iPod and a Starbucks and you're just walking along and then a blinding darkness, the world coming to an end.

She shivered—it kind of put things in perspective.

On the ground before them, she stared at what must have been a family. A man, a woman, and a small child, sprawled, their bodies captured forever for millions of tourists to stare at, wonder about. What had they been doing before the sky went black? Had they been eating? Maybe the mother had asked about their day. Maybe the little boy, because Jessa thought it must be a boy, maybe he'd had a good day at school, had found the lost toy he'd hidden in his school things. Then the sky blacked out.

She followed the group through the rest of the tour, her head clouded with the sprawl of that boy, the way his arms were up by his ears in protection, the mother's hand in despair over her eyes, turned away from her family.

Jessa found a place to sit where she could see down into the amphitheater. The people of Pompeii had performed plays, had gone to see their favorite actors just like they did at Williams Peak. She thought of her Ophelia costume, all gauzy and like a dream. If she were going to be taken down by a thought-to-be-dormant volcano, she would want to be in her Ophelia costume, drowning in ash.

Someone settled beside her. "OK, you've got that look." It was Tyler—and Cameron, who curled gracefully next to him, crossing her tan legs at the ankles. Cameron, who looked way too cute for the eighth day of a grueling tour: Bermudas with a tank and a cap pulled over two braids that dusted the top of her shoulders. It was totally and completely unfair that a person should make braids look that sexy.

"What look?" Jessa asked, her voice careful.

"The contemplating the inequalities of the world look," Cameron said, taking a long drink of her water. The girl was certainly well hydrated. Cameron noticed Jessa's face. "What? Am I wrong?"

"No."

They sat for a minute, staring down at the amphitheater. "Sorry there was yelling." Tyler leaned a little into her, a body apology.

"You were right. About all of it." Jessa leaned too, her own body apology, the knot in her belly unwinding a bit. "I'm a bad friend. Though, I'm not a fan of the yelling."

"I should have talked to you earlier."

"I'm sorry I've been such a train wreck on this trip." Jessa rubbed her eyes, studied the green blades of grass shooting through bits of stone on the ground.

"I think you're holding up pretty well considering." Cameron nodded to where Sean sat by himself at the edge of the amphitheater. "But he looks worse than you do."

"Good," Tyler said, nudging a smile out of Jessa. "OK, we should really just enjoy the rest of this trip. This place is nothing if not carpe diem. Not subtle."

The girls nodded.

Cameron pulled her legs up to her chest. "Speaking of enjoying the rest of the trip, I heard you totally trashed Borington's wife!"

"Who?"

"Cruella," Tyler said, helping himself to Cameron's water. "They call him Mr. Borington because their last name is Corrington. Get it, *Boring*-ton."

Jessa felt their ease creep its way back in. "Um, yeah. I get it. It's not hard math."

Cameron giggled, a sound maybe a touch too much like bells for Jessa's taste—little golden fairy bells. But she was being really cool, and Tyler was over the moon about her. "Hilarious." Cameron offered her the water bottle.

Jessa took the bottle. "Thanks." She took a short sip. "I don't know. It was actually kind of sad. She's just so…"

"Pathetic?" Cameron suggested.

"Trollish?" Tyler offered.

"Just sad, I guess." Jessa thought about it. "And pathetic. And, yes, trollish."

Cameron leaned against Tyler, his arm circling her. "She's a freak show," she said. "We went to England with them last year and she totally pitched a fit and went home early. It's her MO." She paused. "*This* place is sad."

Pompeii was a strange landscape—the ruins, the cobbled streets, the lush green of the hillsides. Jessa's brain kept snagging on the casts of the ancient dead, their fright. "It makes me want to go home."

Tyler slipped his other arm around her, something—Jessa noticed—Cameron didn't seem to mind. Instead, Cameron reached over and cupped her hand over the top of Jessa's shoe. Gave her a sweet, quick pat.

. . .

It was an impromptu creativity salon of sorts. Jessa, Tyler, and Cameron wandered over to where most of the group sat in a large circle on a patch of lawn outside the city walls. The bus would be picking them up in a couple of minutes for their ride to Sorrento. Jade had her guitar and was playing an old Aimee Mann song that Jessa loved. Something about "driving sideways"—Jessa felt like that most of the time.

Jessa settled on the grass next to Hillary and pulled one of Carissa's reasons from her pocket. She told herself she was done. She didn't really want to open any more of the envelopes, but it was just sitting there with a big #15 on the front. What was it about her that made her want to follow the rules all the time?

She ripped it open.

It read:

Friendship

And there was an old picture of them. Carissa and Jessa in seventh grade, dressed as Danny and Sandy from *Grease* for Halloween. Jessa was Danny. A fake cigarette in her mouth, dark hair slicked back, her black leather jacket arm slung around Carissa's bare shoulder because Carissa *had* to go as slutty

Sandy—the Sandy who Jessa always thought sort of sold out in the end. Underneath it, it read, "We Go Together!" And underneath that, "No Matter What (Ask Tyler)."

Jessa tossed the note in his lap. Tyler whistled a few lines of a *Grease* song—"like shama-shama-shama-she-bomb."

"Shama-she-bomb?" Jessa laughed. "Those aren't the words. OK, this one isn't even a reason. She's losing focus. This has nothing to do with Sean."

His dark eyes settled on Jessa. "Doesn't it?" She could feel them on her face like some sort of tracking device, dissolving her smile. "No matter what?"

Jessa fiddled with the hem of her shorts. Jade was handing the guitar to Dylan Thomas. "Does she mean he threatened our friendship? Is that the reason? Come on, instruct me. What is she talking about? Manual me."

"I'm not reading the manual anymore, Jessa."

"Right." Jessa folded the note back up.

"Ask Cameron."

"He's not." Cameron did that pity-tilt thing with her head that Jessa usually hated, but somehow Cameron's version held all the intended sympathy in its tilt without the condescension. How did she do that?

"Carissa told me you already knew." Tyler pulled blades of grass up, twirled them in his fingers.

His words seemed layered with something shadowed,

something slick and razor edged. Her mouth went dry. "Knew about the *Hamlet* kiss? Is that what she's talking about?"

Tyler shook his half-filled water bottle slowly back and forth, the water sloshing inside. He wiped his sleeve across his mouth. "The other one."

"What!" Her screech stopped Dylan Thomas mid-strum. Jade looked alarmed. Actually, everyone did. No one wanted a repeat of the first creativity salon. Jessa tried to smile, leaned back on her hands—totally relaxed. "Nothing to see here" she hoped her very relaxed lean showed the group.

Dylan Thomas started to play again.

Tyler brushed grass from his pants. "That's what I thought this letter was about."

"Tyler, seriously, what are you talking about?" Her skin rippled with icy bumps and she flashed back to the curled body of the stone boy, his hands by his ears in defense, frozen. The air seemed suddenly full of ancient Mount Vesuvius ash.

Tyler blinked at her. "You really don't know? During Summer Festival."

"When I was in Santa Barbara?" Jessa's head filled with haze. She hadn't wanted to go to her cousin's wedding in Santa Barbara. She'd wanted to go to the Williams Peak Summer Festival for the Arts. She didn't even know her cousin, had only a floating image of an older girl who ate Wheat Thins out of the box with a jar of Nutella and used the word *swellio* a lot when you told her something, but her mom had gone through one of her whole we-have-to-keep-the-family-together things, and before she knew it Jessa found herself monitoring a purple satin guest book that was shaped like a heart and staring out at the Pacific Ocean next to a woman who was about a thousand years old playing Pachelbel on a harp. She had written "have a swellio life" in the guest book and not signed her name.

Tyler flipped quickly through the instruction manual pages. "Oh." He flipped the page around to face Jessa. At the top of the page, it said:

For # 15.

She doesn't know about it. I repeat, she doesn't know. If she finds out, make her understand. You were there. Jessa will understand about the improv. She understands that I get caught up in things. She gets me. Tell her. That's all it was.

Jessa forced the haze out of her head. "What happened?"

Tyler held up his hands. "Jessa, I swear I didn't know she hadn't told you. She told me you knew. That you guys figured it out."

Jessa studied her hands. "She told me she did a weird improv with Sean. She didn't say anything about kissing him."

"It was in front of a bunch of us. Just your average 'freeze' game…But…it was kind of intense. It wasn't part of the sketch.

We were all a little weirded out." Tyler reached out as if she might fall, even though they were sitting, like she might fall into nothingness. "I'm sorry, Jess, honest."

"And no one told me." Jessa's head began to throb. "Again."

"Yeah, that's not so good." Tyler scrambled for Cameron's water again who passed it to him, wide eyed. "We…We really thought she told you."

"She said, if I find out…"

"I really, really had stopped reading it, Jess." Tyler looked like he might cry.

"It's not your fault." She took a shuddering breath. "Are there any other Carissa and Sean kissing-for-no-reason moments that I should know about? Anything else in that little manual of yours?"

He flipped to the last page. "Nothing. Not that I know of. I swear. Do you want to see it?" He held out the index-card pages to her.

"No."

Tyler did that squinty thing with his eyes when he was really, really worried, like when he was taking a geometry test or right before an audition. "Don't freak out, Jess."

"Please stop saying that to me." Jessa sat up, tucked her knees under her, folded her hands in her lap. Freak out? She was actually, suddenly, inexplicably calm. She studied Dylan Thomas as he launched into another song. He was pretty good on that travel guitar of Jade's. She lassoed her vision to him, found herself wrapping her ears around the lyrics—a Rhett Miller song she had always really liked.

You've got terrible vision if you don't see…that I'm in love with you…

Jade giggled next to him. Jessa sighed. She was just missing things right and left, clearly. Wandering about in her little pity bubble. *Not* freaking out, she wanted to point out to Tyler. But then maybe that would just be its own brand of freaking out—that assertion that she wasn't. Maybe this trip was just one epic freak-out.

And really, could Jade throw herself any more at Dylan Thomas? She was practically swooning, her face all bright and staring up at him, winding all that great hair around her finger. Guys tended to look like asses around Jade, not the other way around. Jessa thought maybe she should say something to her on the bus.

Gears shifted and whined, and Jessa saw the bus ambling around a corner to fetch them.

Another bus ride.

Jessa wanted to scream, wanted to ride on the top of the bus, ratcheted down with bungee cords so she could feel the wind in her hair and not have to spend five more minutes pressed into those velour seats with that liar—that liar! Sitting right there down the aisle listening to his liar iPod and reading his liar magazine. Carissa and Sean? She felt sick. Perhaps she should take a quick survey on the bus: "Excuse me, please—anyone here who *hasn't* made out with my ex-boyfriend?"

Instead, she flipped open the letter from Carissa, the instruction like a suddenly illuminated sign:

Forgive Me.

She took a black pen from her bag, scribbled out the instruction, then added to the title across the top a line of question marks.

Friendship????????

Then she got on the stupid bus.

#16: the beat before and after

Jessa texted Carissa on the bus:

I know about u and S. BOTH TIMES. The REAL story. U lied. How could u? And I know about your stupid Jessa instruction manual! WTF?! U don't know me at all! I do NOT forgive U!!!

She turned her phone off and stuffed it as far to the bottom of her bag as she could, jammed it between her sweatshirt and a couple of *torrone* candy wrappers still a bit sticky with the nougat. Yuck.

Her fingers grazed the edge of the novel. She needed to finish it, to find out what Stephen did when the world went all dark and wrong.

For a moment, she studied the shifting landscape, turning more pastel as they headed south, then flipped open her book, but the words just swam on the page, and it felt like years before she could lose herself in them.

. . .

The bus pulled into a dusty parking lot in Naples.

"Here is the cameo factory." Francesca stood the frog at attention at the front of the bus. She pushed her sunglasses into her curls, rubbed her fingers quickly beneath her dark-circled eyes. Where was Giacomo? Jessa hadn't seen him at Pompeii.

Out the window, she saw the small, squat building. Factory? Every factory she'd ever seen was the size of a football stadium and spewing smoke or something into the sky through huge stacks. This could be someone's house.

Jessa closed the novel she hadn't quite finished, her eyes dazed and readjusting to Italy, lost for so long in Stephen's green Ireland. She wished she were in Ireland now. Then she wouldn't have to watch Sean's long, muscled back take the bus steps in two quick strides, see Tyler stealing sheepish glances at her, or watch Jade's arm linked through Dylan Thomas's arm like she owned it or something.

Inside, rows and rows of tables stretched room length, covered with thousands of small round cameos. Jessa wandered the narrow aisles, her eyes slipping over the creamy, delicate pieces. She sneezed in the dusty air. The room seemed to block out all outside light, all the natural, peach-colored Italian late afternoon. Instead, the light in the room seemed to be fighting a losing battle with shadow, straining against it to cast a yellow glow on the tables. She sneezed again. Or the room was losing its light to all the dust in the place.

Her eyes landed on a small oval. Three women draped in robes, twirling together against a creamy shell pink background.

"The Three Graces." Madison stood beside her, following her gaze. Her red hair was tied into a head scarf and she wore a clingy tube top and short skirt. Huge silver hoops glinted in the dim lighting. No camera in sight. "Faith, Hope, and Charity." She picked up the delicate piece. "This is very you. I'm getting it for you." She marched toward the cash register.

Jessa followed, dazed. "What? Oh, no. You don't have to do that…"

Madison turned on the tiny heel of her silver flip-flops. "Don't worry about it. I mean, I want to. Besides," she waggled a Visa at Jessa. "It's on my dad."

Jessa followed her to the register, watched as the Italian man placed it in a slick, dove-gray box. Handed it to her in a slim blue bag with gold script. "Thank you," she said softly and then said it again, louder this time, to Madison.

Madison's eyes darted to her face and then over her shoulder as if unsure where to land—hummingbird eyes.

"You know what?" She flipped her head a little, sending her earrings swirling about. "It's too bad the trip's almost over. We could have hung out." Madison nodded toward the door. "We're having a group meeting or something. Anyway, see you later."

And like a hummingbird, she disappeared, leaving Jessa holding the blue bag and the tiny, gorgeous Graces.

• • •

It took them a minute to realize the bus was gone.

Just a minute, blinking into the fading light.

Francesca stopped, the frog dipping to the ground, her eyes searching the vacant lot. All of them stood there, some with their little blue bags, staring, turning circles in the dusty parking lot, some with their hands to their eyes as if the bus was a ship lost on the horizon.

Ms. Jackson pinched her lips together, her eyes squinting down the road. "Did he go for gas?"

Francesca whipped out her phone and started dialing.

It was Christina who noticed that the other group was gone too. She pointed it out in her cool, whispering voice that always made Jessa think of snow.

Cameron shot her hand in the air. "But I'm here. Dylan Thomas is here. Mr. Reynolds is here." Quiet Guy didn't look up from his BlackBerry, but the group seemed momentarily reassured. Those three were standing right here. Where were the others?

"They wouldn't have left," Cameron said, her voice starting to fray at the edges. "They would have noticed…" The air seemed to swallow up the rest of her voice, carried it off into the sky that was just starting to turn toward evening, splinters of pink shooting through blue.

Devon and Tim looked stricken. "Um," Devon said, rubbing his hand across his belly. "Will we miss dinner?"

"No concern," Francesca said, clicking her phone shut. "Another bus. It is twenty-five kilometers. No more."

"Is that a lot?" Tim unwrapped a candy bar, ate the whole thing in two bites.

"It's like fifteen miles, Einstein." Dylan Thomas peeled the wrapper from a stick of gum.

Jessa saw Mr. Campbell's face shift, redden slightly. He was getting the angry eyebrow he would get in class sometimes when someone said something inappropriate or mean. But she didn't think he was mad at Dylan Thomas.

"They left." She heard him say. Then he leaned and whispered something to Ms. Jackson, who just shook her head over and over as if she just couldn't believe what he was saying, didn't want to believe it. Quiet Guy joined them, showing them something on his BlackBerry. Mr. Campbell's face fell.

What had happened suddenly seemed to dawn on the rest of the group at same time. "No way!" Natalie's face turned an alarming shade of purple, and she let out a string of names for Jamal.

"Natalie!" Ms. Jackson's voice sounded more shocked than angry. Jessa was pretty sure all their ears would now need a good washing out with some Italian soap.

"How could he leave with them? You didn't leave with them!" She pointed an accusing, manicured finger at Dylan Thomas who simply raised his eyebrows at her. "I'll kill him!" Natalie flipped open her phone and began to type furiously. She waited. The group waited, watching her. A few seconds later, her face melted, returning to is normal color. "They're in Sorrento. At the hotel. He didn't mean to go without me." She smiled as if the world had suddenly whisked itself out of a storm tunnel and righted itself on a flowering meadow.

Blake raised his hand. "Um, does anyone want to go get a soda or something?" He motioned to the little store near the factory.

Mr. Campbell gave the OK, and most everyone wandered off, back into the factory, into the little store, over to the little lip of shade the factory's roof provided, sitting cross-legged, sharing iPods with people who'd left theirs on the bus.

"It is half-hour drive at most," Francesca said to the remaining travelers. She shrugged and re-collected the frog, but her cheeks held red spots of color.

Cameron still steamed. "I'm calling my dad. I can't believe they left us here! I mean, how irresponsible is that? The guy might have a loony pants for a wife but that doesn't mean he gets to abandon us in a foreign country."

Dylan Thomas shrugged. "I didn't think Borington had it in him. I have to admit I'm borderline proud of him."

Cameron glowered.

"What did he think he was accomplishing?" Tyler rested his hands on Cameron's shoulders, started to massage her neck, massaging the glower out of her face at the same time. "I mean, it's like a half hour."

Which struck Jessa as really funny, not just sort of ha-ha funny but totally and completely hysterical. She started to giggle, just a little at first, but suddenly Dylan Thomas was laughing with her. "What a sad, sad little man," he choked out through his laughter.

"His one big act of rebellion," Jessa sputtered through her laughter. "We'll miss the appetizer!"

And then Tyler was laughing, and finally Cameron too.

Already another bus was pulling into the lot.

. . .

The Mediterranean coast leapt into Jessa's view—not there, and then suddenly everywhere, a sweeping expansive blue, curving white beaches, houses clinging to hillsides. Pressing a palm to the bus window, she felt someone settle into the seat next to her: Tyler. He wore the bowling shirt he loved so much and wore more often than he probably should. The blue one, with the circle that read "Gary" over the chest pocket.

"Hi, Gary," she peeled her eyes from the water, studied her friend.

"I have a two-part apology." He picked some lint from Gary's sleeve.

"OK."

"One. I'm sorry I didn't tell you about them kissing—*Hamlet* or the festival."

"OK." Jessa waited.

"And two. I'm sorry about the instruction manual. I thought," he paused. "I thought it would be fun. Helpful, even." Tyler pulled the stapled sheets from his pocket. "But...you know Carissa was never going to come on this trip."

"Because she had to baby-sit." Only as she said it, Jessa knew that wasn't the reason at all. Carissa would have never come to Italy, Santa Cruz or not. And Jessa realized, her stomach sinking, that she'd never even asked Carissa if she wanted to go. "Was she jealous of me? Because of Sean?"

Tyler shook his head. "Jess, I think she was jealous of Sean. Because he took up any time you had left over. I mean, you're a busy girl—don't get defensive," he held up his hand to quiet her response. "You take on a lot. Especially the last year or so. I think Carissa felt like she was starting to lose you."

"Well, you know what? Instead of kissing my boyfriend, she should have talked to me."

"In a weird way—and this is Carissa we're talking about, so it's very weird—but in her own messed-up way, I think that's what these envelopes were. Her trying to talk to you about it. When she knew you wouldn't be distracted."

Jessa swallowed her reply. Tyler was right. She took in her friend's face, his dark skin and eyes, the flop of his black hair— she was reminded of all the times he picked Carissa up when she got in trouble with a boyfriend or brought them both a latte to rehearsal, or the time Carissa got really drunk at Scott McKinley's party and he carried her all the way to Jessa's house, tucked her quietly under Jessa's quilt. Or the time he typed Jessa's honors paper for her at eleven at night when she sprained her finger playing volleyball. Tyler had spent most of his Italy trip so far making sure she didn't throw herself in front of the bus. She and Carissa owed him a Pantheon-sized thank-you card. "Why do you put up with us?"

Tyler shrugged a smile. "Entertainment value?" He held the manual out to her. "What do you want me to do with it?"

"I'm still trying to decide what to do with these." Jessa peeled open envelope #16. "I mean, if she's trying to tell me something, I can at least read the rest of them and figure out what kind of conversation she and I will be having when I get home."

Tyler looped his arm across her shoulder and read #16 with her.

Reason #16: The Beat Before and After. Sean never considers the before or the after. Doesn't consider why things are the way they are or where they are going. He never loved you in the complete way that needs the beat before and after to make sense of what's now.

We were friends then (before), we are friends now (after).

I'm sorry.

I love you.

Chills lit up and down her arms. Carissa knew she'd find out. So why hadn't she just told her? If the kisses didn't matter, didn't mean anything, she should have just told her.

Tyler tucked the manual back into his pocket. "Think Carissa realizes how ironic this is?"

"Probably not."

"Didn't think so."

Jessa folded the letter back into its envelope, watching the water, wishing she could believe her friend, not knowing what to believe, about anything, anymore.

• • •

The beat before and after.

In theater, Mr. Campbell always talked about the beats of a scene. The tiny little pieces that made up the whole scene, and how each beat had its own little world, its own intention, building blocks. And when they did scene work in class, he always talked to them about the beat before and after. What came right before you enter the scene, what came right after. Those two beats are just as important, if not more so, than the ones in the scene being performed. The actor needed to know them, even if she wasn't performing them. They establish and conclude. Establish and conclude.

This was something Jessa loved about theater, about a play and scenes within a play. They started. They ended. So clean. Clear beginning, clear ending. No fussy, messy strings and roads that led nowhere. Life, real life, didn't always make for very interesting theater. The beats weren't always where they were supposed to be.

"You coming?" Ms. Jackson waited in the bus aisle next to her, resting a hand on the seat edge.

Jessa hadn't even realized the bus had stopped at the curb of a tall, pink hotel resting over the ocean, hadn't noticed Tyler's silent exit.

"Yeah. Sorry." Jessa pulled her bag onto her shoulder and followed her teacher off the bus.

• • •

The Mediterranean Sea at sunset was something that Disney must have tried for in all its princess tales, all its Disneyland ads, and then just simply failed at, instead landing in a slightly blurrier, slightly more metal version of the sweeping view in front of her. Jessa was certain she'd never seen anything like it, never would again, the sea a mix of every possible blue and the sky stained pink, bleeding to purple. Everything both muted and striking, hushed but full of clean, dynamic lines.

Jessa leaned on the hotel railing and stared out at the shifting water, the melting sky. The other students had gone to the beach or into the busy bustle of downtown Sorrento, but Jessa had decided to stay at the hotel. She wanted to finish her book, marinate in the view. Plus, she had three texts from Carissa she wanted to read. And she didn't want to look at Sean, who had tried, unsuccessfully, to smile at her during dinner. She didn't want to throw soda in his face anymore, but she sure didn't want to smile back.

Instead, she had slurped her pasta and craved a really big plate of nachos. At one point, Dylan Thomas had watched her over a spoonful of lasagna, but she couldn't meet his eyes.

She felt like she'd been in Italy for ten years.

She heard voices on the veranda behind her and she shuffled down the railing a bit, hid behind an ivy-covered pillar. The sky turned dark alarmingly fast.

Francesca and Giacomo were arguing, intensely, in Italian, their bodies in shadow. Jessa couldn't understand a word of it, but with all the mad gesturing, she knew it wasn't a polite conversation. And Francesca still had that stupid frog with her. She must sleep with the thing.

She was brandishing it like a wizard, and for a brief moment, Jessa expected a streak of light to emerge from the frog's mouth, like something out of *The Lord of the Rings*, something green or maybe even electric blue that would turn Giacomo into some boggy animal or to dust.

Then without warning, Giacomo grabbed it from her, smashed the frog into the cement of the veranda, and stormed off, his shoes slapping against the stone, growing faint, and then gone entirely.

Francesca stared down at her shattered frog, shards of green plastic fanned out around her. Jessa slipped out from behind the pillar and, without a word, knelt down to start picking up the pieces one by one.

"Grazie." Francesca dipped beside her, picking up a chunk that held the black orb of the frog's eye. "I am sorry for that. My son—my son is very confused."

"I don't know what I'd do if I was kicked out of school." Jessa placed a small handful of plastic shards into Francesca's delicate hand.

Francesca stood up suddenly. "Is that what he told you? That he was kicked out?" Her eyes probed Jessa's face.

Standing, Jessa bit her lip, averted her eyes. "Um, he said because of narrow minds."

Francesca shook her curls, her eyes slipping out over the water. "He left school, all of his own accord." Her voice was a sigh, all breath and water. "No one wishes him to leave."

"Oh." Jessa's eyes searched the stone for any stray pieces, mostly because she couldn't look at Francesca's face—her tight skin, her eyes such sad, dark pools. Several feet away, Jessa saw a small folded piece of tissue, a glint of metal poking out of its folds. Had it come out of the frog?

Jessa made a move toward it, this glinting fragment that had gone undetected, but Francesca was already slipping away into the shadow of the small hallway leading to the hotel lobby.

Jessa picked it up, a key poking from the thin skin of tissue. Frowning, she slipped it into her pocket, then turned back to where the sky had bled to ink.

#17: the dream about nothing

Dawn was even more beautiful than sunset. Maybe—or maybe it was just sprawled in front of her and last night's sunset had already become lodged into that hazy place of memory that diminished things.

Jessa shook her head. She was starting to sound an awful lot like Stephen Dedalus from *Portrait*. She finished it last night on her tiny balcony by the light of a candle she'd found in the bathroom, and the whole thing—the night full of gathering storm clouds, the candle's flickering light, the ending of the novel that had left her sobbing into the air, the dark, dark roll of the sea—had almost been too much for Jessa. Stephen's words echoed through her head, *I will not serve that in which I no longer believe…I will try to express myself in some mode of life or art as freely as I can and as wholly as I can…*

Jessa thought about the holes in herself, the patchy places that didn't seem formed yet. She craved being able to express herself wholly, as wholly as she could. As an artist, sure, but mostly just as a girl. Whatever girl she was and would be, not just what school or other people expected. But it would also mean expressing herself in her friendship with Carissa. It would mean dealing with Sean in a *whole* way, figuring out what she wanted from him. How did she feel about him? The actual him and not just the cheating part.

And it would mean figuring out which road to take from now on, the busy bustle of her current schedule—the obvious well-traveled path toward success—or the one, like in the Robert Frost poem they'd read in English last month, the one less traveled, the one that would feed her need for beauty and light and words. *I will not serve that in which I no longer believe…*

Italy had given this to her—the time to sort it all out, the time to stop, think, dream, decide, to figure out why she kept trying to stuff all her holes full of activities and classes and events—why even after she kept filling her life to the brim, she still felt empty at her center. Standing here, watching the silvery water, she was reminded of a scene from that eighties movie *Ferris Bueller's Day Off*, the part where Ferris says something about life moving fast and making sure you don't miss it. Had she missed her life so far?

Last night, she'd read all three of Carissa's text messages.

The first two said how sorry she was, that they should always tell the truth, that their friendship was so important to her. She was just trying to help with the envelopes, with the manual. Normal

Carissa—excuses and love and moving forward. The kisses meant nothing—stupid drama. She was truly, infinitely sorry.

But the third had said:

Did you love him?

Jessa had texted back:

I don't know anything anymore.

Behind her, she could hear Christina rising, moving about in the early light of the room, getting ready for their ferry ride to the island of Capri. Last night, a thunderstorm had rocked the hotel. Flashes of lightning illuminated the room, and the sea had turned chunky and aggressive. Now the morning dawned clear and fresh.

But Jessa's text repeated over and over in her head like a mantra or an old-fashioned record that skipped and skipped: *I don't know anything anymore.*

• • •

"Let me see the manual." Jessa grabbed Tyler by his sweatshirt sleeve on the docks as they waited for the ferry. "If you still have it."

"You sure?"

"Yes." Jessa pulled her hair into a ponytail and waited.

He handed her the pages. She flipped to the instructions for Reasons #16 and #17.

This looks bad. I know it does. But she doesn't know the history. I'm sorry. Make her know that. That's the most important thing. Here's the truth. Sean and I had a little thing. During *The Breakfast Club*. It didn't last and it was totally stupid freshman backstage stuff. It resurfaced. Twice. It will not happen again. I never meant to hurt her. Please, please, Tyler. Make her understand. She'll listen to you.

Jessa saw the boat approaching. Everyone shifted on the dock, jockeyed for position. Jessa handed the manual back. "Why didn't I know? I worked on *The Breakfast Club* too."

The boat docked, and Jessa and Tyler fell into line. "I think it meant more to Carissa than it did to Sean. When he talked about it, it was just sort of a backstage thing they had. It didn't mean anything—to Sean."

Jessa hoisted her bag onto her shoulder as they began to move forward.

Tyler tucked his hands in his sweatshirt pockets, stared out at the water. "When you two started hanging out, Carissa was sure it wouldn't last, didn't want you to get all mad about nothing for nothing." He frowned, his eyes shifting to the students climbing onto the boat. "And then it did last. And then it was too late to tell you."

"She should have told me." She blinked at her friend. "You should have told me. Or Sean should have."

"We all *should* do a lot of things," Tyler said quietly. "But I think, most of the time, we don't."

. . .

Capri was cold and wet when they arrived, washed by the previous night's storm, but the sky and water engulfed them in a shocking, blue world, haloed with golden light. The sea stretched out like melting silver encircling the famous *Odyssey* rocks off the island. Sorrento had been so bustling, buzzing, but Capri simmered with tranquility, the hum of the surrounding sea, the fresh smell of last night's rainwater. The sun had won its battle with the few remaining storm clouds and only the most stubborn remained, silhouetting the floating lines of seagulls. Against the cliff, peppered spots of white houses and palm trees stood out amid thicker, denser trees. The sun played hide and seek with the clouds, casting layered patterns of light and shade over the island.

Jessa closed her eyes, wanting the sea in her ears forever, her face bathed in salt air, cooled by mist. They had walked from the main square, past the incredible Quisisana Hotel to the Giardini di Augusto, a park with striking views of the Faraglioni rocks. Jessa wished she'd paid more attention when she had read the *Odyssey* in freshman English. She would have appreciated it a lot more now facing this expanse of sea. Odysseus had sailed and sailed across it, alone on the raft. She flipped open her journal and chewed the end of her pen.

After a moment, she wrote:

Can I be alone, lashed to a raft in a drifting sea, but still surrounded by the whole stupid world?

Ms. Jackson had given them an hour with their journals to prepare for their final creativity salon in Rome. It was hard to imagine they'd be heading home tomorrow.

She took a breath. What had Francesca said about these gardens? That they had once been a school for revolutionaries? Something like that. Jessa would have trouble mustering up a revolutionary spirit here; this place seemed more spiritual, more suited for meditation—or full-on napping.

She turned at the rustle behind her. Natalie froze in mid-descent down a little grassy slope, her own journal clutched in her hand. "Oh, sorry. Didn't know anyone was here." She started to retreat, tugging at the strap of her red tank top.

"Natalie?" Jessa closed her journal.

Natalie turned, her face wary. "Yeah?"

"Did you think about what being with him, like that, would do to me?" Jessa's heart raced and her hands sweated onto her journal cover, dimpling it. "I'm just wondering, actually, if you thought about me at all? I mean, I know we aren't friends or anything but…we've known each other. A long time. You came to my birthday party in fourth grade, helped me build a castle out of Popsicle sticks." Jessa felt the revolutionary spirits shift beneath her after all, and their shadowed energy buoyed her. *I will try to express myself in some mode of life or art as freely as I can and as wholly as I can...* Stephen Dedalus tapped at her skull, thumping her brain.

Natalie made her way down the slope, settled herself down next to Jessa, and blew a strand of blonde hair from her eyes. She appraised Jessa, picked blades of grass, brushed imaginary dust from her tight white sweatpants.

"I did." She kept her eyes on the grass. "But I believed Sean."

Jessa's stomach churned. "What do you mean?"

Natalie fiddled again with her tank-top strap. Jessa tried to keep her eyes from the swollen chest straining in the tank, the lacy edge of bra cup also struggling. Her boobs really were alarmingly huge. How could she just grow them in one summer? Just one summer? Natalie finally said, "That you two were over. That it was over. That's what he told me."

"We weren't."

"Yeah, I kind of know that now. Why do you think I broke it off? But you know what, Jessa? You haven't been very nice to me. I mean, Popsicle-stick castle or not, it's not like I used Miracle-Gro or had an operation or something. The same thing happened to my grandma." Her large eyes pooled.

A wind chilled Jessa's bare arms. She grabbed her Williams Peak sweatshirt from her bag, pulled it quickly on. She pushed her sunglasses to the top of her head, stared until the other girl met her eyes.

"I'm sorry, Natalie."

"Me too," Natalie whispered.

Jessa nodded, said again, louder this time, "I'm so sorry."

The spirits settled beneath them.

• • •

Reason #17: The Dream about Nothing

Sean Does Not Support Your Dreams!

Remember our dream. From when we were twelve and used to sleep in the tent in your yard during summer break after we dug all the fairy holes for Maisy for when the fairies came. The dream where we both woke up and couldn't remember anything at all. Couldn't remember if it had been about the fair or about the water-slide you might get for your birthday or about Tim, the older boy across the street who was so cute and worked on his truck and who sometimes bought us ice cream from the scary ice-cream-truck driver and ate them with us in the driveway. It was just blurry, like fog. And we used to say, "Let's make up a dream to stick where we had the dream about nothing." Remember. Can we do that now? Can we make up a dream?

Instruction: What will you stick into your dream about nothing?

Jessa wrote three things at the top of her journal page: *Dream, Fairy Holes, Love.*

. . .

Giacomo waited for her at the entrance to the Villa San Michele. He seemed perfectly in place, leaning against an arch covered in vines, as if perhaps Odysseus had given in to Capri after all, surrendered to the siren call, threw on some designer denim and a tight black T-shirt and waited for Jessa all those years under a flowering archway.

Light slanted across his face, and he smiled when he saw her. "Buongiorno, bella."

She flushed with sudden sunburn. The Capri sun had nothing on that smile. "Hey, stranger." She was sure she sounded five, all high and hiccupy. "Where've you been?"

He frowned, drawing the stray storm clouds into his face. "My mother and I...had a disagreement."

"I saw you." She brushed a piece of windblown hair from her eyes, shaded them as she studied his face.

He squinted down at her, his eyes growing dark like his mother's. "Last night. On the balcony. I'm sorry."

"Why are you sorry?"

"Because I know what it feels like to be that angry." She licked her lips, let her eyes take in the sea. When he didn't say anything, just let his dark eyes wash the landscape, she added, "Besides, we've all been wanting to work over that frog since we got here.

You have no idea how liberating that was watching you smash it to pieces." She glanced up at him, attempted a smile.

His face broke back into light. "You are a funny girl. Yes, it did feel good in the moment. Not today though. She will not give me what I've asked for."

"Which is what?"

He gazed out over the sprawling grounds of the villa, didn't meet her eyes. "Look at Capri. What do you see?"

"Another world," she said, her eyes falling on spots of red and white, all the flowers amid the green of the landscape.

"It's a special place here," Giacomo said, tucking his hands in his jean pockets. "A siren call for artists, bohemians, seeking beauty, a different life, with no rules—no idea of what is the right way to live life, to love."

Jessa wanted to ask him what he meant, who they were, these artists who were Siren called to Capri, but Ms. Jackson whistled at the group to meet under a flowering arch.

"Giacomo?"

"Yes?"

"After you, uh, left last night, I helped your mom pick up the pieces of the frog. I found this." She handed him the thin, silver key. His eyes widened. "Could you give this to her for me? She's been a little busy." Jessa nodded to where Francesca flipped through a folder, talking rapidly into a cell phone.

"This was in the frog?" Giacomo's voice was a ghost whisper.

Jessa frowned. "You know it?"

Giacomo clasped the key in his fist, his eyes full. He glanced at his mother, his face collaged with emotion, then his eyes rested back on Jessa, who was quite sure this was what it felt like to be caught in a tractor beam. "Thank you. You have no idea what you've just given me."

Before she could reply, Ms. Jackson's voice cut into their stare. "Jessa!"

Giacomo dropped his gaze, and Jessa hurried over to where Francesca stood, looking a bit naked without her frog.

No one mentioned him, that frog they'd followed through the streets of Rome, through Florence, through Venice, but who was suddenly, noticeably gone. Francesca's phantom limb. Actually, Jessa missed him a little, bobbing along on his stick, his bulging black plastic eyes staring, telling them which way to go.

Jessa's eyes strayed to Sean. Her grandmother told her once, when she was seven and they were sitting in front of a frog exhibit at the San Diego Zoo, that she'd have to kiss a lot of frogs before she found a prince. She had stared through the glass at an odd little waxy tree frog and secretly hoped she'd never have to kiss any frogs. She'd been seven and not really grasping the whole frog-prince metaphor, but now, here, staring at her frog across the gauzy air of Capri, she realized that maybe the whole kiss-a-frog thing wasn't just about finding a prince. Maybe you had to follow your own fair share of frogs on a stick through busy streets without really knowing where you were going. And maybe sometimes, you needed them smashed on the cement so you could find your own way.

"The Villa San Michele," Francesca was saying, her voice tired but still floating across them in that now-familiar lilt, drawing them into the place she was about to share. "The original owner was Axel Munthe, a Swedish physician who built the villa out of remains of Roman ruins."

Jessa followed her class through the grounds, watching as Giacomo fell to the back of the group, checked his phone, texted something. A trance seemed to be taking over her limbs, the world here seeming a thousand years old, all green and varied, white buildings, fountains, the sea a breathless vastness. Running water from the fountains mixed with the sea crash filled her ears with a noise that sounded mostly like silence, like hours stretched out and made into taffy, sweet, with no sense of time or distance.

All around her, beauty from ruins—beauty from ruins.

• • •

She found a railing with a straight view of the sea, a blooming vine nearby smelled of apple candy. The edge of the island fell away beneath her. She could be at the end of the earth. She hadn't felt this kind of ease, this kind of melting simplicity since the way the costume barn used to make her feel. Before—B.C.B.

What would happen if she didn't go home?

She could get a job in one of the shops in the square, finish high school with distance learning, live in a small studio with a view of the sea. She could write things, or paint things. She could read every book she had wanted to read but couldn't because there was always school, where they made her read other books, the ones not on her shelves. She would stack them all around the small room, spines out, use the stacks as tables, as places to rest her coffee cup, her pictures of home, the ones in the etched silver frames that had been her grandmother's.

"Careful," said a voice behind her. "Those Siren songs get in, fill you up. You'll never want to leave." Mr. Campbell joined her at the railing, his eyes shadowed by his Giants cap.

"Too late."

He chuckled, taking in a deep breath of sea air. "You ever finish *Portrait*?"

"Last night." Her stomach hummed with the memory of the incoming storm as she finished Joyce on the hotel balcony, the flickering light of the candle. "Mr. Campbell?"

"Yeah?"

"I'm screwed, right?"

"What?"

A seabird found a hollow in the sky that stopped its flight, just drifted out there on the air in front of them. Jessa closed her eyes, imagined trading places with that bird, to dip and sail, glide, passing time in sunbeams, in gusts of sea air—floating, a slave only to migration, knowing to come or go. Birds were so lucky.

"That guy at the end says to Stephen. 'You poor poet, you.' He pities him."

Mr. Campbell leaned on his elbows. "Yes. He does say that."

"I'm screwed. That's the point of the novel."

"I'm not sure Joyce would agree with you."

"Now that I've figured out that I see the world a certain way, that I might not want that big, big future I had so steadily been planning, so blindly. Now I'm destined to wander the world always feeling too much, noticing too much. Crying and hurting and in despair while other people just live normally, happier. Not wondering so much, feeling so much."

Mr. Campbell adjusted his hat and leaned on the railing. "OK, I can see how you'd get that, but, listen, you're not giving up anything. You're just figuring out how you see things. And those people—I don't know if they're happier, Jess. Maybe they just seem that way to you. But sure, having an artistic sense about you can make things difficult sometimes, feelings can be more extreme, like all of our nerves are always open to the elements. But that's the secret."

"What is?"

"We get to *feel* those things. Some people—they get comfort and ease, maybe. We get complexity and really messy feelings that make people uncomfortable. It's a trade-off. There are people who don't get to look at this sea and wonder what you're wondering."

She pushed up the sleeves of her sweatshirt, felt the sun warm her forearms. "You mean that I could live here forever and read and write and never need to be part of the real world. Practical people don't wonder that, huh?"

"Practicality can be its own prison." He pulled off his hat, ran his fingers through his messy hair. He had dark stains beneath his eyes. The trip had been long, too much drama.

The kiss on the bridge in Florence felt like years ago, another life. What an idiotic maneuver that had been.

She shivered a bit. "You know how in the novel Stephen has to choose? Between the life he thought he was supposed to live and the one he discovers, his artistic path?"

"Yeah."

"How does he know he makes the right choice?"

Mr. Campbell frowned, his eyes searching the horizon. "He doesn't. But he vows to himself to live life on his terms, to not serve that which he no longer believes in. I think the vow itself is what matters. It will inform each choice he makes in the future."

"But Joyce didn't write that part of the book, right? The part where we see how it informs him."

Mr. Campbell laughed. "No. No, that's the thing about books. We don't get to see the fallout after the happily ever after—true."

"Mr. Campbell?" Devon, Tim, and Sean had come up behind them, a little army of drama boys. Devon watched her with interest, his eyes slipping back and forth between her and Mr. Campbell. Lovely—one more rumor to cart home from Italy. "Ms. Jackson says it's time to start rounding up the troops," Devon told them. "There are many roads to Rome." He cracked himself up.

"How long you been waiting to say that?" Mr. Campbell pushed himself away from the railing and followed Tim and Devon back toward the entrance.

Sean lingered behind.

"I'm warning you," Jessa told him. "I'm contemplative and emotional and I didn't sleep well last night. Approach at your own risk."

He risked it, leaning next to her on the rail, staring out at that huge sprawl of water. "What I told Natalie was that we were pretty much over. That's what I told her."

"I guess a lie is as good as the truth if you can get someone to believe you." Jessa pulled her sleeves down again, tucked her hands inside the cuffs. A wind had come up suddenly, the air chilly and full of salt.

"I didn't think I was lying."

"You didn't tell me you thought we were pretty much over. You didn't tell me a lot of things."

"I guess I forgot to make an appointment." He jammed his hands in his shorts pockets, hopped a bit up and down to keep warm.

"Whatever, Sean. That's not fair. I'm a busy girl. No get-out-of-jail-free card for you because I'm ambitious. You know I have a lot on my plate. It doesn't give you an excuse to kiss Carissa or Natalie or anyone else."

His eyebrows shot up, but he didn't deny it or try to explain it. "I just hope you get something for all of your busy, Jess. All that you put yourself through." He set his hands on the railing, squinted out over the ocean. Clouds were starting to gather again. It would be a rocky boat ride back. He smelled like cinnamon and sea air. His face had gotten tan on the trip. Looking down at her, he said, "I do love you, though. I know I sort of have the world's crappiest way of showing it, but I do. For what it's worth, I think a lot of people will love you. And maybe you'll love one of them back."

His words spattered her body with microscopic pin pricks. "I loved you."

He stood very close to her now, his body long and solid next to her, and maybe it was just because it would be warmer to hold him, or maybe she just wanted to share this feeling with someone, even him, or maybe she wanted something to stick into her dream about nothing. Whatever the reason, she reached out and grabbed his shoulder, pulled him in to kiss her, the wind cold against her cheeks and his arms warm as they wrapped around her back.

#18: frodo

Giacomo was gone. Not on the boat back and not on the bus now. She debated telling Francesca about the key, but maybe she'd already caused a problem. No need to draw attention to it. She fiddled with *Wicked* playing on her iPod, kept skipping songs before they finished. Restless, annoyed, she chewed a Frutella candy and folded the wrapper into tiny squares. She offered one to Kevin, who was sitting next to her. He shook his head, his eyes on the spy novel in his lap.

No more buses. No more buses. She never wanted to see the inside of a bus again. Next time she came to Italy, she would ride a bicycle along the Italian roads with the wind in her hair. She barely looked at the world outside as they hurtled down the highway toward Rome, tired even of the view out the square bus window.

Sean thought she didn't love him. But she did. She did. She just couldn't be one of those girlfriends who built their whole world around their boyfriends. That was too dangerous, too stupid. She had her life to think about, the life stretching out before her like a highway. No, not like a highway. Something more twisty, with bends she couldn't see around and fallen trees and no center divider. Her future road was more like that. But she had loved him with every cell in her body, so much so that at night falling asleep, she would hold one of his shirts to her face and breathe him into her. If he couldn't see that, couldn't see how he had made her feel then he wasn't paying attention and the last thing she needed was a boyfriend with some sort of emotional ADD.

"Switch me," Dylan Thomas said, motioning for Kevin to move. Kevin barely peeled his eyes from his novel as he slid into the empty seat across the aisle. Dylan Thomas reached over and pulled her earbuds out. "You kissed Sean?"

Jessa wound the cords of the earbuds around her hand, the way a boxer must tape up his hands before a fight. "Who told you that?"

"He's telling people."

"Like he's taken out an official announcement?"

"Um, he told Devon and Tim. And Kevin." Dylan Thomas hooked a finger at Kevin.

"That's true. He did tell me," Kevin mumbled, still not looking up. Must be a good book.

"It was nothing." As she said the words, she knew them instantly to be true. Nothing left there. Just a view and an island known for false promises, for escape. An attempt to conjure a love back out of a bottle that had been too tightly capped.

Dylan Thomas held her eyes. He unwrapped a stick of gum, popped it in his mouth. Chewed. "You sure?"

Jessa shrugged. She wasn't really sure "nothing" existed—everything was about something. Carissa had said the kisses were nothing too. Maybe they meant more to her than she was willing to admit. Maybe everyone lied a little to themselves right in the moment because it was easier than looking like the one who wasn't wanted. She had asked Jessa, "Did you love him?" Maybe Jessa should have asked Carissa the same thing. What Jessa had said was, "I don't know anything anymore."

She repeated this to Dylan Thomas.

"Because you are not a stupid girl. Don't act like one." He leaned a bit toward Kevin. "I'm going to keep this seat, OK?"

"Help yourself," Kevin said.

"Smart girls can act stupid." Jessa said, plugging her ears up again with her music. Turning her eyes to the sweeping caramel hills flying by outside, she whispered, "We are all more stupid than smart, I think."

• • •

Reason #18 was a picture of Frodo. Well, two pictures of Frodo. One of the actual Frodo or that actor who played him—what was his name? Elijah Wood. And the other picture was of Sean's car, the green Honda she'd named Frodo. She set the letter on the bedspread in front of her. Her last hotel room in Italy, and she wouldn't even sleep here since they all vowed to stay up until they left for the airport.

> Reason #18: This probably seems stupid now after everything else, but he is really weird about his car. You know I'm right.

Carissa was right. Sean was a freak about his car. But Jessa knew that was just a place holder, that this envelope was really about the instruction:

> Let's think about the other Frodo for a minute—the hero's journey and all that. So think about it. What did you learn on your journey?

Jessa had checked her phone in Rome. No more texts from Carissa—total text silence from her end. She would wait Jessa out. Sighing, Jessa scanned her things, her suitcase, her dirty clothes, the presents she bought: the Murano glass frame she'd selected for her mom and dad, the leather journal for Maisy. After tucking all the ticket stubs from their museum visits and church visits into the small blue cameo bag so she could make a collage for her photo book, she picked up the cameo Madison bought her. The Three Graces: Faith, Hope, Charity. She knew she would need all three in her immediate future, supersized versions.

Someone knocked on her door. Jade poked her head in, her curls tied back at the nape of her neck. "You coming?"

"Almost done." Jessa placed everything in her suitcase, zipped it shut. Would she really go home tomorrow, walk through the red door of her parents' house and back into her old life? Her bed with the quilt her grandmother made her, the white furniture she had desperately wanted in seventh grade and now seemed sort of babyish, the view of the pine trees out her window, her huge calendar bulging with activities, events, responsibilities, checklists—the tried-and-true path she was laying like bricks out in front of her, solid, predictable bricks. Would everything be just as she had left it? Or would her normal life now seem foreign and strange?

Jade leaned her head against the door frame. "Ms. Jackson wants to start right at midnight. Ugh, I'm so tired."

"Me too." Jessa ran her hand over her closed suitcase, fingering Maisy's little hair ribbon tied to the handle. "But we can sleep on the plane." Jessa set her suitcase on the ground. "It will be better to just not sleep at all now."

They had to leave for the airport at 3 a.m.

Jessa followed Jade down to the lobby. The other school group waited there, sitting on their suitcases or on the floor. Jessa didn't see Cameron. She was probably somewhere saying good-bye to Tyler. The whole room seemed filled with shadows, people saying good-bye in dark corners.

Jade cuddled up next to Dylan Thomas, who was sitting propped against a far wall of the lobby. He whispered something to her. She laughed, brushed some hair out of his eyes. Jessa clutched her journal, searching out where they'd be meeting for their last creativity salon. Ms. Jackson and Mr. Campbell sat alone on some couches in a dimly lit room right off the lobby. She didn't want to be the first one there.

A patch of night sky loomed outside the crescent windows above the hotel doors, and she found herself pushing through the heavy doors and out into the cool night. The air filled her lungs, the sweet smell of Italy, flowered and musty. She could hear airplanes in the distance. She wished she was on one.

"What, you bad with good-byes or something?" Dylan Thomas stood in silhouette against the open hotel door. It hushed to a close as he joined her on the sidewalk.

"I was going to say good-bye." Her whole body began to shiver, her skin crawling with goose bumps.

"Sucks I'm missing the last salon," he said. "But we're leaving now. Our plane leaves soon."

"I wish we were leaving now."

"No you don't."

Jessa felt tears wetting her cheeks. What was wrong with her? Dylan Thomas moved close to her, pulled her into his sweatshirted chest. She realized she'd never hugged him before, which was weird because she was such a hugger. He smelled great. Like mint gum and aftershave, something musky and soft. He smelled the way velvet should smell.

"I'll miss you," he said. "You poor poet, you."

Her breath caught; she looked up at him. "What did you say?"

He smiled, his eyes dark but full of hotel lights. "What? You're not the only one who reads."

Dylan Thomas took a step back. A bus idled near them. The other group filed out of the hotel, bags over shoulders, wheeling suitcases, a wilted, travel-weary brood. They'd lost a bit of the shine they'd walked into the Pantheon with that first day, but it looked good on them, the dull rub of these past ten days. Madison waved to her as she climbed on the bus, took a quick snap of a picture. Jessa waved back.

"Oh, hey," Dylan Thomas grabbed her left wrist. "You should tell people the truth about that scar of yours. The truth is always more interesting anyway. It has rougher edges."

"What makes you think I'm not telling the truth?" But she knew her smile gave her away.

He gave her wrist a little squeeze, his eyes warming hers. "You know how to find me." He wiggled his phone at her.

"Bye," she whispered as Dylan Thomas climbed on the bus behind Cameron, her face tear streaked. Jessa felt Tyler next to her, the weight of his arm on her shoulder.

"Well, that's lugubrious," he said, finally, as the bus pulled away.

"Lugubrious?"

"I'm trying it on for size."

Jessa leaned into the curve of him. "It's perfect, actually. But I don't really see it catching on."

Shrugging, he gave her shoulders a little squeeze, waving again to the bus disappearing into the Italian night.

• • •

Jade played Green Day's "Time of Your Life," which seemed totally perfect even if it was so completely overused in these kinds of situations. They all sang along.

"Thing is, this song is really titled 'Good Riddance,'" Tyler whispered. Jessa gave him a good-natured poke with her elbow and sang loudly over him.

Jade finished, red cheeked, adding a little flair at the end just for fun. The room burst into applause. Next, Devon, Tim, Hillary, and Kevin did a funny scene with Tim miming a frog on a stick. Kevin played an alarmingly accurate Cruella outside the Uffizi with Hillary as the dithering, clueless Borington, who couldn't, literally, find his ass with both hands.

"OK, OK," Mr. Campbell said, cutting them short of an ending sure to turn inappropriate much too fast. "That's enough of that. Accurate. But enough." Laughing, they fell into their seats. Kevin took an extra bow, smiling at the boos and hisses.

"How very *Commedia* of you all," Mr. Campbell said proudly.

"Next?" Ms. Jackson asked.

"I'll go," Jessa said, standing up. "And no drinks in the face—I promise."

Kevin gave Sean a good-natured thump on the back. "Want my rain jacket just in case?"

Sean's eyes locked on Jessa. He looked a little sick to his stomach.

Jessa opened her journal. "OK, so you all know that Carissa gave me those letters with all the reasons why I shouldn't be with Sean. And number 18 is called 'Frodo.'" A couple of whistles for Frodo sounded out. Sean's Honda had its own little following. Jessa continued, "And this is, of course, a nod to your Frodo, Sean." He managed a queasy smile. "But the question really is, What did I learn on my journey? Well, I learned a few things here in Italy, but one in particular that I'd like to share."

She paused. "This is called 'Instructions for a Broken Heart.' And it's for Sean."

Sean's smile vanished. Silence poured into the room or else all the noise, the small whispers and fidgets and feet shuffles, were sucked out suddenly with a superpowered sound vacuum.

Jessa read into the silence.

Instructions for a Broken Heart

I will find a bare patch of earth, somewhere where the ruins have fallen away, somewhere where I can fit both hands, and I will dig a hole.

And into that hole, I will scream you, I will dump all the

shadow places of my heart—the times you didn't call when you said you'd call, the way you only half listened to my poems, your eyes on people coming through the swinging door of the café—not on me—your ears, not really turned toward me. For all those times I started to tell you about the fight with my dad or when my grandma died, and you said something about your car, something about the math test you flunked, as an answer. I will scream into that hole the silence of dark nights after you'd kissed me, how when I asked if something was wrong—and something was obviously so very wrong—how you said "nothing," how you didn't tell me until I had to see it in the dim light of a costume barn—so much wrong. I will scream all of it.

Then I will fill it in with dark earth, leave it here in Italy, so there will be an ocean between the hole and me.

Because then I can bring home a heart full of the light patches. A heart that sees the sunset you saw that night outside of Taco Bell, the way you pointed out that it made the trees seem on fire, a heart that holds the time your little brother fell on his bike at the fairgrounds and you had pockets full of bright colored Band-Aids and you kissed the bare skin of his knees. I will take that home with me. In my heart. I will take home your final Hamlet monologue on the dark stage when you cried closing night and it wasn't really acting, you cried because you felt the words in you and on that bare stage you felt the way I feel every day of my life, every second, the way the words, the light and dark, the spotlight in your face, made you Hamlet for that brief hiccup of a moment, made you a poet, an artist at your core. I get to take Italy home with me, the Italy that showed me you and the Italy that showed me—me—the Italy that wrote me my very own instructions for a broken heart. And I get to leave the other heart in a hole.

We are over. I know this. But we are not blank. We were a beautiful building made of stone, crumbled now and covered in vines.

But not blank. Not forgotten. We are a history.

We are beauty out of ruins.

Jessa stopped, closed her journal, turned her eyes on her silent friends. Then, Jade jumped up, threw her arms around Jessa. Over Jade's shoulder, she saw Mr. Campbell and Ms. Jackson clapping; she saw Hillary smiling, nodding. She let her gaze slide to Sean, who sat very still on the couch, watching her with heavy, Hamlet eyes.

"OK," Devon said, "That was kind of a downer, Jess. Can we do our scene again?"

#19: air, not just for breathing anymore

Everyone, it seemed, had Jessa's seat. Or was it the other way around? Jessa had already moved twice. First, a ridiculously tall German woman told Jessa she had the wrong seat. She wasn't very nice about it, probably because she was used to being able to squash people like grapes. Then it was a grandma in an "I Was Romed" T-shirt, which didn't make any sense, who didn't act very grandmotherly. Now, a short, blue suited Italian man sitting next to Jade looked apologetically up at her. The flight attendant tried to tell Jessa that she would have to find her another seat, but the man stood, gathered his newspaper, ushered her into the seat, the kind of gentleman they didn't seem to make in California anymore.

Already, Jessa felt coated with a thin film, dust or sweat or some sort of hybrid body excretion that rears its head only on airplanes. She settled her bag on the floor in front of her, nodding at Jade, whose pen scritch-scratched across the pages of her journal. Jessa's eyes surveyed the plane. A row up, a gorgeous couple sat thumbing through magazines, probably on their way to be Armani models or something, one giant advertisement for why the rest of the world was just too ugly to breathe. They whispered quietly, he in what sounded like German, and she in Italian. Nothing like a Europe trip to make you realize how stupid you were when it came to languages. Jessa vowed to pay more attention in Señor Allen's Spanish class.

Italian filtered out over the speakers, announcing their departure—instructions never sounded so beautiful, and Jessa took another peek out the window but it just looked airporty.

Ciao, Italia.

• • •

Jessa checked the big envelope again, pulling out all the smaller envelopes. One by one, she set them on her pull-down table, trying not to wake Jade who slept next to her with tiny, purring snores. Eighteen envelopes. She knew she'd left one at the place where she'd had dinner with Giacomo, but where was #20? She hadn't opened #19, thought she'd just open both and then maybe sleep the rest of the plane ride. It would be so like Carissa to just forget to put in #20 or maybe it would be waiting for her on her pillow at home. Dramatic flair.

She peeled open the last envelope.

Big Fat Reason #19: Air, Not Just for Breathing Anymore
He took you for granted.

Air: Not Just for Breathing Anymore
Breathe it, fly through it,
spill our dreams into it,
color it with rain. Air—necessary
and totally taken for granted.

No instruction with this last envelope. Maybe the poem was the instruction even if it was more like a decree. The world according to Carissa. Did Sean take her for granted? Did Jessa take Carissa for granted? Probably. Maybe air was a lot like love, or friendship. It was noticeable when you suddenly lost it and were left gasping. But up until that loss of it, did she notice it? Jessa had the horrible feeling that she'd yet to scratch the surface of all she'd been taking for granted her whole life. She'd sure taken Tyler for granted on the trip. Rolling her head from side to side, Jessa folded all the notes back into the larger envelope and tucked them back into her bag, then sat back into her seat. Breathe—breathe air.

Sean turned in his seat several rows up, caught her staring. They hadn't talked since her reading, but the crackling bridge of ice between them, the one that held her from him but also fastened her to him, had thawed, melted, leaving only a few icy tendrils, ones that could be seen only in direct light, tiny diamond sparkles. She felt like she was seeing him for the first time. Teenage boy in bone-colored shirt, great hair, slightly crooked nose, long limbed—far from her, miles from her. She smiled, and with their history framing his face, he smiled back, then returned to his magazine.

Jade stirred next to her, mumbled something that sounded like, "Rwar awr me?"

"The polar route over the ice caps," Jessa said, pointing out the window. Both girls pressed their faces to the window. Below them, the beautiful blinding ice stretched out, rippled and textured, rolling away into vastness and then sudden glimpses of blue sky shot through thick as paint.

"It's like *The Golden Compass* or something," Jade breathed. "We can imagine we're bounding over it in a huge, red balloon."

Jessa nodded, wanting very much to imagine that. "Do you think there is life there?"

Jade's eyes sparkled, taking in the ocean of ice below. "I imagine dozens of ice creatures living in tunnels beneath the snow, eyes like slits, creatures who use smell the way we use sight, who can feel the difference between snowflakes, who have a million nerve endings at the end of their fingers." Her eyes darted quickly to Jessa. "Oh, God. You probably think I'm such a total freak that I just said that."

"No way." Jessa leaned closer to the window. "It's just that the creatures in my head have huge orb eyes instead of slits. And they live in cavernous glass domes beneath the ice."

"Oh, that's good." Jade smiled, her white teeth even, organized squares. "I'll have to text Dylan Thomas when we land. He'd love that."

"You two had a good connection, huh?" Jessa felt an icy pool gathering in her own belly, felt Jade's creatures taking refuge there.

Jade nodded. "He's a really sweet guy, so smart and funny. We had fun."

Jessa hesitated. "Are you guys, um, together now?"

"What? No! I've been with Trevor Johns for, like, two years."

Trevor Johns! Jessa had totally forgotten about Trevor—senior, president of Project Green, long-distance runner, overall crunchy-granola cutie pie. He basically wanted to marry Jade and live in his Eurovan. How had she so easily popped him right out of her mind?

"Oh, yeah. Duh."

Jade pulled her curls off her shoulders, tying them into a knot with a strip of cloth at the base of her neck. "Trev's in Mexico building houses this break. This trip's just a little too consumer splurge for Trev. Can you imagine him with that other group?" Jade giggled. "He'd be all, like, um, Cruella, are you aware of your global consumer impact?" Jade's love for her boyfriend wrapped each word with music. "That would be hilarious."

"He's very earnest, your Trevor," Jessa smiled.

"Oh yeah. He'll change the world." Jade pulled her journal out of her woven bag. "But I wanted to see Italy. Because it's really, really pretty."

"So pretty," Jessa agreed.

Jade held her journal up. "Gonna write about our glass-dome cave creatures. Might make a good song."

Jessa nodded, the ice pool in her belly evaporating. The in-flight movie blinked on, and she pulled on the headphones, curled into her seat, cradled in all the air surrounding her, buoying her, as they hurtled through the sky above the wide expanse of ice, the frozen ocean below.

#20: addendum

Jessa peered into the bleary light of the Sacramento airport. Was it just her or did the light here seem beige, so unlike the fairy wing light of Italy? All around her, beige people wheeled beige bags, sat on beige chairs, ate beige food.

"Culture shock." Mr. Campbell rolled his suitcase up next to hers. "It passes in, oh, well," he shrugged, "never."

"Once Italy gets in…" she started.

"It never leaves," he finished, nodding. "Good trip." With a tired smile, he wheeled his bag away from her through the glass doors to where a bus idled outside.

Jessa scanned the airport, desperately wanting a Starbucks before she climbed on another bus. Maybe a little caffeine would pop her out of her funk.

She blinked. Did Sacramento have a problem with mirages? Was she just that tired that she was imagining beautiful Italian men standing by the Cinnabon shop? She probably rubbed her eyes, because people in movies rubbed their eyes when they thought they were seeing things that couldn't, under any circumstance, be standing right in front of them. Of course in the movies, the thing in question was always there.

"Is that Giacomo?" Tyler rolled his suitcase up next to her.

They couldn't both be having the same hallucination. Could they? Her stomach back flipped.

Giacomo saw her. His face lighting, he strolled over. "I knew that your flight was coming in. I flew in last night, left Capri, and headed out. Thanks to you." He nodded at Tyler, who studied him with some skepticism but nodded back.

Jessa's mouth felt stuck together with paste, cemented. What was he talking about?

Giacomo held an envelope in his hand. "You are missing one, no?"

#20.

The mouth paste turned to sand. Jessa nodded, took the envelope in trembling fingers, stared at it, turning it over and over in her hands.

"It's sort of random that you're here, dude." Tyler raised his eyebrows, waited for an answer.

Jessa's heart was suddenly like one of the neon smoothie machines from the airport food court, all swirls and churning. "Why do you have this?"

"I found it on the boat leaving Capri. I almost threw it out, but I wanted you to have all twenty. If you are still opening them?"

He squinted his dark, liquid eyes at her, cocked his head to the side. "You did something for me. Now I do something for you."

"So you came all the way to California? To give me this letter? Just in case?" All the airport sounds, the voice in the speakers, the beeping of carts, the whirl and whine of weary travelers, all of it heightened, pounded Jessa's ears like it was being pumped into her head through earphones.

Giacomo's eyebrows jumped. "Oh, what? Oh, no. I should have explained…" Then he laughed—hard. Held a hand over his belly, even wiped a tear from his eye.

Tyler cleared his throat. "You can see where she might get that idea. Since you are standing here in the Sacramento airport holding an envelope. Since you are standing right here."

Jessa could kiss Tyler.

Giacomo got himself under control. "I flew here yesterday. Because of Aaron."

"Who?" Jessa and Tyler asked at the same time.

On cue, a tall, blonde boy of maybe nineteen joined them, a bag slung over his shoulder. He had face dimples and eyes like the ice capped sky they had just flown over.

Giacomo put an arm around him. "This is Aaron. He attends UC Davis. For art. He is…" he paused, his eyes locking on Jessa's. "He is the reason I left. To come here. Like we talked about."

"Ohhhhhh." Jessa could just imagine the light bulb blinking on above her head right about now. Narrow minds, he had said.

Narrow minds. He had to leave. His whole cryptic discussion of love in Capri. She held out her hand. "It's nice to meet you, Aaron."

"Nice to meet you," he said, shaking her hand and then Tyler's.

"That key was to my…What do you call them?" Giacomo was all ease around Aaron, his smile without its edge of sadness.

"Safety deposit box. Where his passport was," he explained. "Thanks, by the way." And if it was at all possible, his smile might have outwatted Giacomo's. Jessa let herself take a little bath in it for a second.

"Jessa! Tyler!" Ms. Jackson stood several feet away, her own suitcase behind her, watching them curiously. "The bus is here."

"You have my email," Jessa said quickly to Giacomo, giving him a hug. "Congratulations," she whispered into his ear.

His strong arms engulfed her.

Waving to him over her shoulder, she followed Tyler through the sliding doors of the airport.

•   •   •

Another bus.

As they pulled out onto the highway toward home, she studied the bulky northern California landscape—beige.

Had it only been ten days?

Tyler sat next to her, polishing off his last bag of gummy bears.

She studied the envelope in her lap. #20. The last one. She peeled it open.

Empty.

"He's kind of stealing my thunder," Tyler said through a mouthful of bears. "Showing up here with the envelope I thought you'd lost. Stupid, charming Italian guy."

"What are you talking about?"

Sifting through her airplane-mussed bag, Tyler pulled out the copy of *A Portrait of the Artist as a Young Man*. He opened the front cover of the book, plucked out a different, smaller envelope that was nestled there, held it up like a visual aid. "Reason #20," it read. Only it wasn't written in Carissa's purple pen.

It said "JESSA"—in thick, black pen. Boy-writing pen.

"Tyler..." Jessa's voice edged a warning.

"Carissa wanted the last one written by someone I thought should write it. You know, based on the trip." He flipped black hair from his eyes and as much as he was trying not to, he couldn't quite mask his grin.

Jessa shook her head. "I saw the manual. She didn't say anything about this." She took the envelope as if it might burn her, or sing to her, or spill infinite light on her, something like that.

Tyler shrugged, his smile winning over. "There may have been an addendum."

"Tyler! Seriously, you and Carissa..."

"Just stop," Tyler interrupted. "You know, he's right—for a smart girl, you can be a real dumbass sometimes. Good thing we love you so much."

Jessa's skin rippled with sudden heat.

Dylan Thomas.

Tyler kicked his knees up on the bus seat in front and pulled the hood of his sweatshirt down over his eyes. "Just read it."

She opened the envelope, extracting a piece of stationery, the top emblazoned with the swirled script of the hotel name from their last night in Italy.

> This is not a reason, not an instruction, not a memory
>
> of something to unfold for you so you can hold its mirror self
>
> up to your face, study it for answers; it is not advice or
>
> judgment or laughter or a history of us.
>
> There are no answers.
>
> It is simply this:
>
> You are human—flesh, blood, bone, soul, heart,
>
> dreams, memory.
>
> But you are so much more, Jessa.
>
> You are an artist, a poet, a dreamer.
>
> I stand at a window, looking out at a dark world streaked
>
> with light. And I see what you see,
>
> my eyes filled with a constant threat of tears,
>
> at all the desolate beauty in the world.

Her heart flushed with air, with all of the Italian sky at once in her soul, with the words in black and white in her lap. Dylan Thomas—a poet. How ironic and wonderful and obvious.

She read the poem again. "Oh, Tyler."

Tyler studied her from under his hood. "I know."

As the landscape of her normal life whirled by the window, her own mind flashed to the day at Pompeii, everyone sitting on the grass, Dylan Thomas playing guitar. *You've got terrible vision if you don't see that I'm in love with you…*

She did. She really, really had terrible vision. Terrible, sucky missing-the-point vision.

Her mind filled with pieces of him, a little Dylan Thomas mind collage: dancing around her singing *Mamma Mia!*; walking alone on the beach, his face bathed in a sheet of light; chatting with Mr. Campbell at the front of the bus; his brow pinched in anger about Sean's kiss; last night, outside the bus, the weight of his hand on her wrist like a familiar bracelet whose metal had grown warm against her skin.

I'll miss you, you poor poet, you—said in the way only another lonely artist could say it, another soul finding its way through the fog.

Tyler already had her phone in his hand. Grabbing it, she clicked to Dylan Thomas's number.

She texted:

Is there room at that window for another pair of eyes?

A minute later, her phone rang.

acknowledgments

Twenty Reasons I'm a lucky author:

1. I have so much gratitude for my agent Melissa Sarver at the Elizabeth Kaplan Literary Agency for all her love, love, love.

2. My writing group: Kirsten Casey, thanks for your wit and friendship and for using language in the most inspiring (and often irreverent!) ways. Jaime Young, thanks for your compassion and honesty. Ann Keeling, thanks for your heart and integrity, especially for the early read of this manuscript.

3. I'm grateful for my other early readers: Rachel McFarland, Tanya Egan Gibson, and Sands Hall—this book would not be what it is without your insight and encouragement.

4. Mom, Dad, Krista (who puts up with my constant questions about the web page)—thanks for always believing.

5. It's not often a book gets three amazing editors to love it. Thank you to Daniel Ehrenhaft, who first loved Jessa's story.

6. And next to Kelly Barrales-Saylor, who nurtured Jessa through so much of her journey.

7. And to Leah Hultenschmidt, who came in toward the end and helped bring her home.

8. Paul Samuelson, a terrific publicist—thank you for spreading the word.

9. Thanks to Kristin Zelazko, Aubrey Poole, and all the people who make the Sourcebooks Fire books so beautiful!

10. Michelle Litton—Italy guru! Thank you for the attention to my Italian details. Any oddities in the book are errors in my memory and my inability to Google correctly.

11. Thank you to my friends (all of you!) who ask, "How's the book going?" and listen patiently to the answer, and especially to Dawn Anthney, Erin Dixon, Emily Gallup, Crystal Groome, Lillian Lacer, Caryn Shehi, Gary Wright, Michael Bodie, and Loretta Ramos. Oh, and Todd McFarland, of course!

12. Thanks to the Sagebiels and the Culbertsons, all of you, who always root for me.

13. My students, past and present, especially the ones who went to Italy with me oh so long ago—you are an inspiration.

14. Marnie Masuda, thanks for asking me to go to Italy in the first place—you make a most wonderful travel partner.

15. Forest Charter School (everyone there!)—I feel lucky to be a part of your school.

16. I'm so grateful for my daughter's caregivers during the writing of this novel: Tall Pines, Karen Slattery at Pine

Mountain, Sydney Lewis, Vienna Saccomano, Bethany Anderson, Daisy Sagebiel, Christie Allen, Mom and Dad (again!), Erin (again!): all of you provided such amazing care of Anabella so I could write with a clear head knowing she was in such good hands.

17. Thanks to the cafés that indulge my presence when I can't write from home, especially Broad Street Books, Summer Thyme's, and Flower Garden.

18. Whether it was to the same lake each summer with my parents and sister or to Europe, Peru, Mexico, Italy, Hawaii, travel transforms me, and I come back slightly altered by a place and the people I interact with there.

19. Most important in my little sphere, thank you to my husband, Peter.

20. And to my sweet daughter, Anabella.

about the author

Kim Culbertson technically writes for teenagers, but there are some grown-ups who like her work. She is the author of the award-winning young adult novel *Songs for a Teenage Nomad* (Sourcebooks Fire, 2010). When she's not writing for teenagers, she's teaching them, and she currently teaches English and creative writing at Forest Charter School. The fact that she's a published author doesn't seem to dazzle her students, who still complain about how much homework she gives them. She lives in the northern California foothills with her husband and daughter and travels as often as she can. Visit her website at www.kimculbertson.com.